AFTER BERLIN

Also by Martin Corrick

THE NAVIGATION LOG

AFTER BERLIN

Martin Corrick

SIMON &
SCHUSTER

London · New York · Sydney · Toronto

A VIACOM COMPANY

First published in Great Britain by Simon & Schuster UK Ltd, 2005
A Viacom Company

Copyright © Martin Corrick, 2005

Photographs are used with the permission of
The Trustees of the Imperial War Museum, London

The right of Martin Corrick to be identified as author of this work
has been asserted in accordance with sections 77 and 78 of the
Copyright, Designs and Patents Act, 1988.

1 3 5 7 9 10 8 6 4 2

Simon & Schuster UK Ltd
Africa House
64–78 Kingsway
London WC2B 6AH

www.simonsays.co.uk

Simon & Schuster Australia
Sydney

A CIP catalogue record for this book is available
from the British Library.

If the author has inadvertently quoted from any text or verse in copyright, the
publisher will be pleased to credit the copyright holder in all future editions.

ISBN 0-7432-2018-8

Typeset by M Rules
Printed and bound in Great Britain by
Mackays of Chatham plc

To Molly

One

I stand still and clutch my hat to my head, my coat flapping. The sun, low-angled, picks out the autumn blaze of the limes along the Queen's Ride and casts a deep shadow across the lake, whose silver surface is brushed by falling gusts of air. My eye is drawn up the limestone track to the summit of Beacon Hill, to the stand of seven beeches by which it is crowned, to the ragged clouds that chase across the bright horizon – oh yes, Waverley is always the same, no matter how many years have come and gone.

If I stand still for long my right knee begins to ache. I turn and go into the house. The girl at the desk issues a ticket and eyes my walking-stick, my gnarled hands, my stoop. 'If you find the stairs difficult,' she says, 'there's a lift at the end of the hall.'

'Thank you,' I say, standing a little more upright. 'I know about the lift. I've been here before.'

'Oh good,' she says. 'I'm so glad! It's so nice when visitors keep coming back!'

She smiles brilliantly and makes a small clapping gesture,

evidently of genuine delight. I feel somewhat ashamed: she is not merely a girl at a desk but a young woman of character and enthusiasm, and her smile warms me. How open the English have become, how free to display their true natures!

I turn towards the lift. It was installed when the house was a military hospital, and is an Otis lift – no, an Otis *elevator*, I should call it – beautifully engineered and panelled in oak. The doors admit me with a soft hiss and I am elevated, humming to myself and still thinking of the charming girl at the desk, a dark-haired girl, strong and trim in her uniform, a new girl whom I haven't seen before.

The season is near its end. The house is quiet, the library empty. As I step through the door the floorboards creak sharply as they always did, a sound like the croak of a pheasant in the woods. Ranks of Beevors stare down from the walls, bland, comfortable, some a little pop-eyed, and lines of books sleep on the shelves – agriculture, ancient history, Anglicanism and animal husbandry, the improving reading of an English landed family in the nineteenth century. Beyond the bookshelves, at the far end of the room, tall windows allow the slanting light to fall upon the chair that was my grandfather's – a club chair, a warm and commodious chair.

I unhook the red rope and walk towards the windows. In my early childhood I sat here each day with an old man while he told stories about India – I remember particularly the slow, mesmerising sway of the howdah as my grandfather, holding me at his hip, re-enacted a solemn procession. His voice was husky, his breathing weak, and I came to think of India as filled with hypnotic mystery and gentle sighing.

One day I waited in the chair for a long time but my grandfather did not appear. I never saw him again. I was not told what had happened, since I was not considered old enough to know of death; but I knew anyway, from the faces and the whispering. I was a quiet child, inquisitive but inward, and always marginal to a family in which silence was peculiar. My father and brother liked to be damned sure of everything; it was fortunate that I was only a younger son, and hence in training for no particular role. 'Young Charlie? That wretched book-reader! He'll be dreaming in the library again. We'll start without him.'

After his death my grandfather's chair became my own. It was the early nineteen-thirties, uneasy years. I could read, or dream, or lift my head and watch the labourers setting out with their forks and scythes, my brother out and about on horseback, the gradual dimming of the light, the dusk, the setting of the sun, the coming dark. I found the details of the world, its patterns and colours, quite delicious, and sketched continually in the margins and end papers of my books, thinking that I would one day be a painter. Ridiculous! Such a notion was inconceivable in my family, of course, and I never dared speak of it; but many years later I did find myself concerned with images – not the painted kind, it's true, but nevertheless I had a sort of revenge.

I lower myself into grandfather's chair, place my stick upright before me and support my chin on my hands. A grand sweep of the estate is illuminated before me, from Home Farm in the west to the lake and the classical bridge in the east, an enormous stage that is framed by hills and occupied, from time to time, by small figures going about their business. I am enchanted, as I always am, by a world that is open to inspection yet remains at a certain distance.

I no longer need the chair's sanctuary, nor have any rights here, but the house and its grand estate still excites me as nothing else. It was designed to display itself, and it does so. It moves me, and lifts my spirits, and draws me into the past.

Beyond Beacon Hill is Rookwood, the house in which my father's secretary, Ernest Bowman, lived with his wife and their three children. Elizabeth was born there. I knew Ernest well, of course – indeed, he had replaced my grandfather as my principal adult friend. But at first I rarely encountered his family, and it was from this high vantage that I first took real notice of Elizabeth. I was reading Stevenson, awaiting the next tap of Pew's stick and absorbing the book with cautious delight. The library windows stood open to the early morning, admitting the falling song of a lark and a drift of scent from the honeysuckle in the garden below. I heard the call of a child, glanced up from my book and watched the girls strolling with their father to the meadow gate.

Elizabeth must have been twelve years old, her sister Ruth two years younger. They were dressed in sandals, white ankle-socks and cotton frocks printed with bold flowers, while their father wore his usual bowler and three-piece black suit, the jacket slung across his shoulder. In his youth Ernest had been a Thames waterman, and he was still square and strong. At the gate he hung his jacket on the fence, bent down and in one movement lifted both children from the ground, one in each arm, as if they were a couple of sacks of grain. Turning his head from one to the other he began to kiss them, and they laughed and wriggled as if they would never stop.

I forgot about Blind Pew and watched until at last Ernest placed each child carefully on the ground, turned away from them and became the man of business, putting on his coat, checking his cuffs and striding towards the house. Yes, I can hear the clink of the latch as the gate swings behind him, the crunch of his boots on the gravel, the cries of the girls calling to each other as they run away down the meadow, their dresses fluttering like seaside flags. Elizabeth is the taller, her legs longer and her knees knobblier, and she runs like a deer, easily and lightly, swerving this way and that for the fun of it. She spreads her arms wide and makes a great leap, then another as if she were flying, and then Ruth does the same, the girls elated at being alive and together and running in the sunshine.

The figures are distant now. They reach the stream at the foot of the slope, cross the bridge and turn uphill, toiling up the steep limestone track, their hands pushing their knees. They stop once or twice for breath, go on again and at last reach the top. They glance back at Waverley, turn and are gone.

Every morning, as soon as I wake, she comes back to me. She slept on her left side, facing away from me, and she was a good sleeper, a highly committed sleeper. I always woke first and turned towards her. Though I knew I must not disturb her, I had a strong desire to touch her immediately, as if to assure myself of her warmth and life. She lay very still, seeming hardly to breathe. I made myself wait for a quite unconscionable length of time, and when I could wait no longer I would reach out and stroke her spine, following her vertebrae into the dip of her waist, past the two faint dimples that lay in the small of her back and ending at the set of fused bones that are known as the sacrum.

'I'm asleep,' she would whisper. 'Charlie, I am still asleep.'

'Darling Lizzie,' I would say, and she would wriggle a little deeper into the mattress, murmuring, 'That's as maybe, but I am still asleep, and I am not to be woken for hours.'

We staged that little play, I suppose, hundreds of times, and through such caresses I learned her with my hands. Now, when I wake, I can recall her precisely, from the planes and angles of her cheeks to the crinkled soles of her feet. I knew that I lacked something, and Elizabeth had sufficient for both of us; she completed me and remained herself, energetic, resistant to fashion, careless with clothes and make-up. Her dark and wiry hair was the sort that requires nothing more than brushing – each morning she would sit naked on the edge of the bed and work at her hair fiercely, her head bowed – I remember that, and I remember much else, and if I could I would remember everything.

While I'm dozing in that chair in the library a dream comes upon me, its subject annoyingly elusive. It has something to do with that phrase of Milton's, 'No light, but rather darkness visible'. Was there ever such a poet of light and dark, flying and falling, as Milton? In my dream there is a sense of flight among gathering shadows, shadows that soon become darkness, blank and black. I wait, and soon a few pinpoints of light appear; they might be stars, but they are nearer and more fiery than stars. Some of them move slowly, swaying together as if in some strange dance, a slow and formal dance, and there is a kind of music, all on one note, low and unvarying, a curious kind of thunder. Time passes, and many more of those seeming stars come into view until I can see thousands of them, multicoloured, some of them flying upwards or sideways, others falling slowly like rain, all of them making patterns of great beauty.

The dream makes me afraid, and I force myself awake, feeling ashamed. I had let myself fall, and for those moments had lost contact with the truth. Only memory remains. Elizabeth is dead. Waverley has been a museum for more than twenty-five years. Its gardens are open all year. The house may be visited between March and October for five pounds per head, and there are special rates for parties. That is the truth, which must be set against memory.

The floorboards creak a warning and I turn away from the sunlight into the dimness of the library. It is the uniformed young woman from the reception desk.

'Oh, sir,' she says, 'I don't think you ought to—' and then she stops and looks at me, her head on one side. She comes closer, inspects me again and looks up at the portrait on the wall above us.

'That's my grandfather,' I tell her. 'He's sitting in this very chair, and when I was a little boy he used to sit here with me beside him. I liked it very much, sitting here with him. I still like it. You get such a lovely view, don't you think? I'll show you something.'

In my wallet is the yellow, cracked photograph that I took with my first camera. I show it to the young woman, who looks from the picture to the window and back again.

'It's this view, isn't it? The same view from the same window?'

'Exactly the same view.'

'And it hasn't changed at all!'

'I don't think it has.'

She peers at the two tiny figures in the picture. 'Who are those girls?'

'One's my wife, Lizzie, and the other is her sister Ruth. They were young when I took that. It must have been the early thirties, I think. The nineteen-thirties.'

'I wasn't born then,' the girl says. 'My *mother* wasn't born. My *grandmother* wasn't born, even.'

She gives me back the picture and I turn away from her and look out of the window. A dark cloud is passing, and spots of rain patter against the glass.

'I'm so sorry,' the girl says. 'We'll have to go downstairs now. They're locking up.'

'Of course.' I begin to get up, but the chair is soft and deep. She helps me. Her hands are warm and strong.

'Thank you,' I say. 'Do you know the word *sacrum*? It's the name of a bone in the lower back, at the point where the hips join the spine. It's a Latin translation from the Greek *hieron osteon*, meaning "sacred bone". The Greeks believed it was the place where the soul resided.'

She considers this information for a moment, then reaches round with both hands under her uniform jacket and feels the base of her spine with her thumbs.

'It's a funny place to find a person's soul,' she says.

'Yes,' I say. 'I suppose it is.' I am about to say more, but the story is too long for the moment.

She's waiting for me to leave. I ask her, 'Would you mind if I had a few more moments to myself? I'll be down in two or three minutes.'

She smiles. 'Of course. I'll see you downstairs.' The floor creaks as she walks out through the door, and I look round at the books, the pictures, and then back to the window, thinking that I may not come here again. Slowly I start to make my way to the lift. There is surely something of Lizzie about that girl – the same purposeful air, the same directness, isn't there? But maybe I'm imagining it.

Two

During the last year of the war I did not see Elizabeth at all. It was three months after VE Day when I suddenly glimpsed her among the crowds in Charing Cross Road. It was a Friday afternoon, the pavements jammed, queues straggling from the bus-stops, traffic nose-to-tail. She was in uniform, stepping briskly along the edge of the opposite pavement with her skirt swinging. I stood on the kerb, called her name and in a moment she saw me and waved eagerly, both hands over her head, grinning at me between the passing buses. On her head was a forage cap, the strap of a briefcase over her shoulder and on the left breast of her jacket, bright against the dark blue cloth, the winged badge of the Air Transport Auxiliary.

We gestured at each other, signalling the impossibility of crossing the road, and she called out, 'Charlie! I can't stop now! I'm going to Berlin in the morning! I'll see you soon!'

'Berlin? Oh, Lizzie!'

'Yes! Isn't it terrific! I'm going down to Limehouse, and then we're off to Berlin! I'll see you soon!'

She waved again, then turned away. I saw her pause at the

corner of Cranbourn Street with one foot in the gutter, the other cocked behind her on the kerb while she looked for a gap in the traffic. She wasn't tall but she seemed so, because she stood up straight and looked people in the eye. She glanced right and left, dashed in front of a cab, brakes squealed, the cabbie tooted his horn and then she had gone into the crowd.

Limehouse was the home of Alice Attwell, who had been Elizabeth's flight engineer for most of the war – they both served in the ATA, which was the only wartime organisation to employ women as pilots. When I saw her, Elizabeth would have been on her way to Leicester Square and the tube to Mile End.

The underground would no doubt be jam-packed and foul with cigarette smoke, but I knew she wouldn't be thinking of that; she'd be thinking of flying, as she always was. She'd be thinking of the grey expanse of the North Sea and the yellow dunes that mark the Dutch coast, the black cross of the aircraft's shadow flickering over estuaries and lakes, fields and forests and then, beyond the low hills, the enormous plain of northern Europe, stretching a thousand miles to the east. Already she would have pencilled the course on a half-million map, a line through cities whose names were familiar from years of war: Bruges, Ghent, Brussels, Cologne, Düsseldorf, Essen, Dortmund, Hanover, Magdeburg – and at last, lying deep in the heart of the plain, that great capital, Berlin.

Lizzie had been a country girl, brought up in a tied house on a great estate. Now she was a First Officer in the Air Transport Auxiliary with five years' service and nearly two thousand hours in command. She considered herself robust, fit to take knocks. She owned only what she could carry in a green fibre suitcase and a kitbag, and for five years had been content to make her home wherever she was. She wanted nothing but to fly, and the motto of the ATA could have been her own: *Aetheris avidi*, eager for the air.

Elizabeth's friend Alice was born in Limehouse, in Mafeking Street, not far from the river. As is the usual way of things, Limehouse, one of the poorest areas of the city, suffered most grievously both in the Blitz and in the later attacks by flying bombs and rockets. There were gaps in every street – many of them, as their residents liked to tell you, were more bloody gap than bloody street. The route that Lizzie took, from Mardon Street to the Regent's Canal and along the towpath to Limehouse Basin and Mafeking Street, was a journey through ruins.

But Lizzie was not thinking of that. She was thinking of her friend Alice and the news she was bringing her. Dearest Alice! Alice, tiny Alice, whose hair bristles in every direction, Alice with her astonishingly capable hands and the toolbox that she lugs everywhere, the toolbox she made herself from selected beechwood, each drawer carefully dovetailed and lined with green baize! Oh, Alice and her skilful hands, her capacious toolbox! How fortunate she had been in her dearest friend!

Indeed she had. Between 1941 and 1945 Alice spent hundreds of hours at Lizzie's side, listening to the beat of the engines in Blenheims and Beaufighters, Halifaxes and Hampdens. The aeroplanes they flew were often damaged and unreliable, but Alice had the temperament of a good doctor and would spot the slightest irregularity in temperature or pressure, the smallest change in sound or vibration. She was prepared for anything. Her toolbox contained a selection of taps and dies for Whitworth and British Standard Fine, reamers, a clock-gauge, ring-spanners, feeler gauges that opened like miniature Japanese fans. In one drawer she had a set of tiny BA open-enders and watchmaker's screwdrivers for magneto work, in another she kept wire brushes and rat-tailed files and in a third was a hand-drill and a set of bits from a thirty-second to half an inch – there was so much in Alice's toolbox, and Alice was so skilled, that any difficulty was quickly resolved. Dear Alice, lovely Alice!

Lizzie turned a corner and there was the viaduct and the Attwell house, still unharmed, thank goodness – and beyond Mafeking Street, under brisk clouds and sunshine, the grey water of the London river. Cranes dipped and rose over lines of moored ships, dipped again and swung. Her father had told her stories of his childhood on the river. She stopped and listened. Mixed with the cries of gulls were the shouts of stevedores and crane-drivers, cries whose meaning was taken by the wind. Out on the water a tug whistled, a rag of steam drifting from its funnel, and somewhere a sledgehammer clanged on steel plate, its beat as slow and steady as a tolling bell. Oh, the great river and what it might mean!

She was drawn to the quayside and along the planks of a rickety pier. The tide was ebbing with sluggish force, swirling beneath her feet – she felt suddenly dizzy and stood still, watching the water, staring downriver towards the pale glimmer of Greenwich. A minute passed, another, and she was steady. She took the forage cap from her head, ruffled her hair, replaced the cap and turned away, thinking again of the news that she would bring to Alice Attwell, the news of the last journey they would make together, their journey to Berlin.

Three

Through Limehouse, in a wide sweep, first east from Stepney, then north towards Bow, runs what was once the London & Blackwall Railway. A dip in the landscape required a high-arched viaduct of dark blue bricks, the sort called 'engineering brick' that lasts more-or-less for ever. The houses along one side of Mafeking Street were knocked down to build the viaduct. The houses were a loss, but not a total loss, because the viaduct immediately found its uses. If a workshop was needed, a stable, or a secure place for some private purpose, nothing was easier than to occupy one of the arches. Strictly, they belonged to the L&BR, but the railway never claimed them and they were quietly received by the people of Mafeking Street as compensation for their lost homes and the clatter, smoke and dust of the railway. Those high brick arches are spaces of their own kind, neither properly indoors nor out, with the primitive mystery of caves; even now, when standing beneath one of them, I feel impelled to cry out, and to listen for the echo.

The occupants of the archways came and went. People kept trying, as people do, and when one enterprise failed another took its place, the arch given a lick of fresh paint to fit the new purpose. Big money has never been made round here, and to survive was difficult enough.

Because of the slope of the ground, the arches vary in height. The lowest arch, number 2, is at the top of the street. Number 2 had always been used for storing coal. Old Ben Yossakin kept his pony and cart in the front of the arch and the rest of it was full of coal right up to the roof. Most days, if it wasn't raining, Ben sat outside on a milk crate covered with a folded blanket. On the door he'd chalked 'Best Welsh Steam Coal – 6d A Sack'. From time to time someone would stop by and ask him to deliver a sack or two, or maybe they'd just stand and chat. Once a month he took his cart down to the wharf at the end of the street and brought back half a ton of Best Welsh. When you stood talking to old Ben Yossakin you could hear the pony moving behind the door, the clop of its heels as it took a step, the regular munch of its jaws. It was no good looking in there – it was pitch black, but you could hear the pony was in there all right.

At the other end of Mafeking Street, in the house that stood beside the canal and opposite the last arch of the viaduct, lived the Attwells. They moved here in 1919. Roy Attwell had been a corporal in the Royal Artillery in the Great War, and by some miracle survived unharmed. His wife, Lily, bore their daughter Alice that same year, and many years later, unexpectedly, they had a son whom they called Arthur.

Roy Attwell was determined not to waste his reprieve. He took over the house, and the timber business in archway 14 that had been his father's and kept them going through hard times; it was one of the few local businesses to survive the thirties.

Number 14 is the highest arch. Many times before the war, standing and staring up at its vault, Roy Attwell spread his arms wide and told Lily that number 14 was as big as a bleeding cathedral, straight up it was. The arch had been occupied by his family for the best part of seventy years and Roy looked after it with due care, just as his father and grandfather had done, whitewashing the grand radius of the roof every two years and keeping the floor spotless. The high windows faced south-east and on a clear morning sunlight poured in from dawn onwards, yellow bars of sunshine lying sharp across the dusty air. Roy extended the timber racks along both sides of the arch, painted the doors white and the number 14 in black, big and bold. In the years between the wars the racks were filled with softwood – pine, fir and spruce that came off the boats from Norway and Russia. 'You put your nose up against that timber,' Roy used to say, 'and tell me you don't smell wolves.'

The baulks lay drying in the lower racks. After a year or two, when the moisture content was right, Roy hauled each one down and sawed it into stock sizes – six by four, three by two, eight by four. Nominal sizes they were, rough-cut on the big circular saw and allowing an eighth all round for planing and finishing. The circular saw stood like an altar in the centre of the arch. Roy said nobody was to touch it save him. It was an unnecessary warning: even at rest the saw's hooked teeth were savage, and when the blade began to tear its way through a baulk of Norwegian pine its scream forced everyone to step back and clap their hands over their ears.

Roy wasn't afraid of the saw. He sang along with the wailing blade. When she was old enough, his little girl Alice helped him. She only went off to work for Harry Nicholls because they needed her wages when Arthur was born. Roy's timber business didn't make much money. Alice was a big help until she went to work for Harry.

Number 8 was Harry Nicholls's garage in those days. Alice

began working there when she left school at the age of fourteen, a little mop-head girl. Harry was tall and gloomy, a bachelor who needed help. Roy Attwell knew that his daughter would be a bloody good apprentice, better than any bloody boy, just see if she wasn't. The Attwells needed the money; the timber business was bad then, and Arthur had just been born. There was a long-running argument between Harry and Roy.

'You don't understand, Harry old lad. This girl fixed my busted watch at the age of seven. She's a natural mechanic.'

'Huh,' Harry Nicholls would say, bending under the bonnet of an Austin and tugging at something.

'And what's more, she's a lively child, a cheerful girl and a willing worker. She'll cheer you up no end, you miserable bugger.'

Harry would turn his oily face for a moment towards Roy, then go back to his study of the Austin's plug leads.

'Now come on, Harry. Be reasonable. Try her out, is all I ask. See if she doesn't get the hang of it, quick as you like. You don't have to pay Alice nothing to start off. She's got clever hands, she has.'

'Clever hands be buggered. Ain't got no ladies' toilet.'

Roy would laugh at that. 'She can nip home for a pee any time she wants, as you know bloody well.'

The argument followed its laborious course and eventually Harry was persuaded to try Alice out for half a day. She stayed for the rest of the day, then for a week, then a month, then six months. Harry discovered that the girl was indeed a natural, and he employed her for four years. It wasn't a bad training for her, as it turned out, and the money was useful. She started at ten bob a week in 1934 and finished on two pounds in the autumn of 1938, when she went away for training as an aero-engineer in Manchester.

Harry Nicholls never did admit that he had been wrong about Alice. When she went away he was sad to see her go; he didn't say so, but everyone could tell. The garage in number 8 was quiet after that, and it stayed that way through the war. The war wasn't a good time for garages, since there was no petrol worth speaking of. They were making tanks and guns, not cars.

And then, in 1941, Roy was called up. He was a reservist but he'd assumed he was too old; when the letter came it was a surprise but he was glad to go. He was an old artilleryman and if they wanted him to teach new boys how to lay and aim, well, that's what he'd do.

After he'd gone the great saw lay silent and dusty, the arch and its store of scented timber still and calm, sparrows fluttering in and out of the gaps round the doors and squeaking high up in the roof. Children found their way in, climbed the racks and built dens in corners where a few bone-dry lengths of red cedar still remained – cedar, that deliciously aromatic timber whose scent conjures up some hot, faraway, unknowable land. Alice's yellow-haired little brother Arthur, who was nine at the time, was up among the red cedar when Lily got the War Office telegram – *Dear Madam, We regret to inform you that Sergeant Roy Attwell, 4097723 Royal Artillery, has been reported killed in action.*

Lily knew her little boy was up in the racks somewhere and she yelled for him, but for a long time Arthur was too scared to move, looking down and seeing his mother pacing below, in and out of the sunlight, sobbing and raging and wrapping her arms round herself. Eventually the boy came down and she grasped him so fiercely that his arms bore the marks for weeks. That was strange; somehow the bruising was a kind of proof, a necessary confirmation. He told his little friends that his dad had been killed in Italy at a place called Monte Cassino, and then he showed them the bruises his mother had given him. That shut them up all right. The fury of his mother and the sight of those bruises kept those boys quiet, and that was useful in a funny kind of way.

As for Lily Attwell, she knew the minute she saw the telegraph boy. She had been a quiet woman, well organised, loving her husband, bringing up the children with care. When she saw the telegraph boy she was filled with rage. She finished telling Arthur, went back into the house, filled a bucket and started scrubbing the floors from the attic downwards. She pulled all the carpets up, took them into the garden and beat them with a length of bamboo. She washed all the family's clothes, cleaned the windows, swept the chimneys and dug over the patch of garden at the back. When she had run out of household tasks her rage drove her to start up her husband's business again. Supplies of new timber had been cut off by the war, but timber can be salvaged and demand was strong. Lily hired Ben Yossakin's cart for five bob a day, scrubbed it out and took herself and Arthur round the bomb sites collecting lengths of floorboard, joists and rafters that smelt of smoke and were stuck full of nails, odd lengths of soffit, skirting board, stair treads, pieces of dado and broken banisters.

Alice got compassionate leave and came home for a week. Lily told her, 'Get away, girl. You get on with your life. Never mind about us.'

Lily worked all hours and the power of grief even overcame her fear of the circular saw, though she kept her distance. She bargained for timber with the demolition gangs, carted it back to number 14, pulled out the nails with a claw-hammer and ripped it lengthways on the big saw, sorting and stacking it with the chain hoist according to size, just as her husband had done.

She worked like a tiger but she was no businesswoman. If it was a good cause – and it usually was – she'd give the timber away, likely as not. She supplied all the six-by-fours they used to prop up the west wall of the chapel in Lane End – dozens of them – and never sent a bill. Arthur stopped going to school, but the Attendance Officer was warned off by the headmaster of St Mark's, who needed three dozen twenty-foot six-by-twos for rafters in the school hall. Lily didn't talk much to anybody else, but she wanted the company of her little boy and she liked knowing he was somewhere nearby. She had to hear his voice, and after Monte Cassino she brought him to sleep in her bed. Alice was away at her flying. She hardly ever took any leave except once or twice. In the tall terraced house in Mafeking Street and under the grand arch of number 14 it was just Lily and her little boy, just the two of them.

Near the end of the war one of the last of the V2s wrecked St Mark's School for the third and final time. In the Lamb & Flag that night the landlord, George Honeysett, banged his glass down on the bar and shouted, 'It's always us what cops it. How many bloody bombs fell in bloody Surrey? How many bloody bombs fell on Buckingham bloody Palace?'

'One did, Pa,' said the smallest Honeysett child, who was washing glasses behind the bar, 'I saw a picture in the paper.' But nobody took any notice of him, since he was only a little feller after all, and didn't know no better.

Elizabeth Bowman walked up from the river and went looking for Alice. When she found her working high up in the timber racks of number 14 she called out, 'Alice! I've come to get you –

we must go at once – we're off straightaway to White Waltham, and then – oh Alice, tomorrow we're going to Berlin!'

'Lizzie! It's you! How lovely!' Alice lifted her dusty hands to her face. 'Berlin! Crikey!' She turned and slid backwards down the long, springy ladder, her dungarees fluttering with the speed of her descent. 'Well now! That's something, isn't it! Berlin! Blimey!'

Four

The tall windows lacked glass. They had closed the shutters the night before and lain in darkness. Early in the morning something had woken her. It was still dark. She kept still and there was silence for several minutes, save for the faint sound of Alice's breathing. Then it came again – a long, low sound, the melancholy whistle of a train miles away, the other side of the city. It was only a train. Moments later there were footsteps and someone spoke in German, a man's voice in the corridor outside their room. Torchlight flickered under the door.

'Die englischen Engel,' the voice said, closer now, then he laughed and another man said something unintelligible. What did that mean? Oh yes, it was a joke – 'The English angels'. It was a joke, that's what it was, a pun in German. Both men laughed again, then one of them coughed and their boots creaked on the floorboards. Elizabeth listened to the men walking away, the sound of their boots diminishing into silence. They had gone, but now she was awake.

She yawned, stretching her arms up into the darkness and opening her eyes wide. The shutters kept out every trace of light, but somewhere a bird had begun singing a repetitious phrase, so dawn couldn't be far away. She sat up, the ancient bed creaking as she moved, pushed the blanket aside and swung her legs to the floor. Alice had begun to snore with her usual thin, fluttering whistle. Collecting her shoes and clothes from the end of the bed, Elizabeth felt her way to the door.

In the corridor a thin grey light had begun to illuminate the scarred wallpaper, empty picture-hooks and broken furniture. This had once been a grand building: the ceilings were high, the plasterwork elaborate, the windows carefully proportioned. She walked cautiously to the room where they had eaten their sandwiches the night before, a splendid room with a white marble fireplace and curtains of red plush. Someone had covered the furniture with dust-sheets and swept the glass from the shattered windows into neat piles. Outside was a low stone balcony with a dozen steps down into the garden. She pulled on her uniform jacket and opened the door to the balcony. It wasn't locked. Nothing was locked in Berlin any more. You were lucky if the place had a roof, a door that fitted, a tap that worked. The flagstones were cold. Elizabeth put on her shoes, leaned on the balustrade and looked at the shambles that had once been a garden. Before the shelling there had perhaps been an arbour and a decorative pond enclosed by a gravel path and box hedges. The garden was still littered with slates, rubble and shattered branches that had fallen during the final battle. At the foot of the steps were parts of a white marble statue – an arm, the upper half of a woman's torso, a foot broken off at the ankle.

She looked up. High in the sky were thin strands of cirrus, diaphanous and widely scattered: there'd be no problem on the way home. There was the usual horrid Berlin smell, the usual drift of smoke in the air, but no sign of mist. When the sun got up it would be calm and clear as it had been yesterday, an ordinary morning in late summer. To the east the low, ragged skyline of the city was becoming visible, and just above the horizon lay the crescent moon, large and lacy.

Again there was the whistle of a train. She stood still. Was there something wrong with her? Was she ill? In the last few days a malaise had come over her. Surely it could be nothing, and she would soon feel perfectly well. After all, they had come all the way to Berlin, she and Alice, and that was certainly a great adventure. Nevertheless, something was not quite right, something had unsettled her. How odd.

That persistent bird was singing again. A small, high fluting. A musical sound, and familiar. Possibly it was a thrush. She had never been good at small birds. In their childhood her brother Edmund used to laugh at her – 'You can't recognise so much as a starling, can you Lizzie? Everything's just another LBJ to you.' He meant 'little brown job'.

Her big, handsome brother was proud of his knowledge of the countryside and he would have been interested in this place. Yesterday she and Alice had circled the airfield at Gatow for fifteen minutes, waiting for a gap in the stream of American C47s. Here and there the sun glinted on water. All around the city were forests, lakes and rivers. Somehow when you said 'Berlin' you didn't expect this enemy city to be set in pretty countryside. They had looked down upon fields and forests, lakes, the glittering crescent of the Wannsee, the silver Spree jutting into the city – oh yes, this was the setting for a fine civilisation. Good hunting country, her brother Edmund would have said, looking round for a horse.

So it was, so it had been. Good hunting country, and at its centre a gigantic ruin, a city absolutely smashed, wrecked, eradicated. There was no comparison with London, which remained functional, still itself. As for Berlin – Berlin had surely been destroyed, and the number of its people who had died must be beyond counting, soldiers and women, children, old people, shopkeepers, bus drivers, teachers, plumbers, aunts and uncles, grandparents, babies – hundreds of thousands of them.

She stood up and pushed her hands through her hair. She and Alice had searched the house last night but had found no water in the whole bloody place, no electricity, nowhere to wash. Somewhere there must surely be a bathroom that still worked. She took out her handkerchief and blew her nose, but the smell was still there.

Columns of smoke had reached up towards the Anson all the way from the Belgian border. That was when they first noticed the smell, even at five thousand feet on a clear summer's day. Ruins everywhere, smoke everywhere and a stink that was still laden with corruption and death, three months after the fighting had finished. Düsseldorf, Essen, Dortmund – the crushed cities passed slowly beneath their wings, so many of them: another, another, another. Nothing prepared you for such sights, the evidence of such vengeance, and it was surely impossible that a country could recover from such damage. Minden, Hanover, Wolfsburg and down through the Russian zone to Brandenburg and Berlin they had seen only the skeletons of cities, nothing but ruins, and here was Berlin, that mighty capital, absolutely destroyed.

Elizabeth looked again at the insubstantial moon. *Berlin.* The name rang in her mind like a solemn bell, so long had it been haunted. *Berlin, Berlin.* On the BBC they spoke the name with special gravity, and for the millions listening in their kitchens and parlours the city was the lair in which evil dwelt. *Berlin.* The name meant hatred and darkness and fire. For years we had dared to come here only at night, a few hundred of us filling the night with our engines, letting fall fire and turning for home. Now the war was finished, our task complete, Germany and its capital ruined, justice done.

After the Anson had landed, Elizabeth and Alice had borrowed a jeep from the American sappers who were working on the runway at Gatow. The two women drove cautiously into the city and discovered places that bore some resemblance to the Tiergarten, Unter den Linden, the Brandenburg Gate and the Kaiser Wilhelm Gedachtniskirche, half its spire slid into rubble. At the wrecked Chancellery they were photographed with a crowd of laughing Russian soldiers, young soldiers who made jokes they could not understand. They watched the women of Berlin – 'Trümmerfrauen', rubble-women, already famous – stacking bricks with their bare hands. The dust and the smell lingered everywhere. They wandered the streets and became lost among the devastation, unable to make sense of their map.

Eventually they stopped the jeep and asked for directions from a young woman in a dusty black dress.

'Hier ist das Tiergarten,' the woman said.

Berlin Zoo. They gazed at the heap of stones. It was impossible to know what it had once been.

'Ich arbeite beim Zoo,' the girl said, talking urgently and moving her hands. She stood there in her dusty black dress and told them she had been a secretary at the Zoo and that her name was Anna Schwartz. She moved in an agitated way, shifting her weight from one foot to the other, not wishing to speak but compelled to do so. Two years ago, Anna said, in the middle of the night, hundreds of English bombers had come. 'Der Zoo wurde zerstört' – the Zoo was destroyed. It was odd, the way she said that, as if she was apologising for its absence.

'Es gab einen orang-utan. Ihr name war Cleo,' Anna said. 'Sie entging in eine Baum.'

'Baum' – that meant a tree. They worked out the girl's meaning: an orang-utan called Cleo had escaped from her enclosure and climbed into a tree.

'Sie entging in einen Baum mit ihrem Baby.' She had escaped into a tree with her baby.

The young woman stepped back and then forward again, gesturing in an awkward, tense way. 'Das Baby heißte Muschi.'

The baby was called Muschi. That was clear enough.

'Cleo hatte einen Herzangriff. Sie starb.'

Something had happened to the baby's mother. 'I'm sorry,' Elizabeth said in English to the young woman, 'We don't understand.'

The woman explained again, placing her hand above her left breast and bending forward as if fainting – no – not fainting – dying. That was it. Eventually they grasped the whole story. Cleo, the orang-utan, had escaped into a tree with her baby but had died from a heart-attack. Soldiers had brought her baby, Muschi, down from the tree and sent her to Copenhagen Zoo for safety.

Anna raised her arms to the sky and swivelled on her heels, demonstrating that the soldiers were 'Gewehr-Mannschaft' – they were gunners. The men who saved the baby orang-utan had been the crew of an anti-aircraft gun. She pointed at the enormous concrete blockhouse that stood beside the wreckage of the Zoo, many storeys high, pock-marked and massively scarred but still intact: it was the Zoo flak-tower, one of the massive gun towers built to defend Berlin against the British, the Americans and finally the Russians.

'Gewehr-Mannschaft.' Anna said the word for 'gunners'

again and then was silent. Having finished her struggle with the story, she watched them, assessing its reception, standing very still and staring at the two Englishwomen in their blue uniforms, the taller woman with a winged pilot's badge on her tunic.

Elizabeth looked at Alice, knowing that the German girl's grief was next to rage, the same rage that possessed Lily Attwell, her friend's mother. The German girl did not wish to display her anguish but it emerged despite herself, in her awkward stillness, in the tension of her body, in the angle of her head, in the way she held her arms, and it was a grief entangled with fury.

'There isn't anything we can do,' Elizabeth said, and Alice shook her head in support.

Elizabeth said, 'I'm sorry. We're both very sorry, but we can do nothing.' Words had to be said, and they could have no meaning. She looked at Alice again and saw the anguish of the German girl reflected in her friend's face. 'We're going now,' she said curtly to the girl, feeling angry with her for no reason that she could understand.

'It's not our fault,' Alice said to Anna Schwartz. 'We know it's not your fault either. It's Hitler's fault.'

When Alice said the name 'Hitler', the German girl made a small involuntary movement, as if someone had raised a hand to strike her. Then she stood still again, upright and determined, her eyes suddenly full of tears.

It was difficult to leave. They had listened to her, but that was not enough; they could not appease her grief and anger. Nothing more could be done, nothing more could be said. Elizabeth and Alice climbed into the jeep and drove away. The girl stood and watched until they were out of sight, standing very straight and still in the centre of the road, staring after them and wiping the tears fiercely from her cheeks with the back of her hand.

That was enough of sightseeing. They had searched for somewhere to stay the night and found this house on Unter den Linden, a fine house that must have been an embassy or the home of some great personage. Elizabeth looked up. The Russian soldiers were at their high window overlooking the garden, just as they had been yesterday, smoking and talking and gazing out across the city. We just walked in and nobody challenged us, because we are the victors. It is as simple as that. We have won and we will do as we like, though it is hard to see what can be done, what should be done, amid such destruction.

She looked at her watch: it was six o'clock. It would take perhaps seven hours to fly home, including an hour for refuelling at Brussels. The Anson was easy and gentle to fly, like a great soft bird, a quiet bird like an owl, but it was very slow.

Something was certainly wrong with her. She must be sickening for something. Perhaps it was flu. She shook her head, yawned and stretched her arms upward.

Behind her, Alice's voice said, 'Lizzie? What are you doing out there? You haven't got no trousers on.'

Elizabeth looked up again at the sky. It was getting lighter and the high cirrus was dissolving.

Alice said again, more tentatively, 'Lizzie?'

Elizabeth stepped down into the garden and the dusty grass rustled beneath her shoes. Oh yes, this had certainly been an elegant garden, as befits the diplomat or party official or whoever he was, the owner of this grand place. All the houses along Unter den Linden were mansions like this, but grandeur had been no defence against the Red Army. The fighting had gone from one house to the next, foot by foot, yard by yard: snipers, mortars, tanks, rockets. Perhaps those Russian soldiers, the ones guarding the place, were those who had taken this house and killed its defenders one by one. You heard stories about the ferocity of the Russians that were hard to believe. Those young soldiers had been bold with the two Englishwomen to start with, whistling and calling to them, but when they got up close they became polite. They were only boys, after all. They said they had marched all the way from Stalingrad, which was remarkable. Last night they had brought glasses and insisted that both women drink with them. The Russian boys sat politely beside them all evening, struggling to tell them how it had been in Stalingrad and then in Berlin, drawing diagrams with one finger on the dusty floor, showing where the enemy tanks had been, the Russian artillery, the snipers, and late in the evening they went back to their lookout on the top floor, having caused no difficulty at all.

'Now look, Lizzie,' Alice said, coming up close behind her, 'you can pretend you're not hearing if you like, but you've got no trousers on and those soldiers, those Russian boys, they're getting an eyeful.'

'Oh, Alice,' Elizabeth said, turning round. 'I'm in a bloody awful mood. I don't know why.'

'You're bloody daft, that's what,' Alice said. The two women put their arms around each other, standing in the ruined garden while the Russians looked down from their high window, the smoke from their cigarettes drifting up into the calm dawn. Elizabeth held Alice's face between her hands and said, 'Dear Alice. It's so silly. Why should I feel so funny all of a sudden? It's all over, we've won, we can go home now, and I feel so tired. It's ridiculous.'

Alice said, 'Lizzie, you're very clever, but sometimes you're just plain bloody stupid as well, you really are.'

At Gatow their Anson had been pushed to the back and was hidden behind half a dozen Dakotas. An American dispatcher drove up as they were doing the daily inspection. 'You ladies are late,' he said, waving his clipboard at them. He looked lean and fit. 'We gotta get that baby airplane of yours out of here right now.'

'Never mind,' Elizabeth said, wiping her hands on a rag. 'Hard to be on time when nobody's told you when you're due.'

The dispatcher stared at her for a second and then laughed. He had very white teeth. 'OK, OK,' he said, 'I guess I earned that.' He looked at the Anson's registration letters and checked his list. 'Are you the skipper?'

'Yes. My name's Bowman.' Elizabeth pointed at Alice, who was kneeling on the wing and closing one of the engine cowlings. 'She's the flight engineer. Her name's Attwell.'

'Bowman. Attwell.' The dispatcher checked the names and flipped through the sheets on his clipboard. 'You got four POWs, a child, a nun, a motorcycle in pieces and six bags of mail, all for London. Your gas is on its way. I'll get you a ground crew when you're ready to go.' He looked at his watch. 'Take off at ten hundred. OK?'

'A nun, did you say?'

'Yeah. A nun and a kid. What it says here. Guess the nun's a nurse, maybe.' He looked an untroubled man, easy with himself, wearing shorts and an open shirt and being so brown.

'And a motorcycle in pieces.'

'You got it. The bike's in a coupla boxes.'

'We'll need two or three quarts of oil.'

'On the bowser with the fuel.' The American waved his arm

in a half-salute and drove away, dust spurting from the wheels of his jeep.

Elizabeth looked up at Alice. 'Well, there you are,' she said. 'Just like that, and we're ready to go. They somehow make things simple, the Americans, don't they?'

She paused and wrinkled her nose in the way she sometimes did. 'But it's odd. A nun and a child? Somehow you don't expect nuns to fly.'

Alice laughed. 'We won't come to any harm with her on board,' she said.

Elizabeth began with the port undercarriage while Alice went to work on the engines. The tyre was worn and would have to be changed when they got back. The starboard tyre was fine. No oil leaks. Ailerons, rudder, tailplane, flaps, all OK. When she had worked all round the Anson she sat down on the grass, leaned against a wheel and filled in the daily inspection book. She wrote the date, 7th August 1945, the third month of peace in Europe. Five years of flying, soon to be over. Just short of two thousand hours and more than eighty different types of aircraft flown. How extraordinary that she had done such a thing, such a very great adventure, and got through to the end, very nearly to the end!

She looked up. Alice was sitting on the wing, swinging her legs, waiting for the fuel bowser.

'It's going to be funny when it all stops,' Alice said.

'I was just thinking that. Do you remember, on the way out, when we climbed up through the rain and popped out into the sunshine and there it all was, all new and fresh and gleaming in the sun, the sea below and the land ahead?'

'Clouds towering all around. Lovely!'

'And the sun, too. The deep blue sky. Immensely blue.'

'Yes,' Alice said, swinging her legs. 'Really lovely, it was. All that blue, all that white and the green of the land.' She looked up. 'Here comes that Yank again.'

The dispatcher's jeep skidded to a stop. He leaned out and shouted to them, 'Hey, you ladies! You heard the news?'

Elizabeth shook her head. 'What news?'

'We bombed the Japs to hell yesterday. Atomic bomb. Some town don't exist no more. A helluva lot of Japs too.'

'An atomic bomb?'

'Yeah. Some kinda new thing. Atomic bomb. Bigger'n anything you ever seen. Place called Hiroshima. Town in Japan.' He said it again, practising the name. 'Hiroshima. That's the place. Jap town. City, I guess. Hiroshima.'

'Hiroshima?' Elizabeth stood up. 'What's happened? Have they surrendered, the Japanese? Will they give up now?'

He waved his clipboard. 'Sure they will. One bomb, and a city's gone. Goodbye Hiroshima. They gotta give up now. Matter of time before they all gets blowed clean away, else.'

The American put his jeep into gear and jerked a thumb over his shoulder at the fuel bowser behind him. 'Here's your gas now. On your way, ladies,' he said, and drove away.

'An atomic bomb,' Alice said. 'I don't know about that.'

'It's when they split the atom,' Elizabeth said. 'Atomic fission. Something in the atom splits. Heat comes out, and a terrible lot of it, too.'

'Are you sure that's right?' Alice asked

'Oh yes,' Elizabeth said. 'I've read about it.' She thought for a moment. Why had she attempted that ridiculous explanation? A single bomb had destroyed a city called Hiroshima, and that was all she could know about it. Goodbye Hiroshima: the American's words made perfect sense, but could be taken no further, since such a thing was beyond understanding. There had been London and Coventry, but that had only been the start. Stalingrad, Hamburg, Stuttgart, Auschwitz, Dresden, Rotterdam, Berlin – there was a long list of names that stood like grave markers, and now there was another, a set of gentle, whispering syllables, far away and brimming with sorrow: Hiroshima, Hiroshima, Hiroshima.

'I'm sorry, Alice, what did you say?'

'We'll go on flying somehow,' Alice said. 'I mean, after the war. Won't we, Lizzie?'

'Of course we will. Think of all the work there'll be for people like us. Goodness, Alice, there's so much to be done! They'll always need aeroplanes, and people to fly them, won't they? What would people do without aeroplanes?'

The ex-prisoners of war were RAF officers, and their newly issued uniforms hung loosely upon them. They looked at their flight crew and one of them said, 'Johnno, get an eyeful of this, and just you remember what you see. This is how it's going to be, post-war. We'll sit back and let the ladies do the driving.'

'Suits me,' the man called Johnno said. 'It doesn't bother me who's in charge. I can find room for a bit of luxury.' He leant on a stick and his eye-sockets were deeply recessed.

'You've had such a tough time, you poor bastard,' one of the others said to him. 'If your kids ask what you did in the war, at least you can say you played a hell of a lot of bridge.'

'And at the end of it some girl picked us up and drove us all the way home,' Johnno said.

'I'm not some girl,' Elizabeth said. 'I'm probably older than you are, and my name is First Officer Bowman.'

The POWs laughed a great deal at this. One cried, 'Put you in your place, Johnno!' Another clapped Johnno on the back and said, 'Never mind, old boy. You've been locked up a long time. You've got a few things to learn about post-war ladies.'

Post-war ladies. She was a lady, of course, but perhaps she was an incomplete lady, an unfinished lady. The person who had learned to fly in 1938 had been a girl, not yet a lady, and in the intervening years she had somehow missed any chance to become one. A lady wore cocktail dresses and had lovely manners. Men sprang to open doors for her, and in the films the screen grew misty when she appeared. She wore a fur coat and high heels, kissed men goodbye at railway stations and had a certain way with a cigarette-holder.

But perhaps that was a *pre-war* lady? Would a post-war lady still have to do those ladylike things? Would she wear high heels as well as flying her aeroplane or whatever she did for a living? Assuming she did something for a living, that is. Assuming she had a job. It would surely be an awful bore if she didn't have anything to do except being married, and had to wear high heels all the time. It was true that she had once waved goodbye to a man at a railway station, but she had never quite kissed him and had never worn high heels. Come to think of it, there were all sorts of ladylike things that she'd never done. Would they be fun? It wasn't awfully clear.

The components of the motorcycle were contained in two ammunition boxes with rope handles. The POWs loaded the boxes into the Anson and when they had finished the American dispatcher arrived with a nun in a black habit. The nun carried a sleeping child.

'I thought you said she was a nurse,' Elizabeth said. 'She looks more like a plain old nun to me.'

'She sure is a nurse,' the dispatcher said, 'and she's a nun too.

A French nun. Speaks no English. Don't ask me why a French nun is going to England with that kid. It's a war. Anything happens. I've learned that much.'

Elizabeth looked at him. 'Four POWs, a child, a French nun, bits of a motorcycle and a sack of mail,' she said. 'Gotcha.'

The dispatcher nodded and Elizabeth began to laugh. After he had stared at her for a while the dispatcher began laughing too. Alice slid open the cockpit window of the Anson, looked out and asked what was so funny.

'Oh Alice, don't ask,' Elizabeth said. She was still laughing. 'I don't know why I'm laughing. It's just – '

'It sure is one helluva crazy thing.' The dispatcher had stopped laughing. He shook his head and looked again at his clipboard. 'Says here that she's a Red Cross nurse. In that get-up? Red Cross? OK, let that go. The motorcycle? Let that go too – some guy wants a souvenir, so what. And the child is a girl. On the list she's 409.'

'409? What do you mean?'

'I guess she's got a name, but I ain't got it here. I just got the number. Child 409, female, accompanied, care of the Red Cross. I never heard of a child with no name before, but I guess no one knows it. Hey, somebody should've asked her name, shouldn't they? A little girl oughta have a proper name.'

They took the nun up the creaky aluminium steps into the Anson and placed the sleeping child in a nest of folded blankets behind the rear seats. Elizabeth showed the nun how to strap herself in. When she had finished the nun crossed herself. 'You don't have to do that,' Elizabeth said. 'You're going to be perfectly safe.'

The nun looked up at her and smiled a broad, vague smile of incomprehension.

'That's it,' the dispatcher said. He was leaning against the edge of the doorway, his arms folded. His legs were so very brown that one kept noticing them, his brown muscular legs and his big hands.

'All loaded up,' he said. 'All present and correct, ma'am.'

'OK, sir,' Elizabeth said, 'Yessir, OK sir, sure thing.'

'Maybe I could look you up, if I ever get to England,' the dispatcher said.

'Look me up? Heaven knows where I'll be. I haven't the faintest idea.' She laughed.

'OK ma'am. But no harm looking to buy a drink for Miss Bowman some day, I guess.' He grinned at her.

'I guess not.'

The dispatcher put his head a little on one side and looked at her. 'Sometimes I can't exactly tell what you mean, you English,' he said.

'I'm sorry – I didn't mean anything in particular.'

'My name's Frank. I'm Frank Oldfield. That's me. If you hear that name sometime, you just remember it's that guy you met in Berlin. Sergeant Eugene Oldfield, US Air Force. I'm Frank, see, but I ain't so old and this here is a field.' He waved his arm at the bustle of Gatow and grinned at her. 'Frank Oldfield. That's me. Easy, ain't it?'

She laughed. 'All right. I'll remember you, Frank.'

'You folks have a good trip.'

The nun watched impassively from the scratched and yellowed window. She was in the hands of God, and all would be well. The yellow, worn grass of the airfield at Gatow behaved as it always does when aero engines begin their bellowing, its separate blades streaming into a blur in the shadow of the Anson's wings. The aircraft lifts at last and a hedge flashes beneath, a burned-out farm, the glimmer of a lake, a wood of larch and beech, a twisting road, a broad river with a raft of geese getting up – and as the aircraft climbs, the frantic pace grows less, the earth steadies, broadens and becomes itself. The aeroplane, launched steady and alone into the limitless space of the sky, makes a slow circle and then another across the vast wreckage of the city, contemplative circles in which to observe the evidence, so that it will be remembered. The two uniformed women sit at the controls and stare down upon victory, and then they turn away towards the west, taking the aeroplane steadily and surely westwards with its cargo of mailbags, motorcycle parts, ex-prisoners, the nun in black and the sleeping child.

Five

Even in 1945 the Avro Anson was an elderly aeroplane. It had a comic look, inspiring in its crews and passengers amused affection. It was sturdy but had little reserve of power. If an engine failed during take-off the Anson struggled to maintain height, let alone climb. But it was stable in flight and its two Cheetah engines were known for their reliability.

The wheels and flaps of this particular Anson have now been raised and its throttles set to cruise. Nicely trimmed, the Anson flies steadily towards Brussels at its most economical speed, one hundred and twenty miles an hour. The journey will take something over four hours. First Officer Bowman has established a compass course that allows for the effect of a light south-westerly wind. She has ensured that the aircraft and its engines are functioning normally. Now she settles back into the worn green leather of the pilot's seat and begins to examine in a systematic way the various sectors of the empty sky.

Accidents, say bar-room philosophers, always have multiple causes, and that's reassuring: at least a crash won't be caused by one or two things going wrong. However, the complexity of an aeroplane means that a number of causes may be present already.

Order always tends towards disorder, and an aeroplane is an extreme example of an ordered system; it follows that flight can only be sustained by extreme discipline on the part of engineers and pilots.

In fact it was the discipline of flight, rather than, say, the grace of a seagull soaring along a cliff, that first caught Elizabeth's attention. Her father had always believed an answer could be found for everything; it only needed common sense, as he often said, and a bit of determination. You had to sit down and work things out, and Lo! all difficulties could be resolved.

Elizabeth loved her father and accepted his philosophy completely. It clearly worked. Ernest was particular and predictable, which was endearing. He caused laughter to echo along the corridors of Rookwood, the secretary's house that stood beside the Long Avenue at Waverley. She'd push up the sash and gaze at the avenue of limes that marched away over the hill, knowing that beyond lay the great house, Waverley, grey and permanent. There was Rookwood, there was the Queen's Ride, there was the folded green of the park, there were the scattered oaks, their lower branches trimmed parallel to the slope by the nibbling of cattle and deer; the air was warm, and behind her, as she gazed from her window, was the trill of Ruth's voice and the deeper sound of her father – her life was ordered and secure, and her father had made it so.

It was getting misty ahead, no doubt of it. Elizabeth nudged the throttles forward and the note of the engines rose a little. Was there something amiss with the port engine? There had been a slight fall in revs, a touch of unevenness. The engine's oil pressure and temperature were perfectly normal. She checked the throttles, then leaned forward and looked out at the engine. There was no sign of oil or smoke. She sat back and looked at Alice, who shook her head and pursed her lips, meaning that the cause of the problem was not obvious and hence no action was possible, but the matter was being watched.

During the winter of 1928, while Rookwood was snowed in and chickenpox required her to stay in bed, the ten-year-old Elizabeth began reading *How Man Conquered the Air*. She already knew, in the uncaring way in which one knows such things, that Orville and Wilbur Wright made the first powered flights at a remote place in America. Now, under the influence of a fever and the enormous snowflakes that were drifting past her window, she discovered the highly rational science of aeronautics. It was created more-or-less from scratch by the Wrights in an extraordinary intellectual effort. The Wrights made the first powered flight because no other result could have crowned such meticulous and determined work. On page 147 of *How Man Conquered the Air* there was the classic photograph by Jacques Henri Lartigue of Wilbur Wright in his baggy cap, expressionless as always, inward, entirely self-possessed; and later that night, as Elizabeth tossed and turned under too many blankets, the hawk-faced man strode through her dreams.

The Wrights succeeded because they had applied their minds unswervingly to the problem, and realised that *control* was the key. They studied birds to find out how they flew in turbulent air, built gliders, made numerous test flights, devised instruments to measure aerodynamic variables, built a wind-tunnel and solved the problem of control by changing the shape of the wings, as birds do. At 10.35 a.m. on 17th December

1903 the Wright Flyer ran smoothly down its launching rail, lifted into the air and flew steadily for twelve seconds, covering a distance of one hundred and twenty feet.

Wilbur knew they would succeed, and had set up a camera. The photograph shows the Wright Flyer four or five feet above the ground, banking slightly to the left. Orville lies prone on its lower wing and Wilbur, having run twenty yards after the machine, is frozen by the camera in a stance that is wonderfully expressive of hope, excitement and anxiety. He is wearing a dark suit, a tie, a baggy cap and black boots, his jacket is flapping open in the breeze and his arms are half-raised.

In the foreground is the outline of the Flyer that was drawn in the sand by the Wrights' footprints as they worked around their aeroplane. Here are some of the simple tools they'd been using – a coil of piano wire, a rickety stool, a long-handled shovel with a heart-shaped blade – an American shovel, a pioneer's shovel.

The child propped the book open on her bedside table. Every time she turns her head the graceful, delicate Flyer is five feet above the earth, turning slightly to the left and departing from this very spot at this very moment. It is not history but reality: the Flyer departs and the child is drawn after it, taken from the earth. Twelve seconds: she counts slowly and watches the Flyer as it floats away across the sand. It straightens, starts to descend, smoothly alights, comes to a halt. Wilbur, clutching his baggy cap to his head, starts to run towards his brother.

Oh yes, it was obvious why the Wrights succeeded. They removed all emotion from their task and applied a ferocious and detailed concentration. It was just the sort of thing that Daddy did. Flight was a wonderful thing, and surely the only thing to do!

There was one small difficulty: there were only a handful of references to women in *How Man Conquered the Air*. The Frenchwoman Raymonde de Laroche was named, and there was a picture of an American journalist called Harriet Quimby, a woman who modelled her own flying suits, whatever that might have to do with it. A Russian princess, Eugenie Shakovskaya, was probably the first female military pilot. Women of society, models and princesses – but that was all.

Clearly, people hadn't yet realised how well matched were women and flying. Sensitivity, intelligence and courage, which flying required, were the natural characteristics of women, were they not?

When her father came to see her that evening Elizabeth sat upright in bed and said, 'Daddy, I would like a model aeroplane.' Her cheeks still pink from fever, she looked at him expectantly.

'Aha,' Ernest Bowman said, looking over the child's head at the photograph of Wilbur Wright. 'A model aeroplane! What an excellent idea! Very well, my darling, I shall see what can be done.' He sat on the bed and held her hand.

'Or possibly a kite,' Elizabeth said, placing one finger on her lips and leaning her head a little sideways, 'very possibly a kite, to start with.'

'A kite can be arranged even more easily,' Ernest Bowman said. 'I shall look into it tomorrow, and I shall explore the possibility of a model aeroplane in due course.'

As he said these words in the measured style that he had developed since his days as a waterman, he had no consciousness – although in view of his philosophy he should have done – that a lever had been pulled and a long chain of events set in motion; he simply felt a pleasurable warmth, thought what a very fortunate man he was and bent forward to kiss his little girl on the top of her hot little head.

*

The following Friday Ernest brought a sizeable box kite home from London and his elder daughter began flying it on Beacon Hill. Now Elizabeth began to discover the live nature of flight. Her kite swooped and soared and tugged ceaselessly at its string, giving the strong impression that it might lift the child from her feet and carry her away – and how would it look, the earth from way up high? Her father and herself, Rookwood, the lake, those tiny workers in the fields, all so very small, and chained to the earth!

It was not long before Elizabeth found out that the tugging of the kite was explained by the laws of aerodynamics. Chapter Two of *How Aeroplanes Fly* said that the lift generated by a wing was proportional not to the airspeed but to its square: in other words, if the wind blew twice as fast the kite tugged four times as hard. How odd. Flying was absolutely logical, but graceful and intriguing too. There seemed no limit to its possibilities. In the course of her reading Elizabeth discovered that a woman pilot was called an *aviatrix*. Well! An aviatrix! There was something deliciously exciting about that word, something nearly wicked.

When Alice returned from checking the comfort of the passengers she leaned against the back of Elizabeth's seat and placed her mouth close to her ear so she could be heard above the steady roar of the engines. 'That girl,' she said.

'The German girl,' Elizabeth said. 'The girl in Berlin, you mean.'

'Yes. The girl at the zoo.'

'Anna, her name was.'

'I've been thinking about her. I feel cross with her.'

'Do you? Why?'

'She still thinks it's our fault. Berlin's smashed to bits and she still doesn't know why.'

'Yes,' Elizabeth said, looking ahead. The western horizon had become less distinct and there was a swirl of cirrus high above. 'You're right. I've been thinking about her too, and the thing is—' She wrinkled her nose, reached forward and tapped the altimeter, which remained steady at five thousand feet.

'What?'

'It's not our fault, of course,' Elizabeth said, 'but it's not hers either.'

Alice considered this unsatisfactory reply. Eventually she said, 'It must be somebody's fault, mustn't it? Not just one person, either. Lots of people, not just Hitler. They let him get away with it. Somebody did.'

'I think the weather's getting worse,' Elizabeth said. 'Look. See that murky stuff ahead?'

'What's the forecast?'

'They say there's a warm front coming in, but it shouldn't be here yet. I think it's all right. We'll be fine as far as Brussels, anyway. We can wait there overnight if we have to, or we can go a bit further south and get round it. Nip across from somewhere south of Calais.'

'All right,' Alice said, and looked at the fuel gauges. 'We've got plenty of fuel at the moment.' She leaned on the back of the seat, looking past Elizabeth at the cloud ahead.

'And there's another thing,' Elizabeth said. 'Exactly *when* could the Germans have stopped him? When was the moment it was possible? And who could have done it? Who? That girl couldn't have done it on her own, could she? I don't see who could have stopped that man.'

'Twenty gallons left in the port outer tank,' Alice said. 'Twenty in the starboard outer tank. The other two are full.' She tapped her teeth with the end of her pencil. 'I don't know who could've stopped him, but somebody should have. That's all I say.'

From time to time the events of Berlin came back into Elizabeth's mind, particularly the girl in the black dress and, for some reason, the American at Gatow, Sergeant Frank Oldfield. She had no idea why she should recall that man – he was just another American, a lively and cheerful man of medium height with sharp creases in his shorts, brown arms and legs, very white teeth, big hands and a dark complexion. He appeared in her memory but she was not touched by him and she would soon send Frank Oldfield into the darkness of forgetting that enclosed all the other young men by whom she had not been touched, these last six years.

In wartime some things must be postponed. Elizabeth considered her attitude entirely rational, a matter of duty and of common sense, as she said when questioned by Ruth or her brother Edmund – not that it was any of their business. Some people seemed to think that a woman who wanted to go flying was a curiosity. An avoidance of affairs with men – not avoidance of men as such, but only of close relations with them – was also considered odd. Pish! Tosh! She looked down at the compass and nudged the Anson a little to the southward.

It is certain that Elizabeth had never considered her own desirability, and was unaware that many men took one look at her and imagined their tongue in her mouth, their hands upon her breasts and so forth. None of these young Englishmen betrayed their imaginings to the young woman herself, since young men of those days did not speak their minds. Their ardour was ultimately feeble and dissembling, and when they got no encouragement they retreated to the far side of the room and stood there, feeling slightly hurt.

During the war, Elizabeth's contacts with the Royal Air Force ensured a continuing supply of interested young men. For male pilots she was an intriguing study – a striking and intelligent woman who could fly and had things to say about flying, just as they did. Wasn't she already, in some sense, one of us? How sympathetic a companion she would be to an airman! What a partner she would be, what a team they could make! A lovely female flyer!

Those young pilots were entranced by her energy, her upright carriage and her graceful nose, but rather too easily daunted. Their lust lacked conviction and their social skills were insufficient to overcome her coolness. They did not consider the meaning of her unavailability and what in consequence might be an effective strategy for its defeat. They were nothing but silly boys, brimming with awkward and short-lived urgency and having no awareness of the importance of the brain in matters of the heart.

Elizabeth would have been dismayed and revolted by a knowledge of the thoughts she stimulated, yet the knowledge would have confirmed to her something that she believed to be the truth: passion must be contained. Oh, very well, she might have admitted, there could be a place for passion of a sort, at some future time, in the context of marriage, babies and all that sort of thing – but here and now, passion must be contained.

The air was still and smooth. The Anson's engines, reliably humming, drew the landscape of Germany slowly beneath the aeroplane until the ruins of Hanover lay before them.

Given the good visibility, the navigational work was simple.

The traditional method was to follow a railway, keeping an eye on the compass so that a branch line isn't taken in error. After several collisions early in the war, pilots were ordered to fly not along the centreline of a railway but some distance off to the right, and that is what Elizabeth did. Alice, meanwhile, had moved from her flight engineer's seat into the rear of the aeroplane.

As for that Sergeant whatshisname, he was surely no different from all the other young men who had ever looked in Elizabeth's direction – except, of course, that he was an American, and Americans seemed a little different. There was something fresh about them, fresh and simple and cheerful, like children. They looked at you in a straightforward way, and talked as if they had no secrets.

Elizabeth's commitment to celibacy rested on a single piece of adult experience and a minor event that happened in her childhood.

Five years previously, in the summer of 1940, she had met an unusually persistent young fighter pilot and eventually agreed to a day at the seaside. She put on a pretty dress, one of those simple flowery prints with a wide skirt that she preferred, and caught a train to Margate. There she met the young man – he was a fighter pilot called Tom Anderson – and they had shaken hands. He said it was very nice to see her, and he liked her dress. He bought her an ice-cream on the promenade and strolled along in a white open-necked shirt, looking friendly and at ease.

They talked with increasing eagerness about all sorts of things – about flying, of course, about books they liked, and in particular about the French writer and aviator Antoine de St-Exupéry, whose best-known book on flying is called in French

Terre des hommes and in English – so much more appositely, they both agreed – *Wind, Sand and Stars*.

After lunch and a good deal more conversation Tom escorted her back to the railway station. She departed, waving and smiling from the window as the train drew away, and three days later a lifeboat's crew pulled the boy's body from the English Channel.

His brother had given her the news. William Anderson, Tom's identical twin, walked into the ATA office at Hamble on a misty Monday evening like his brother's ghost; the instant she caught sight of William she knew the whole truth.

As he was leaving, William had asked her if she wished to see the body.

'No,' Elizabeth said, 'no, I certainly don't want to see him, and I will not see him.'

There could be no reason whatsoever to see the body, nor to see his brother again, nor to make contact with anyone who knew him, or might have known him, or was likely to remind her of him, no reason whatsoever.

Tom Anderson proved her case. First of all, there was hardly anything between the two of them; it had been a matter of a few conversations and a day out. There was absolutely nothing between them, and yet, when she heard a rumour that pilots had been lost from his squadron, she had been disturbed. When a day had gone by, and another, without word, she could not sleep. This had eventually to be admitted. And when they found him, and William told her – then she wished she had been with Tom, and had died with him. For two days and a night she sat alone on the floor of her room, crying, hugging her knees and rocking herself. It was the next thing to insanity.

What more proof could one have of the appalling wrongness of her lapse?

It was a simple failure of self-control. The dead boy had been one she hardly knew, yet her command of herself had been utterly lost. And it could have been worse: had they been in love, had they been married – no, don't even think of that. As it was, the thing had been unbearable. No, again the thought was wrong, for she *had* borne it, the disappearance of that boy, and it was therefore bearable. But she would endure no more grief of that kind.

That was the beginning and end of it. She closed iron shutters on the memory of Tom Anderson, shutters that seemed in her mind's eye like the tall doors of an aircraft hangar rolling heavily together, securing that elegantly strolling young man in silence and the dark.

From that time onwards Elizabeth avoided ferrying fighter aircraft. She never took a job that involved that boy's squadron. She neither read nor answered the two letters that arrived during the following year from his brother William Anderson, well-meaning though they probably were. In such a way did she recover from her error, and get back to normal, and come once again to see herself as her own person, completely in charge, at nobody's bidding.

That single lapse was the rock upon which Elizabeth's attitude to men was built. On its own it was incontrovertible proof of the correctness of her position. But there were other arguments that she positioned around herself like the wooden shores and braces supporting a bomb-damaged house. To fall in love in wartime was an obvious dereliction of duty. It could be nothing but weakness to abandon oneself to someone's consoling arms. Indisputably, love diverted one's attention from matters more vital; one only had to ask oneself why Tom

Anderson died precisely as he did, casually and alone. Why had she herself, only the day before he was lost, strayed fifty miles off course into a dead-end valley in the Black Mountains, nearly coming to disaster on a straightforward trip that she had done twenty times before?

The simple answer was that she had set the compass but forgotten to lock it, and the grid had jiggled twenty degrees from the correct course. But why had she forgotten? Why had she not noticed the error? These were elementary mistakes, stupid mistakes, the sort she never made. She ought to have checked the compass, she ought to have noticed the rising ground, the altered angle of the sun. It was incredible that she had not noticed these things, and it proved she had been in a romantic daze.

And so must he have been, that boy, at the instant the enemy fighter fell upon him, the fighter he had not seen. They had brought their fate upon themselves, she and Tom. It was blindingly obvious: you can make love or you can make war, but they don't go together. She had weakened, and let herself go, and for a moment had allowed herself to think that she might, in time, come to care for him; and therefore he had died, therefore she had lost him for ever.

Midday, and the Anson was over the Ruhr. This river valley had received the most relentless bombing of the whole war. Dortmund, Essen, Duisberg, Düsseldorf: the ruins clustered together across hills and valleys, a green landscape painted grey with destruction for mile upon mile.

Alice tapped Elizabeth on the shoulder and offered her a cup of coffee. 'You take her for a minute, Alice,' Elizabeth said, and held the controls steady while Alice slid into the pilot's seat. 'The course is two fifty. Just follow the railway. Keep an eye on the port engine. It lost a few revs a little while ago.'

'I know,' Alice said. 'I've got some sweets in my bag. You could take some to the little girl. She's awake now.'

The child was on the nun's lap, enclosed within the overlapping black folds of her habit. The ex-prisoners were playing gin rummy, somewhat hindered by the racket of the engines and the unsociable arrangement of the Anson's seats. The man called Johnno, the tall POW with the walking stick, put up his hand as Elizabeth went by and asked how long it would be to Brussels. Although his question was yelled against the noise of the engines, its tone contained an apology for their previous jokes. Putting her arm across his shoulder, Elizabeth bent down and said in his ear, 'Only an hour or so. The old Anson's a bit slow, but it gets there in the end.'

The man's right hand lay in his lap. His fingers were all bone and sinew. The detail of his wrist showed through skin that was translucent, as if he were a man of eighty, yet he couldn't be much more than twenty-five. Oddly, for a man only just free from prison, he smelled very clean.

There was a pause and then Johnno turned his head close to her ear and said, smiling in an embarrassed kind of way, 'Wright's Coal Tar. I expect that's what you can smell. They gave us all a bar of it when they let us out. Perhaps they thought it would help with the lice.'

How odd to have been a prisoner of war for so long, locked up for years while the war was fought elsewhere by other people. How irrelevant he would feel in England, amid the flags and parades. Elizabeth reached down and touched his hand. 'My mother always used Coal Tar,' she said.

Indeed her mother, Frances Bowman, had always preferred the most ferocious of household materials – carbolic acid, bleach, salt, blue bags, vinegar, wire wool and scrubbing brushes made of proper hog-bristles. Frances liked Wright's Coal Tar because its pungency told her it was a stalwart opponent of germs and because it enabled her, by sniffing her children, to discover whether they had recently washed.

Elizabeth straightened and patted the man on the shoulder. He looked up and said, 'It's going to be so funny, you know, going home after all this time.'

'Yes,' she said. 'It certainly is.'

There was no more to say about that. She turned away from him. The child was awake and had been looking out of the window, but watched her as she approached. She was perhaps five years old. Elizabeth sat down in the adjoining seat and leaned towards the child. 'Hello,' she said, smiling, 'I hope you're all right.'

The girl remained expressionless and said nothing, just looking at her for several seconds, then she reached out both arms in the powerful appeal of a child who must be picked up and comforted. But the nun's hands grasped her waist and drew her down, and the nun's face, enclosed in the shadow of her wimple, bent over the girl. The child was her property.

There was a remarkable watchfulness about that little girl, Elizabeth saw. She held out one of Alice's mints but the child did not reach for it; instead, she continued to look at Elizabeth as if making an assessment.

'I tell you what,' Elizabeth said, 'I'll leave the sweets here and you can have them when I've gone.' She stood up, and the nun and the child watched as she arranged a small heap of sweets on the seat and walked away towards the cockpit.

Perhaps the nameless girl would live to a great age, and would remember the handful of sweets that lay on the worn leather, trembling with the fine vibrations of the aeroplane. Perhaps, when she thought of the sweets, the old woman would hear the steady humming of the Anson's engines and recall the face of the uniformed woman who had given them to her, the woman for whom she reached but was prevented.

It's curious, the question of memory. There seems no logic in the choices it makes to recall or not to recall, and there's little logic, either, in the power that a particular memory may possess. Something entirely trivial, worked upon by a restless mind, may be more damaging than pain that was real, and has been endured.

In addition to the death of Tom Anderson, there was another factor in Elizabeth's determined solitariness. In childhood she had got into the habit of sleeping with her right thumb in her mouth and the fingers of her left hand pressed between her labia; in that position she felt utterly secure, and it was for years a happy and innocent secret.

Until, one hot summer morning, she awoke late, having thrown off her pyjamas and bedsheets in the night, to find her brother standing over her. A glance at his face discovered, amazingly, some sort of guilt. She yelled at Edmund and he ran from the room. She dressed and went downstairs. At the breakfast table Edmund's head was bent over his cereal. Frances angled her head for a kiss.

'Darling,' Frances said, sniffing as usual, 'you haven't washed, I think.'

Elizabeth went back upstairs, her body on fire. Her mother, following her into the bathroom, said, 'Elizabeth dear, you shouldn't touch yourself, you know. It'll give you an infection, a fungus.'

Into Elizabeth's mind came an image of the yellow-brown bracket fungus that she had often encountered in the woods behind the house, a discoloured and swelling form that might somehow become rooted in her own delicate folds, and with the image of the fungus came the memory of a stench and something dripping.

'Come down quickly, won't you, darling,' her mother said, 'have a proper wash and then come along down.'

When, a year later, dark liquid began to leak from her, it was a confirmation of her sinfulness. Her mother, with her own obsession and a few unthinking words, had created an anxiety that took root, and flourished.

'We've certainly lost a few revs on the port engine,' Alice said. 'Just an oily plug, I expect. I'll check them at Brussels. And look, you're right, the murk's got a lot thicker now.'

'The front's coming in,' Elizabeth said. 'But it's not supposed to have got this far.'

She changed places with Alice, settled into the seat, scanned the instruments and looked ahead. The horizon was now blurred, and overhead some wispy cloud had drawn a halo round the sun. Elizabeth had seen the synoptic chart and it was all obvious enough. Above the North Sea a quantity of warm, damp air from the Azores had collided with cold, dry air from the polar region, forming the sloping wedge of cloud that is called a warm front. It curved north for three hundred miles. At its eastern edge, seven or eight miles above the Anson, the warm air had merely scribbled a few mares' tails, feathery and insubstantial. In the centre of the North Sea the cloud was lower and had thickened into stratus, a grey, solid blanket. Still further westward the cloud had become nimbus, thick and black, from which rain fell heavily. A rising wind had begun to draw lines of foam along the surface of the sea.

'Brussels is only a few miles ahead,' Elizabeth said. 'We'll get there well before the weather closes in.'

Alice nodded without looking up. She was writing in her logbook again, noting the time, their current course and speed, the quantities of fuel remaining in each of the aircraft's tanks and the continuing slight roughness of the port engine.

For a moment Elizabeth watched Alice as she sucked her pencil, bending over her work. On their first flight together Alice's measured carefulness had been immediately reassuring; now it was one of the things for which Elizabeth loved her, and it had several times saved them from harm.

'Look,' Elizabeth said, and Alice glanced up. 'There it is. Next stop Brussels.'

The city lay ahead. Four hours had passed, and five hundred miles. The compass and the railway had guided them safely. The clouds, though they had closed darkly overhead, had caused no difficulty. The Anson, that small, elderly aeroplane, descended towards Brussels and from the airfield a green lamp flashed, inviting it to land.

Six

In the early 1930s, seated in my grandfather's chair, I too became interested in flight. Of course I did: flight was impossible to avoid. Everyone said we were at the start of the Air Age. Record-breakers set off daily for every corner of the earth. Sir Alan Cobham's Flying Circus performed to enormous crowds. The newspapers showed celebrities posing on the flimsy steps that would transport them from gloomy Croydon to delicious Cannes, seductive Rome. I read about the journeys of the solo flyers to Cape Town, Delhi and Darwin and heard again my grandfather's breathy whisper: wasn't this the way to meet the maharajahs and their mahouts? I was not in the least interested in the aeroplane as an object. Flight eliminated distance and time: that was the point of it. As far as I could see, the course of the Air Age was perfectly predictable. Flight was next to godliness, unsullied by the earth. It would enable greater understanding between peoples. It would bring sweetness and light into the darkest corners of the world. It would enable mankind to take off, soar ever upward and become free. I was an impressionable boy.

The advertised benefits, in comparison, appeared prosaic. It was claimed that flight would be convenient. It would save a good deal of waiting about. Soon, very soon, everybody would have an aeroplane and could nip down to Cornwall for the weekend. There were pictures of the new machines in every magazine and newspaper – an aeroplane in flight, in an ordinary garage (its delicate wings neatly folded), or being towed along a road by what was always described as 'an average-sized family car'.

An aeroplane was something that all of us would surely own. That was the accepted view, and one with which, I discovered, my father agreed. In the summer of 1938, on the occasion of my eighteenth birthday, he gave to Gerald and myself a de Havilland Gipsy Moth.

Even in a privileged family an aeroplane was a remarkable present. Lord Waverley was not noted for qualities of generosity or imagination, nor had he previously shown much love for his second son, whose inwardness constantly got under his skin. 'Don't be shy, boy,' he'd say sharply when I stood speechless before a visitor. Maybe, as far as I was concerned, the Gipsy Moth was to be understood as a bribe, a once-and-for-all reminder of the benefits of wealth and of the consequent need to do one's duty as prescribed. Or, of course, it is quite possible that father expected the opportunity to be grasped only by my brother Gerald – the horsey one, the rugby player, the motorist, the sportsman.

Gerald took one look at the Moth and said, 'You'll not get me up in that contraption.' That must have been a blow for father, and his second error was to underestimate the potential of flight to inspire a dreamer such as myself. In essence, the business of the aeroplane went all wrong for St John Beevor, poor man.

*

The de Havilland Gipsy Moth is a famous aeroplane. Amy Johnson's *Jason*, in which she became the first woman to fly alone from England to Australia, was a Gipsy Moth, and the type was used by several other record-breakers of those days – Francis Chichester, for instance, and Bert Hinkler. It was a simple, strong and reliable biplane with two seats in separate open cockpits. It flew slowly but competently and could be maintained with simple equipment. It was pretty. Our Gipsy Moth had been painted red and silver.

They were very light, those old aeroplanes, and seemingly fragile: on a breezy day the Moth quivered and rocked on its wheels as if eager to spring into the air. I walked twice round it to establish that it was not a mirage, and it was not; indeed, father had already got Hawkins secretly to put up a wooden hangar on the edge of the Forty Acre Meadow. Later that same day, with some ceremony, Hawkins hoisted an orange windsock to the top of a tall pole. Lessons had been booked for Gerald and myself at the London Aeroplane Club. I took a photograph of the Moth in front of the hangar, had it framed and hung it in my room. From time to time I would glance up at the picture and remember with joy that the Moth was real.

As soon as I tried it, I discovered, to my delight, that I had some aptitude for flying. The weather was good and I could fly almost every day; in three weeks I had gone solo. Gerald, pushed firmly into the air by father, found himself staggering about in a most precarious fashion. His hands, it seemed, were too large and too strong for the Moth, his thinking somehow unsympathetic; in attempting to learn the important business of landing, he broke several undercarriage struts and three tail skids. He could never remember to observe the way the wind was blowing, a fault that eventually caused him to splinter a propeller in a hawthorn hedge. At that point our instructor advised Gerald to discontinue his lessons, which he immediately did.

I saw that this might cause father to recoup his investment by selling the aeroplane, so I proposed to Gerald that he should keep quiet about his failure and I would serve as his aerial chauffeur, taking him in speed and style to social engagements and to the races. He gave me a great clout on the back and said it was a capital notion. I, of course, did not mind those taxi duties in the least, since they were a useful way of increasing my experience.

What is more attractive, for a young person of a solitary and whimsical inclination, than solo flight? Love? Possibly. Music or poetry? Maybe. I can think of nothing to compare with flight, as it was in those far-off times. It wasn't just the flying, it was the whole damn thing. A very early morning in summer, say, walking down to the hangar in Forty Acre through a light mist, the morning beautiful with birdsong. Or – I can find a hundred examples – let's say a late afternoon in winter, coming home very low to keep out of the cloud, low and flat across the lake, throttle back and into the field with a foot to spare over the fence, heart beating. Alone in the rustling hangar at night, working with an electric lamp among the shadows, preparing the Moth for the following day. Flying high in the evening, still in sunshine while darkness creeps across the ground below and you watch the lights going on, one and then another, another.

Standing high upon the aeroplane's nose, pumping fuel into the tank with a hand-pump, a chamois leather for a filter, the stink of petrol in your nose and the possibility of fire in your mind – oh, all those things and dozens more.

Perhaps the rumours of war made the experience more intense; yes, perhaps so, perhaps so. Rearmament had begun. Diplomatic activity was intense. I felt I must fly at every opportunity, as if I knew that the miracle must end one day, and that it would be soon.

I soon understood, of course, that the Moth was another grandfather's chair, another solitary place upon high, one that was several orders higher, more solitary, more majestic, than I had known before. I felt at once diminished and ennobled by the vastness of the sky and my height above the earth. On a clear day, flying high and banking the Moth into a gentle turn, I was sometimes uncertain whether it was I or the earth that had gently leaned, and was now slowly rotating.

On another summer morning, having taken Gerald to Fontwell Park, I was doing a circuit before landing in the Forty Acre when I saw Elizabeth waving from the gate at the end of the meadow. I landed, taxied to the hangar and switched off the engine. It was delightfully quiet. A lovely day, clouds of gnats, a skylark pouring down its song and a pretty girl waving and smiling – it is, in hindsight, a predictable formula; but since her father died we had seldom spoken, and our first conversation was tentative.

'You didn't tell me you'd got an aeroplane,' she said, running her hand along the leading edge of the wing. She was twenty years old at the time, a young woman with dark hair and a nose that was perhaps a little too big, a distinctive girl but not conventionally beautiful, and wearing a cotton dress printed with yellow and blue flowers.

I laughed and said, mock formally, 'I'm quite sure you knew all about it, Miss Bowman.'

She scanned the aeroplane, assessing it. She had a very direct way of looking at things which she also applied, disconcertingly, to people. 'Yes, I did, of course,' she said. 'It's a good choice, a Gipsy Moth.'

I was surprised by her knowledgeable tone. I knew that she was now a typist, and worked at some factory nearby. It had not occurred to me that she might have any knowledge of flying.

'You perhaps don't know,' Elizabeth said, 'that I work at de Havilland's. I'm a typist in the sales office. To be precise, your Moth is a DH60 Gipsy Moth with the hundred horsepower engine. Amy Johnson flew hers to Australia in nineteen and a half days. I've seen lots of them in photographs and a good many on the airfield. I know all about Amy Johnson and Jim Mollison and all the rest of them.'

'Well, goodness me,' I said. 'You're quite right.'

She said, 'There's quite a family of DH Moths now, isn't there? Hornet Moth, Tiger Moth, Puss Moth.'

She spoke with easy confidence and I heard myself saying, 'If you know such a lot about aeroplanes, why don't you learn to fly? I could teach you.'

Elizabeth immediately said, 'Oh yes, I was going to ask you that. Will you really teach me? That would be terrific fun!'

That was how it began.

Flying was virtually unregulated in those days. One simply took to the air. I didn't even think to ask her mother's permission. We began that same day. I refilled the fuel tank, then got Elizabeth to help. We lifted the Moth's tail and turned her round to face the grass strip.

Elizabeth was wearing only that short-sleeved cotton dress with its pattern of small flowers. I lent her my sheepskin jacket and a spare helmet and goggles. 'You sit in the front,' I said.

'I know that,' she said, and climbed on the wing root and stood beside the front cockpit.

'The Moth's got dual controls,' I said. 'You can fly her from either cockpit.' I started to show her how the stick and rudder worked.

'I know that too,' she said. 'I've read a lot about flying, you know.'

'Have you,' I said. 'Jolly good.' I was a very young man and had myself only just learned to fly. I knew you couldn't possibly learn about flying from books.

'That's the airspeed indicator,' Elizabeth said, pointing at it. 'That's the altimeter, there's the turn-and-slip, the oil pressure gauge, the rev counter.'

She knew a few basic things, I had to admit, the sort of thing one can pick up easily enough from photographs and magazines.

'I'll take you up this once,' I said, 'but if you're going to do any more flying with me you'll certainly need a proper flying suit. In the meantime you'll have to make sure your dress doesn't get tangled with the joystick. Watch out for the wind – it'll swirl all round the cockpit. You'll have to pull your skirt up and tuck the ends underneath so it doesn't flap about. There's not a lot of room to move around. Don't step on anything except the seat or the floor, or you'll break something.'

It was rare for me to say so much at once, and in such a tone. When I thought about it later I was amused at the manner I adopted, but it didn't put her off. I gave her my jacket, helmet and goggles. She put the jacket on, climbed into the front cockpit and slid down into the seat.

'I see what you mean,' she said, pulling up her skirt and tucking it under her bottom. In those days girls rarely showed their legs, of course, and I could tell she didn't much care for me looking at her. Trying to be businesslike, I leaned into the cockpit and showed her how to fasten the Sutton harness.

'You have to keep those straps as tight as you can,' I said. 'We don't want you falling out if we hit a bump.'

'Don't be silly,' she said, tightening the strap of the helmet, 'of course I won't fall out. You don't have to make a fuss about me, you know.'

I always smile when I think of her intent expression, her concentration on the instruments and controls, the way she wriggled in the seat to get comfortable. She looked somewhere between enchanting and absurd. There was a light scent of something, perhaps talcum powder, perhaps some kind of cologne. Her skirt was rolled up of course, so her legs were bare, and she was wearing my fur-lined jacket and the spare helmet, both of them far too big for her.

'I'll show you how to put the goggles on,' I said.

She took no notice, putting them on herself and turning to face me. 'There you are,' she said. 'Will that do?'

'Very good,' I said, keeping a straight face. The oversize helmet, the enormous goggles and her lovely nose made her look like an owl – no, not an owl, something more hawkish than that.

'What's the matter?' she said, putting her head on one side and looking even more birdlike.

'Nothing at all,' I said. 'Everything's absolutely perfect.'

'Good,' she said. 'I had an idea you might think I looked funny.'

'Heaven forbid,' I said. 'Now listen carefully, Elizabeth. I'll explain exactly what we're going to do, because it'll be too noisy to talk when we're in the air.'

She slid the goggles up and looked attentive. I gave her a little talk about not fiddling with any of the instruments or controls, and then began to tell her what was going to happen.

'After I've started the engine we'll wait for a minute or two until it's warmed up, then we'll take off and climb straight ahead. When we're high enough I'll fly in a big square, doing some gentle turns so you can look at the view and get used to it.'

She wrinkled her brow. 'The turns don't have to be *too* gentle, you know.'

'It's always best for a beginner to start gently,' I said, with all the authority of my thirty hours.

'Can't we do a loop?'

'No,' I said. 'Certainly not.' I didn't tell her that I hadn't yet done a loop myself; I was still more-or-less a novice.

'Show me everything,' she said. 'I want to know how it all works. Everything.'

The Moth was not fitted with an electric starter, so someone had to swing the propeller by hand. It's always tricky, starting an engine on your own. The throttle has to be set just right, otherwise the aeroplane can jump forward, knock you down and run away across the airfield, possibly even into the air. If the aeroplane begins to move and the pilot can't get back into his seat – well, the risk is obvious.

I didn't tell Elizabeth any of that. I showed her the throttle and the magneto switches and told her that I would swing the prop myself.

'I'll start her up and climb in afterwards. If she starts moving before I get in, you just shut the throttle and switch off the magnetos. It's quite simple.'

She seemed pleased to be entrusted with this responsibility, and worked the throttle once or twice to get the hang of it.

'When we've flown around for a few minutes I'll give you a shout,' I said, 'and then you can follow what I'm doing with the stick and rudder. Put your hands on the controls but don't hold them tightly. Just follow the movements and feel what happens.'

It all went perfectly. The engine started easily, and when it was warmed up I took off across the long diagonal of the Forty Acre. I levelled out at fifteen hundred feet and flew round Waverley so that she could have a good look. It was a calm evening, the air smooth, an ideal moment for a first flight, and the house looked wonderfully elegant from the air, so serene and eternal beside the lake. After a few minutes I called out, 'Are you all right?'

Elizabeth twisted round and looked at me with a huge grin. 'It's terrific,' she yelled. 'It's marvellous! I love it!'

'Put your hands and feet on the controls.'

She did so, and I flew a few gentle S-turns, feeling a slight resistance as she followed the movement of the stick and rudder.

'Now you try,' I shouted. 'Just keep her going straight and level.'

She tucked her head down, her concentration obvious from the tension at the back of her neck. For a few minutes the aeroplane flew reasonably straight, then I told her to do a turn to the left. That was more difficult, but she got the hang of it after one or two dips and wobbles.

'That's enough,' I called out. 'Hands off now.'

She shook her head and shouted, 'Just one more minute!'

The Moth went into a gentle turn to the right, straightened, turned to the left, then straightened again. 'Hooray!' she shouted, sticking both arms in the air and surrendering the aeroplane to me.

I opened the throttle, flew some steepish turns and then went fast and low past the house, across the lake and back into the Forty Acre. It wasn't a bad landing. In those days I didn't always get it right, but that one was fine. I taxied back to the hangar and switched off.

Elizabeth was singing to herself. I did not recognise the song. She was not a very good singer. We climbed out and I said, 'There you are. I hope you enjoyed that.'

She pulled off her helmet. 'I loved it,' she said. 'You know that perfectly well. Will you really teach me to fly? I can pay for it. Well, I can pay for the petrol. Some of it, anyway. I'll save up.'

'I can't teach you properly,' I said. 'You'll need a proper instructor, and if you want to get a licence, you'll have to join a flying club and take proper lessons. I can give you an idea of the basics, though.'

She was fiddling with her dress, which had got tangled up. Eventually she got it straight and looked up at me.

'I want to learn to fly,' she said. 'There's nothing I want more. I could learn a lot from you. I know I could. Couldn't we have another go tomorrow?'

I laughed. 'No, we can't,' I said. 'I'm busy.' I wanted a bit of breathing space.

'The next time, then. Whenever you next want to go flying.' She was looking at me very directly and was quite impossible to resist.

I said firmly, 'You'll have to wait until next weekend.'

She took a step nearer and I thought for a moment she was going to kiss me.

'Thank you so much,' she said. 'That was lovely. I really do want to learn to fly, you know. I've been thinking about it for years. Whenever you want to go flying, just come and get me.'

I felt an extraordinary tension at that moment. My feelings were enhanced by flight, perhaps, and subject to the lingering elation that always follows flight. No doubt there is an element of relief in that feeling; as I stepped down from an aeroplane I always noticed the remarkable solidity of the ground beneath my feet, the softness of the wind against my face and the sound of birdsong, somehow more musical than usual. And in this case there was a girl before me, a girl I thought remarkable.

She had turned away and was examining the tailplane of the Moth. She's in love with my aeroplane, I thought. It made me laugh, and she turned and looked enquiringly at me.

'I was just thinking,' I said, 'How very much you like aeroplanes, and how unusual that is, particularly—'

I hesitated, and she said, 'Particularly for a girl.'

'Yes.'

'Before long, it won't be at all unusual. Besides, look at Amy Johnson. Look at Amelia Earhart.' She looked at me in a considering sort of way. 'And another thing,' she went on, 'what shall I call you? Shall I call you Mr Charles, like my father used to?'

'Don't be silly,' I said, 'you can call me Charles. Call me whatever you like.'

'Charles sounds rather formal,' she said. 'Would you mind if I called you Charlie? You can call me Lizzie. Everyone does.'

Of course I did not mind what she called me, and we were Charlie and Lizzie from then on.

On the following Saturday Elizabeth turned up at the Forty Acre with a proper pilot's logbook, a helmet and some white cotton overalls that said 'de Havilland Aeroplane Company' across the shoulders. We flew for two hours and climbed to four thousand feet, moderately high by the standards of the time. Elizabeth flew the Moth for more than an hour.

When we landed she was shivering. 'How annoying,' she said. 'These overalls are quite hopeless. I shall take them back and see if I can get a proper furry flying suit like yours. Can we go to Margot's and have some tea? I need to warm up.'

I drove her down to the village and we sat in the sunny garden at the back of Margot's teashop.

'Tomorrow,' Elizabeth said, folding her hands carefully round her teacup, 'I shall bring some better clothes and a pair of gloves. We could go to another aerodrome, couldn't we? I mean somewhere we could land. A proper journey to somewhere and back.'

I thought for a minute, then suggested Cambridge. I had been there with my instructor on practice cross-country flights, and knew the way. It was only thirty-five miles, a half-hour flight.

Elizabeth put down her cup and clapped her hands. 'Oh yes! Cambridge! That's wonderful! Let's look at the map at once!'

Elizabeth's sudden joy was always delightful. She was not an extrovert, but at times she allowed herself to be vivid and naïve, and there was something enormously attractive about that.

The flight to Cambridge went well, despite its being a cold and cloudy day. My navigation skills were not particularly well developed, but I managed to follow the A10 up to Royston and the railway from there into Cambridge. We turned a few circles to look at the colleges and then landed at the airfield. Elizabeth still had no proper flying clothes and was again cold, so I put my jacket round her.

'Next weekend,' she said, 'we could go to Oxford, which would be sort of symmetrical, and that would put another aerodrome in my nice new logbook, wouldn't it?'

We took a cab into the town. She protested, but I bought her a decent pair of leather gloves and a big red woollen jumper to wear under her flying suit. On the way back in the cab I reached for her hand. It was still cold.

She turned to me and said, 'Now look, Charlie, you're being very generous, teaching me to fly and giving me things. But we mustn't get muddled, must we? You're being a wonderful friend, but you've got another life, haven't you? And I'm not part of that.'

I let go of her hand. 'I was just seeing if your hands were still cold,' I said. 'I don't see what's muddled about that.'

'Oh,' she said, 'oh, Charlie, I'm sorry. I just thought—'

'Well, you shouldn't think anything of the sort,' I said.

Of course she was quite right, and I had reached for her hand because I saw an excuse to hold it. I don't quite know why I had denied it; perhaps it was instinctive, a way of defending myself, or perhaps I hoped she would feel that she had over-reacted. If so, it achieved nothing – she didn't clasp my hand in remorse. Odd that one should still remember such a tiny moment. Odd, too, that I was so fearfully tentative with her. I may have been shy, but I knew other girls, and was perfectly at ease with them – or was I? No, perhaps I wasn't. It's hard to know, after all these years.

We never did go to Oxford, but in the next few weekends we flew west as far as Plymouth, and east to the Wash and Great Yarmouth. By that time Elizabeth had a proper Sidcot suit, complete with fur-lined boots, and was proof against any weather. Twice we went to the races, but she grew bored when we were away from the aeroplane, and she disliked having to dress up for the members' enclosure. Small talk was not to her liking, and consequently one or two acquaintances of mine thought her rude and unsophisticated. If she wasn't interested in the conversation she'd fidget, looking up at the sky. She was reading books on aerodynamics and meteorology and wanted to talk about cold fronts, aspect ratios and drag coefficients. At Newbury, between the two-fifteen and the three o'clock, I could see that she was mentally classifying the clouds, looking upwards and murmuring their names to herself.

I presume she simply had no idea how much tension she induced in me. She was utterly different from all the young women I knew – girls who knew all about flirting, who could make entertaining small talk and would laugh delightfully at a man's jokes. One did not flirt with Elizabeth. When somebody tried it, she gave them a blank, puzzled stare.

One Saturday I took her to the flying club at Panshanger. From my point of view that was a mistake. She was flying the Moth most of the time by now, even doing some of the take-offs and landings – that was quite improper, of course, but she was persuasive, and had shown herself to be a capable and confident pilot, or so it seemed to me. When she was flying I kept an eye on the instruments and found that the slip needle always stayed in the middle. That's a good sign. She flew neatly. She didn't skid and stagger about the sky as do many beginners.

At Panshanger I met my old instructor, Jim Taggart. The club had just got hold of a Miles Magister for a trial – it had recently been adopted by the RAF as a training aircraft. Compared with my Gipsy Moth, the Magister was a racy, modern machine, a monoplane. Of course Elizabeth immediately wanted to fly it, and Jim gave her a ten-minute trip. Afterwards I found them talking eagerly together.

She turned to me and said, 'Jim's going to teach me to fly properly! Isn't that terrific? He's going to do it for a special rate. I'm going to join the London Aeroplane Club and get a licence.'

'That's lovely, Elizabeth,' I said. 'That's really good. Well done, Jim, old chap.'

She looked at me and touched my arm. It was a great opportunity for her, and I understood perfectly.

*

There was a fork in the road then. I was unable to avoid it, since her mind was not on me but on flight. We flew together only once more that year, and then the mists and shortening days of November put an end to it. Apart from a couple of racing acquaintances – people of no importance – nobody knew about our flying. But I possess no memories more vivid than that of Elizabeth in her cotton dress, wearing my flying helmet and those enormous goggles, turning round and grinning at me above Waverley on a sunny day more than sixty years ago.

Seven

The Anson had been refuelled and Alice was again working on the port engine. The passengers and their pilot sat on folding chairs in a brick hut, drinking tea. The nun, in a corner of the room, held the child on her lap.

'If the engine's all right and the weather allows, we'll go straight on to England this afternoon,' Elizabeth said. 'We'll nip across Kent and straight up to White Waltham.'

'Kent? I was stationed there in the early days,' said the man called Johnno. '1940 and all that.' He laughed.

Elizabeth sipped her tea.

'They were an awfully good bunch of chaps,' Johnno said. 'We did the daftest things. Wonderful types. Awfully amusing. Tremendous spirit in the squadron in those days. I often wonder how many of them made it through the war.'

He stopped talking and nobody said anything. In a moment he started again.

'In the camps they never told us anything about that sort of thing. Oh, we got letters of course, but all the interesting stuff was cut out. Names and whatnot. Battles. The censors always cut the names out. I never quite understood why they did that, myself. We got the news on the wireless of course, but we didn't get the details. One of our chaps made the wireless. Clever bloke, he was. Rose. His name was Rose. Ernie Rose. He escaped, you know. I think it was in 1943, just before Christmas. We didn't hear any more about him. I expect we'll find out when we get home.'

Johnno paused again, and then said, 'It's amazing what happens. I can't imagine what things will be like in England.' He looked down at the concrete floor and nodded to himself. 'They picked me out of the sea, you know. A German launch, it was. Terrifically fast. They hooked me up with a boathook, took me straight ashore and banged me up. It turned out to be five years without the option.'

He laughed again in his sharp way, then looked up at Elizabeth. 'I say, I'm terribly sorry. I'm talking too much. I've noticed I do that. I do talk a lot. It's a habit I've got into. Blame it on the Jerries.' He laughed again, smiling at her and nodding his head.

'That's quite all right,' Elizabeth said. Through the window she saw Alice waving to her. 'Excuse me,' she said, 'I'm wanted.'

The wind was strong and gusting now, and there was a trace of rain in the air. Alice had removed the cowlings from the Anson's engine so that she could get at the fuel pipes and electrical cables.

'I've checked the fuel pump, the filters and the plugs,' she said. 'I've been right through the electrics and tested the magnetos. I can't find anything wrong. I've changed a couple of plugs that didn't look so good. We'll just run it up and make sure.'

Elizabeth watched from the pilot's seat as Alice stood beside the engine, her overalls flapping in the chilly wind. They ran the engine for several minutes at slow speed to warm it up, then Alice stepped back and Elizabeth opened it up to full power. By wartime standards the Cheetah wasn't a large engine, but when you're close to an aero engine of three hundred and fifty horsepower it seems ferocious; the aircraft strained and trembled against the chocks and the grass behind the engine was battered flat, seeming to flow like water.

After three or four minutes Elizabeth shut the throttle and switched off the magnetos.

'It's fine,' Alice said, speaking too loudly in the silence. She wiped her hands on a piece of oily rag and started replacing the cowlings. 'I reckon it's perfectly all right, Lizzie.'

'Good,' Elizabeth said. She looked at her watch. 'It's four o'clock. We'll leave as soon as you've finished. I'll get everybody aboard right away. I've got the latest forecast. The front's moving away to the north. We can go straight to the coast and nip across the Channel near Calais. We'll be home in a couple of hours, well before dark.'

From Brussels to Calais is about a hundred and twenty miles, and from Calais to White Waltham is the same again. To a ferry pilot, any flight into White Waltham generated a warm feeling of being drawn homewards, since White Waltham was the HQ of the ferry network and always full of old friends. It's still there – a large grass airfield between Reading and Maidenhead, twenty miles west of London.

The Anson climbed away from Brussels in light rain. After an hour the French coast was in sight, and they passed Calais at three thousand feet, flying due west out to sea towards Dover. Elizabeth looked down as they crossed the dunes and saw large flocks of seabirds circling below. Then she became aware of something: there was a strange noise, just audible over the racket of the engines. She looked at Alice.

'Dunno what that is,' Alice said. She got out of her seat and went into the rear of the aeroplane. In a moment she returned and said, 'It's the POWs.' She looked across at Elizabeth and grinned. 'They're singing their heads off because they're coming home.'

The Anson went on its way, the POWs singing 'Abide with me: fast falls the eventide; The darkness deepens; Lord with me abide.'

Across the narrow sea the Dover cliffs gleamed intermittently through the rain and a coaster plugged its way into the gale, white water cascading over its bows. Ahead, the black base of the cloud sagged down towards the water, trailing swathes of rain.

'We'll come down to two thousand,' Elizabeth said. 'I think we can duck under the worst of it.'

Three minutes later the aircraft entered heavy rain that blurred the windscreen and began to drip in through the window seals.

Five miles out from the French coast, at a height of eighteen hundred feet, the port engine stopped.

'Damn,' Elizabeth said.

Following the standard procedure, she closed the throttle of the dead engine and opened up the remaining engine to emergency power. The aircraft slowed to eighty-five miles an hour and began to lose height. The strong westerly wind opposed them: they might continue on their planned course, they might return to France or they might divert to another English airfield. The wind would help the aircraft back to France, but the French airfields were unfamiliar, and besides, there is always a desire to get home, or somewhere near it. Elizabeth had flown into and out of every airfield in the southeast of England; she knew them all, and it would take only ten or twelve minutes to reach the English coast.

'We'll go on,' Elizabeth said to Alice. 'Check the fuel cocks.'

'I have,' Alice said. 'It's not fuel. It's something else. It's electrical, I think.'

The propeller of the port engine was windmilling. Alice attempted to restart it, but it remained dead. For a further seven minutes the aircraft flew on in the rain, slowly losing height, edging somewhat north of its original course and approaching the Kent coast.

Alice asked, 'How high are the cliffs?'

'Three hundred feet,' Elizabeth said. 'We won't go over them. We'll head for Manston. It's got a nice big runway. We'll go straight in. Gear and flaps when I say.'

The Anson flew in a long descending curve over Pegwell Bay and inland towards the runway at Manston. Two miles from the runway their height was three hundred and fifty feet – too low, but now it was simply a matter of whether the runway would be reached before the aircraft touched the ground.

At Manston several people heard the howl of the Anson's overworked engine. In the control tower the Duty Officer went out on to the balcony with his binoculars and spotted the aeroplane coming in low from the east. He picked up his phone and called the emergency crews and then the station commander. Men ran to the fire truck and the ambulance. The DO watched as the Anson crept across the fields and woods, saw its wheels come down and reported that fact to the station commander.

A mile out, and the aircraft was a hundred feet up. Half a mile and fifty feet. Quarter of a mile and twenty feet. At the boundary fence, ten feet, and then the runway, and a puff of smoke as the engine was throttled back, and a second later the skirl of spray sent up by the Anson's tyres as they touched the runway. The Duty Officer puffed out his cheeks and said into the telephone, 'It's down, sir, and all in one piece.'

Thus it was that Flight Lieutenant Johnno Stevens, a pilot who had taken off in his Hurricane from Manston in 1940, had parachuted into the sea and been taken into captivity, limped down the steps of the Anson and stood in the rain on the very same airfield he had left five years before.

Elizabeth came down the steps and Johnno turned and said, 'Thank you, miss.' It was miraculous that he had returned to the very same spot, and there were tears in his eyes.

Elizabeth stood and looked at him. 'Don't thank me,' she said, 'thank the Lord, if you want to thank anyone. It was a close thing.'

Again Alice got out her toolbox. 'I'll have another look at it,' she said to Elizabeth, 'but I think it's had it. We'll have to organise some transport for everyone. I'm sorry.' She began to remove the cowlings from the port engine

'Don't be silly, Alice,' Elizabeth said. 'It's not your fault. You did everything by the book. You couldn't have done any more. We were lucky, and anyway it came out right in the end.'

The passengers were assembled in a draughty hut and given tea. As people do in such circumstances, the POWs felt a strong sense of gratitude towards their pilot, and two of them kissed her. She was unsettled, knowing that it had not been wise to leave Brussels in a hurry and late in the day, in doubtful weather and with a suspect engine. To return to France would have given her more height and time. If Alice didn't find the fault this time, they certainly wouldn't go any further.

The four men stood round Elizabeth, smiling and laughing while she thought how very fortunate she had been, all of them had been. The nun, it seemed, had not been aware of any danger; she sat silently in the corner again, the child asleep on her lap.

Somewhere outside there was the cough and stammer of an aero engine starting up. Elizabeth looked up and listened, knowing that Alice was out on the airfield in the rain, working on the Anson's engine. The engine coughed, roared again and was abruptly silent.

'It's no good,' Elizabeth said, 'the engine's obviously not right. We'll have to find some transport or stay here tonight. We'll organise something. I'll go and find someone.'

'I'll come with you,' Johnno said. They walked across the wet tarmac towards the adjutant's office.

'That was much too close,' Elizabeth said to him. 'I made a mistake. I shouldn't have gone on from Brussels. I had a feeling the weather might be worse than they said. There was something not quite right with that engine, and Alice hadn't found the problem. It's wanting to get home, that's the trouble. You always want to get home, don't you?'

'Please,' Johnno said. 'It doesn't matter. We got back all right.' He gestured with his stick, waving it back towards the hut. 'We're glad to be back, all of us, even if we aren't quite in the right place.' He stopped walking for a moment and looked around. 'I'm so glad to be here,' he said. 'I can't tell you how glad I am to be back.'

The Duty Officer told them there was no spare accommodation on the airfield. 'I'll see if I can find something in Ramsgate.'

As he picked up the phone the door opened and an RAF officer walked in, a man with a lot of braid on his cap. The DO stood up and saluted: this was the station commander.

'I say,' the officer said to Elizabeth, 'that's your Anson, isn't it? The one that landed just now with a dud engine?'

'Yes,' Elizabeth said. 'Is it in the way?'

'No, it's not that,' he said. There was something odd about his manner.

'What is it? What's the matter?'

'I'm sorry. Someone's been hurt.'

'Not Alice?'

'It's a young woman.'

'Alice. My flight engineer. What's happened to Alice?'

'I'm not exactly sure. Nobody saw it. There seems to have been an accident. She was working on an engine. It started. She was hit by the propeller.'

'I'll go to her.'

'No,' the station commander said, grasping her arm. 'No, please don't do that.'

'Don't be silly,' Elizabeth said, pulling away from him.

She went outside and began running through the rain towards the Anson. There was already an ambulance parked there with its doors open, and two men pulling out a stretcher. One of them put out his hand and said, 'Wait, miss—' but she pushed past him. Alice lay face-down in the grass, a great wound across her neck.

'I'm sorry, miss,' the ambulanceman said.

Elizabeth knelt and took hold of Alice's arm. 'Help me to turn her over,' she said.

'No, miss, you can't do that. We'll move her in a minute. We'll get her on the stretcher when we're ready for her. You can't do nothing for her.'

Elizabeth placed her hands softly on Alice's back and leaned awkwardly forwards until her forehead touched the body of her dear friend.

'Please, miss,' the ambulanceman said. 'You've got to let us deal with her, love. You can't do nothing for her now.'

*

Elizabeth took a train from Ramsgate towards London, sitting upright in yet another jam-packed carriage, Alice's toolbox on the rack above her head. The railway line runs along the north Kent coast through Margate, Herne Bay and Whitstable; for Elizabeth, this railway line has significance: it's the way she returned from her outing in Margate with the RAF boy in August 1940, three days before he drowned. Things sometimes gang up on us in that way, strongly suggesting the existence of a malign organising principle; but no, there's nobody in charge, nobody to blame, it's only chance that arranges our lives, sometimes happily and sometimes not.

A woman in the carriage caught her eye and Elizabeth looked away, staring out towards the estuary. From time to time tears crept from her eyes and she dabbed at them with her wet handkerchief, keeping her head turned away so that nobody would enquire or sympathise. Nobody did, since grief was commonplace in those days, and in England grief is embarrassing, like a disability, private and personal.

The train clattered over the bridge at Chatham and there were the same grey ships that she had seen five years before – the same kind of ships, at least, though now there are dozens more of them. On through Gravesend and Dartford, and at last out into the noise and bustle of the Greenwich streets. 'Another Jap bomb,' yelled a newspaper seller.

Carrying the weighty toolbox, Elizabeth walked through the foot tunnel under the river and north through the Isle of Dogs towards Limehouse. The rain had eased but it was dark now, and she walked steadily through the darkness from one dim streetlamp to the next, the sound of her shoes loud in the empty streets. Occasionally she stopped to change hands. As she got nearer she forced herself to stride onward at the same steady pace until she reached the door of 27 Mafeking Street. She banged the knocker twice and heard Lily Attwell yell from somewhere within, 'Come in, whoever you are!'

The door was unlocked. She pushed it open and went down the corridor. Lily was in the kitchen at the back, giving the boy his supper. Arthur looked up, a spoonful of orange jelly poised before his open mouth.

Lily saw Elizabeth and the toolbox, stood up and said, 'Jesus, Lizzie, what's the matter?' She took a step forward, stared again at the toolbox and said, 'Tell me it isn't her, will you? Say it isn't my Alice? Please God, not Alice?'

Elizabeth could not speak. She put the toolbox down. Tears ran from her eyes and her hands folded and refolded her handkerchief. At last she said, 'Yes, I'm sorry, it's Alice.'

Lily fell on her knees and began to cry out, great whooping inhuman noises. Elizabeth sat down on the toolbox and awkwardly attempted to hold her. The boy Arthur put down his spoon, got down from his chair and stood silently beside his mother. After a while Lily saw him and drew him to her, the three of them forming a shapeless huddle on the brown lino.

Some number of minutes went by. The gasping sobs lessened a little. Eventually Lily said, 'You've got to tell me, Lizzie. For God's sake tell me.'

Elizabeth told Lily then about Berlin and the flight home, about the faulty engine, about Alice working on it at Manston in the rain. It was a simple mechanical failure. Something, probably an electrical fault, had caused the engine to misfire and eventually to stop, and then, while Alice was working on it, to start again without warning. She tried to step back, slipped on the wet grass, and one of the propeller blades struck her.

That was all that was known. There was going to be an inquest. They would find out exactly what happened, and whose fault it was, if it was anybody's. When the propeller blade struck Alice, it killed her instantly. Her neck was broken. As Elizabeth talked Lily was silent and absolutely still, her eyes fixed on the floor, her left arm clamped round the boy, who had not yet made a sound.

'Oh God,' Lily said when Elizabeth finished, and then, much louder, she screamed out, 'Oh God, you bastard, why have you done this to me?'

At this point, Arthur, finding a space for his own grief, began to cry too, and his mother pushed Elizabeth to one side and grasped the boy with both arms, enclosing him, and her own howling began again.

The two women and the boy remained kneeling together on the kitchen floor for some immeasurable period. Eventually the eruptions of sobbing grew less frequent. At some time there was a knock at the door and in came Benjamin Yossakin, delivering Lily's three hundredweight of Best Welsh as he always did on a Wednesday evening. The old man, a sack of coal across his shoulder, stood in silence for some moments, looking at the group crouched on the floor. In a few moments he had worked it out and then he got to work. Dumping the sack of coal in the back yard, he went into every room, drawing curtains and turning on lights. He lit a fire in the front parlour, stoked up the kitchen range and filled a kettle. Leaving the house for a while, he returned with Harry Nicholls, the two of them carrying the makings of a stew and several bottles. Harry got on with the cooking while Ben, seeing that Arthur had wet himself, ran a bath for the boy and found him some clean clothes. He made tea for everyone, then sat down and gave himself a large glass of vodka.

The stolidity of the old man had an effect. Lily got up from the floor, sat in a chair for a time then put Arthur and herself to bed. Elizabeth lay on the sofa. Ben and Harry finished the vodka and ate a few spoonfuls of stew. When it seemed that Elizabeth was asleep, the two men switched off the lights and went home.

The following afternoon Lily began to drive herself onward again, just as she had after the death of Roy. She took Lizzie, Arthur and the donkey cart to collect several oak baulks that had been fished out of the river by one of the pilot boats, took it to the archway, ran it through the saw and laid it in the racks.

When they returned home they found another meal cooked by Harry Nicholls, who was proving a good deal more skilful in the kitchen than he was in the garage. Later that evening neighbours began to call, bringing food and staying to drink Benjamin Yossakin's vodka. Arthur was sent to the Lamb & Flag for more alcohol, returning with the Honeysett family as well as the bottles. 'I've shut the pub,' George Honeysett announced, 'I've thrown them all out. Some things are more important than a few pints of beer, aren't they, Lily, my love?'

Lily began to consider the question of going to see Alice, whose body was being held under the orders of the Ramsgate coroner. Harry Nicholls offered to drive Lily and Arthur to Ramsgate the following day. Lily asked whether Lizzie would come with them.

'No,' she said. 'I'm sorry. I can't come. I've already seen her, and I can't see her again.' She held herself very still, but tears began to run down her cheeks, which stimulated another general round of sobbing and a considerable topping-up of everyone's glasses.

The evening passed in this pattern, each wave of sorrow a little less infectious than the one before. Gradually there began to be talk of what to do next, and Elizabeth told the company about the imminent closure of the Air Transport Auxiliary, which was to be celebrated with a fly-past and a speech of gratitude by Lord Beaverbrook.

'I never liked that man Beaverbrook,' Lily said. 'He's all mouth, he is. I don't take to men with too much mouth.'

Her remark, falling into a silence in the conversation, caused a good deal of laughter. Elizabeth thought that the laughter was a sign of the return of Lily's spirit, just like the way the first swift confirms the arrival of summer. Swifts, I noticed a long time ago, often came into Elizabeth's mind when she was searching for a simile.

Eventually the visitors began to leave, until all that remained was the regular whistle and flutter of Benjamin Yossakin's snoring as he lay asleep in the parlour.

Lily began to collect plates and glasses. 'When all's said and done,' she said to Elizabeth, piling crockery on the draining board with a great clatter, 'there ain't no bloody choice and you can't keep on weeping for ever. You've just got to get up and get on with it. What else is there, love? What else?' She went to the window and opened it to let out the stale air.

'Nothing,' Elizabeth said. 'There's nothing else, Lily.' She yawned uncontrollably. It was midnight, and more than a day since she had knocked at the door and walked down the corridor to Lily's kitchen.

'You oughta get some sleep, dear,' Lily said. 'Really you oughta.'

'You ought to as well,' Elizabeth said.

'You go and have a little lie-down upstairs, why doncha? Alice's room, you could use that if you want.'

'Oh no, Lily, I couldn't possibly—' She began weeping again, and so did Lily, but this time it was a comparatively brief relapse.

'It's no bloody good, this ain't,' Lily said, wiping her eyes. She patted the pockets of her apron and looked round the room. 'Now what? I can't have smoked the whole blessed packet, can I? But I must've done.'

She shook her head, then stood up straight and addressed Elizabeth in her most formal manner. 'Now look, Lizzie dear, I knows you, I really do. I've knowed you for a good many years, what with one thing and another.'

'Lily,' Elizabeth said, 'you're going to start me off again.'

'No, I'm not. But I knows what you're thinking, and you're thinking it was all your fault.'

Elizabeth started to speak but Lily interrupted. 'Now be quiet, Lizzie, because I know perfectly well what you think. But as God is my witness, it never was nothing at all to do with you. You always does things right. I knows that, because my Alice was always telling me that, and Alice never did tell a lie, Alice didn't.'

Lily stepped forward and put her hands on Elizabeth's shoulders. 'So make sure you always remember what I'm telling you, love, and that's what a lovely friend you was to my Alice, and it ain't none of it your fault, and that's what I do truly know.'

Both of them cried after this speech, and soon afterwards they went up to Lily's room and fell asleep in her large and creaky bed, each holding the other's hand in a firm grasp.

Eight

Home at Rookwood in her old bedroom and waking in the night, Elizabeth went to the window, pulled back the teddy bear curtains and stared at the stars.

There had been all those ruined cities and then Berlin, a final graveyard. There had been the girl at the zoo and her story about the monkey – no, not a monkey, an orang-utan, more human than a monkey. Then there had been the flight home, the faulty engine, her own errors, their seeming escape, and then Alice. That was how it had gone, that was the sequence.

No – that was wrong. Long before Berlin she had felt something gathering about her, like the creeping chill of an autumn evening. She had felt it in Limehouse, staring at the river, and when she reached Berlin everything had become peculiarly vivid – the girl Anna, silhouetted against the ruins of the zoo; the silent nun and her child; the young POWs with the hands and faces of old men; that energetic American sergeant.

When did it begin? How far back? In her childhood there had been that odd person Auntie Vi, who had lived with them at Rookwood and died in an inconsequential way, like a brown leaf fluttering from a branch. There had been Daddy – why had that happened to him? Why?

Auntie Vi, Daddy, that RAF boy, now Alice. Wasn't that a pattern? And did it belong to the relentless pattern displayed by Berlin, Dresden, Coventry, Hiroshima and now another one, Nagasaki, a name like the gnashing of teeth?

A blight has fallen upon us, she suddenly knew, and has brought a quantity of sorrow beyond understanding and beyond defiance, a stain spreading across the world until we are all touched by it, marked by it and drowned by it. Oh, Alice, dearest Alice – and she put her face in her hands and fell again into the chasm of grief.

Later she forced herself to sit upright and pressed her forehead against the cold glass of the window. This was ridiculous. The stars were unperturbed. What could she have been thinking? There was no connection between any of these things. These fears were fantastic, self-indulgent. All those things had happened at different times and for different reasons. There was no link between them and no mystery about them. As for Alice – the coroner's enquiry had found no fault with her. Alice's death had unsettled her – of course it had – but nothing else had changed. One made one's own destiny, and the worst thing was doubt.

She went to the basin, washed her face and dried it on a towel printed with elephants parading as if on a tiger shoot. She stared blindly at the marching creatures, knowing that she had begun to doubt herself. Standing up straight, she looked into the mirror.

She would go on being herself and she would continue to fly, because she had long ago decided to do so. She looked at the photograph of the Wright Flyer that hung beside her bed. She was confident, capable. With peace would come new opportunities all over the world. She could fly the mail, like St-Exupéry, along the desert coast of Africa, or wing her way eastwards to Burma, Sumatra, Java and all the way to Darwin and Sydney, like Amy in her Moth. A long way in a small aeroplane. The window was misty with her breath. She wiped it with the towel. It was good that she had got it straight in her mind. She folded the towel and hung it on the rail.

The previous day, as Elizabeth stepped into the hall and put down her bags, her mother had cried 'Darling!' from the landing and hurried down the stairs. 'Oh, darling! Oh, it's so lovely that you're home! Oh, my poor darling!' She ran at her daughter, seized her by the shoulders, kissed the air beside her cheeks, let her go and stood back to inspect. Frances Bowman did that sort of thing energetically, yet was never wholly convincing.

'Now, darling,' Frances said, 'we haven't touched your room. It's going to be so lovely to have you home, and everything is going to be just the same as it used to be. Come and see.'

On the centre of Elizabeth's bedroom door was a glazed china image from Beatrix Potter, a duck wearing a blue bonnet and a teacloth. Elizabeth stood in the doorway and looked in. The rose-patterned wallpaper, the coverlet knitted so laboriously by Ruth and Elizabeth, the photographs of aeroplanes, the lines of books and the curtains with the teddy bears.

Her mother opened and shut various drawers. 'I've got you a few bits and pieces I thought you'd need, darling. Dear Bunty has been a terrific help – she has such good taste. Blouses, skirts, socks and stockings, a mackintosh, shoes – you take a seven, don't you, darling? Oh, yes, a lovely cardigan—'

She held the cardigan up: it hung from her hands, brown, knitted. 'What else? Of course, the coat—' She opened the wardrobe and took out a long beige coat with a fur collar. 'Lovely, isn't it?' Holding it against herself, she gazed into the mirror on the wardrobe door. 'Camelhair. Secondhand, of course, but awfully nice. Beige is such a sophisticated colour.' She smoothed its collar with the back of her hand. 'Lovely soft fur. Oh, Lizzie darling, you'll look so smart!'

Elizabeth stood in the centre of the floor and looked at her reflection in the wardrobe mirror, a woman in a blue uniform standing in the middle of a little girl's bedroom.

Her mother had gone to visit her friend Bunty to tell her the happy news of her daughter's return and the sad news of her friend's tragic death. Elizabeth prowled about the house. It all looked the same, but something was missing. Ruth's room – surprisingly tidy, but that was because Ruth was not at home; she was working on the canal boats that carried coal from the mines to the cities. The spare room, still shrouded in dust covers, in which Auntie Vi had lived for two years. Edmund's room, which Elizabeth never entered unless asked. Mother's room, smelling of face-powder. Daddy's room, mothballs and shoe-polish. The stairs creaked. The dining-room, formal and ordered. The drawing-room. She stood still. Of course! Daddy's clock!

She turned. On the mantelpiece stood her father's clock, an old and elegant piece by Macune of New Fleet Street, the kind that plays a different tune every day. Daddy's clock said four-twenty. She looked at her watch. It was eleven-thirty. Nobody had wound the clock. She looked more closely. Nobody had dusted it either. On the base was a silver plate inscribed *To EB from NC, 23rd June 1928: with thanks.*

There was the sound of the front door. Elizabeth stepped into the hall and called out, 'Mother!'

Her mother came in, undoing her coat and reaching up to remove her hat-pin. 'What it is it, darling?'

'Daddy's clock has stopped!'

'I know, dear. I don't think of winding it, I'm afraid. The tunes get on one's nerves so.' She stepped into the alcove to hang up her hat and coat.

Daddy's clock had been given to him by some great personage, possibly a Prime Minister. When she asked about the clock her father always said, 'Aha, little Miss Nosey', and placed his finger beside his own substantial nose. 'Services rendered, services rendered in high places, my lovely.' He laughed and kissed the top of her head, which he much liked to do.

She pushed her fingers beneath the clock and found the key. There had been a ceremony on Sunday mornings which began with Daddy saying to the three of them, 'Who is to be the Keeper of the Key?' – whereupon they clamoured at their father like chicks in the nest. He had taught them to wind the clock with care, so that nothing was strained. She opened the face of the clock, inserted the key and turned it ten times. It was eleven thirty-five; she set the hands, closed the face and stood listening to the clock's so-lazy tick, a tick that each time seemed about to come too late, but never did.

Her mother was calling to her. Elizabeth shut the drawing-room door. At noon she would discover which of the familiar tunes would be played by the twelve delicate bells of Daddy's clock.

The following day Elizabeth sat at her father's writing bureau and typed a dozen copies of her curriculum vitae, which she posted that afternoon to wartime friends and acquaintances.

A reply came by return of post, an encouraging confirmation of her new resolve. It was a weighty, cream-coloured envelope bearing an embossed crest. She opened it carefully, the paper crackling as she unfolded the letter. OCEAN ISLAND AIRWAYS, it said, and in smaller letters underneath, *We Serve The Globe*. This was certainly hopeful. Below the heading was a Douglas DC3 painted in a smart red-and-yellow colour scheme, flying above the inclined palms of a tropical beach.

She read the letter. Mr J M Savage, Company Director, was most interested in her account of her experience, and would be pleased to see her at company's offices in Oxford Street at 10.30 a.m. on Friday 25th September. Along the foot of the page was printed a line of cities: New York, London, Paris, Rome, Berlin, Los Angeles, Buenos Aires, Moscow.

Elizabeth had not heard of the airline, but what matter. She had got an interview at her first attempt, and it was in Oxford Street, which was better than Swindon or some such place. She would wear her ATA uniform. Certainly she would never in her whole life wear the horrid coat that her mother's friend Bunty had chosen, nor the cardigan either.

The office was not precisely in Oxford Street, but down a small alley containing a great many dustbins, and the door was an ordinary back door, in fact, with an ordinary doorbell. Never mind. There was a polished brass sign saying *Ocean Island Airways*, and that was something. She was wearing her uniform despite it being well-worn, and she had checked the straightness of her tie and the seams of her stockings in a shop window.

She rang the bell and waited. There was no reply. She pushed at the door, found it unlocked and entered a hallway full of mops and buckets. On the opposite wall a handwritten sign said *OIA Ltd – top floor – go straight up*. On what must have been the fifth floor she rested for a short time, to avoid arriving breathless. The stairs became narrower, steeper and darker until they ended at a blank door. She knocked. There was no reply. She tried the handle. It was locked. Damn. Somehow she had missed a sign or a turning.

She turned and went back to the ground floor without finding anything. She was now late. How very annoying this sort of thing was!

Climbing up again, she heard a faint voice calling from above. 'Hallo! Miss Bowman! Hallo! Are you there?'

'I'm on my way up,' she called out. When she reached the top she found the door open. A large room, uncarpeted, contained two desks, three chairs and a stack of cardboard boxes. A man came forward. Elizabeth had an impression of a dark-blue pinstripe suit, a red-and-yellow tie, a red face, glasses, a bald head, a cigarette. 'I'm Savage,' he said, and coughed.

'I'm Bowman,' Elizabeth said. 'I did knock before.'

He laughed, puffing smoke. 'My dear girl! Not with tremendous force, evidently. I was on the telephone and heard not a thing. So sorry.'

One of the desks had a telephone, the other a typewriter. Mr Savage sat down at the desk with the telephone. 'Do sit down. Dear me, you look a bit winded.'

'I've been up and down twice,' Elizabeth said. She sat down at the table with the typewriter.

'Up twice and down once, I think you mean.' Mr Savage smiled to show that this correction was mere jollity, not to be taken to heart. He held a cigarette packet towards her. 'Smoke?'

'No thanks,' Elizabeth said.

'Now,' Mr Savage said, 'You sent me a most interesting letter. Yes.' He removed his glasses, picked up the letter and held it close to his face, his lips moving a little.

When he had finished reading he replaced his glasses and looked over the top of them at Elizabeth. 'You've been flying all sorts of things since the start of the war, and before that you were employed at a rather well-known aeroplane factory.'

'Yes. That was when I was young. It was my first job. I was a typist and then a secretary at de Havillands while I was learning to fly.'

'And how well do you know the aviation world?' He drew on his cigarette and looked expectant.

'I've been in it, one way and another, for seven years. I think I know it pretty well.'

'Who do you know?'

'Who do I know?'

'Yes, Miss Bowman. It's not a large world. You must have met one or two significant people. Douglas Bader. Cat's-eyes Cunningham. Geoffrey de Havilland. Air Commodores and Air Marshals. People like that.'

'I don't know young Mr Geoffrey or his father at all.' She thought for a moment. 'I saw them from time to time, of course, but I didn't know them. I don't know anybody important, and I don't really know why you're asking that question, either.'

'My! You're very direct, Miss Bowman. An unusual attribute in a young lady, and so very useful, no doubt, from time to time.'

'I think perhaps I haven't come to the right place. I'm not even sure your airline really exists. I think perhaps I'll—'

He waved her back into the chair. 'Dear me, Miss Bowman, we've got off on the wrong foot. I'm so sorry.' He smiled again. 'Let's begin again, shall we?'

'All right,' Elizabeth said.

'I see that I must explain what an airline is, and how it

works. On the one hand, it's like a bus company – it takes people speedily from one place to another, on time, and without losing too many of them. Secondly, it's a precarious sort of business, a way in which to make a bit of money or to lose a lot. Thirdly, it's something that people enjoy doing – flying, I mean. Quite a number of people in aviation are what might be called enthusiasts. For myself, I have little knowledge of flying. I do the business part, which is essential to the rest of it. Upon my foundations, you might say, the whole jolly enterprise rests. I fly the business, I don't fly the aeroplanes.'

'I see,' Elizabeth said.

'You are right to think that Ocean Island Airways is, as yet, on the small side. It has just begun. But don't worry about that. You'll find that airlines appear and disappear for a pastime. They can grow fast and die fast. And the secret of a good airline, Miss Bowman, is to possess as little as possible in the way of concrete assets, and therefore remain agile.'

'You have to possess a lot of aeroplanes, surely.'

'One certainly needs a number of aeroplanes, but one does not have to *possess* them. At this particular moment the world is full of aeroplanes. Crammed with them. There's an enormous surplus. And pilots, of course.' He puffed his cigarette and coughed again. 'Aeroplanes can be bought for next to nothing. Even so, one wouldn't necessarily want to *own* them, because they're such complicated and troublesome things. Let someone else own them. Ocean Island will hire aeroplanes when it needs them, and we'll also hire pilots from the vast stockpile that is being released on to the market as we speak.'

'That seems a funny way to run an airline.'

'It's not at all funny. It's just sensible. It's the way all business will be run in the post-war world.'

'If you're just going to hire pilots when you need them, I

can't see what you want me for. I think you probably haven't got any aeroplanes yet.'

Mr Savage leaned back in his chair. 'Miss Bowman, I think your idea of an airline is out-of-date and rather romantic. There are those who like the idea of taking a flying-boat down the Nile – breakfast at Alexandria, dinner at Khartoum or whatever. Well, that's dead and gone. Flying will be about getting there quickly, that's all. And in fact I don't need you for the flying side at all.'

'But flying is what I do.'

'It's certainly what you have done, and what you know about. It struck me how useful a knowledgeable woman pilot might be to the business. You're quite unusual, after all. It would be an attraction to have you about, and you clearly have a lot of experience of flying and flyers. You seem to be a bold young woman, and an attractive one. You also happen to have the skills of a secretary.'

He pointed to the other desk. 'Suppose you were sitting there, Miss Bowman, and giving me the benefit of your experience and your ability to talk flying. That would be most valuable to me. I would pay more than the going rate for that.'

'I'm a pilot,' Elizabeth said. 'I don't want to be a secretary.'

Mr Savage looked carefully at the stub of his cigarette, then stubbed it out. 'Oh dear,' he said.

'I have been flying for seven years. I have two thousand hours on a large number of types, including multi-engined aircraft. I have never damaged an aircraft in my charge. I understood you to be looking for pilots.'

Mr Savage sighed. 'Miss Bowman, I respect your determination. The difficulty is that you couldn't possibly be a pilot. Passengers will not accept a woman pilot. That has to be faced, I'm afraid.'

Elizabeth stood up. Mr Savage looked disappointed. 'Oh dear,' he said again.

'I'm going to fly,' Elizabeth said. 'Whatever you say, I shall go on flying.'

As she clattered down the first flight of stairs she heard the telephone ring and Mr Savage begin talking with great warmth and charm. What an infernal cheek the man had, and an absolutely infuriating manner to go with it. An airline that had nothing but a few boxes of stationery! How could he think for a single moment that she would be attracted by such a ridiculous notion? That was the most annoying thing – that he had thought she would be interested. He was completely wrong. They were lovely, those flying-boats, and the idea that somehow the magic of flight had no role in an airline – that was simply absurd!

Her state of mind lasted until she was nearly home, when she remembered Alice and was swept by sorrow; and when she had recovered, she thought how angry Alice would have been about that awful man.

At Rookwood her mother heard her come in and called out from the kitchen, 'How did you get on, darling?'

'I didn't get on at all.'

'Oh dear,' Frances said. 'Still, it's only the first one, isn't it? There'll be lots more, I'm sure. It's time for supper.'

Frances was sixty now, and had adopted the gravity of a widow. Elizabeth watched her remove the tea-cosy and stir the tea. The swelling of her finger joints was due to arthritis, about which she never complained, although she could no longer remove her rings. The teaspoon clinked once, lightly and musically, against the rim of the pot. In a moment Frances would say to each of them, 'Tea, darling?'

Elizabeth asked, 'Where exactly is Ruth?'

'Ruth?' Edmund wrinkled his nose. 'Ruth has gone to the dogs. Utterly gone to the dogs.'

There was a moment of silence, then Frances said, 'That's a very silly way to put it, Edmund, as you know perfectly well. The simple fact, Lizzie, is that some months ago Ruth took it into her head to leave home. She used to come home between her canal trips, but now she wants to make her own way in the world.'

'Yes,' Elizabeth said, 'but where is she at the moment? I want to see her.'

Edmund laughed. 'You tell her, mother. See what Lizzie thinks about that.'

Frances poured a precise amount of milk into each of the three cups, looked up at Elizabeth and said, 'Tea, darling?'

Elizabeth nodded and her mother said, 'We understand that Ruth is lodging with another family. People she met on the canals, I gather.'

Elizabeth half-turned and looked out at the lawn, the plum-tree and the row of poplars that marked the boundary of the garden, their silver leaves fluttering. The conversation weighed upon her, its patterns and tensions familiar. 'I want to see Ruth,' she said. 'Who are they, these people she's staying with?'

Edmund was about to speak, but Frances prevented him with an inclination of her left hand. 'Edmund, it isn't helpful for you to talk about Ruth in that way.'

Edmund said, 'Really, mother, I haven't said anything yet.'

His mother continued. 'Ruth works for a canal carrying company. The company is owned by a family called Mitchell.'

'Mitchell Brothers and Moore,' Edmund said. 'It used to be called that, but the Moores are no more, it seems.'

'The Mitchells live near Northampton,' Frances said. 'They own a boat. A barge.'

'Several barges,' Edmund said.

Elizabeth had a sudden and intense desire to see her sister, whose laughter she remembered and who had the trick of happiness.

'Edmund,' Frances said, 'please do not interrupt again.' She sipped a little tea and went on: 'Ruth likes it. It's hard work, out in all weathers. They take the boats up and down between the Midlands and London. Most of them have motors these days, but a few are still pulled by horses. It's not in the least surprising that Ruth decided to do it. She always liked doing things outdoors, of course.'

'Ruth's barge will certainly be horse-drawn,' Elizabeth said.

'Of course it is,' Edmund said. 'But they don't call them barges, they're called narrowboats. They're built for the narrow canals. Ruth is very particular about using the right names for things. She has a boat pulled by a horse called Major, and she shares it with another girl.'

'Pat Mitchell is the other girl,' Frances said. 'The boat's called *Foxglove* and the horse's name is Major. Ruth might be passing at any time. One never knows when she might appear. You could catch her if you wait by the locks for long enough.'

'Edmund,' Elizabeth said, 'I want you to find me a piece of plywood, some paint, a brush, a hammer and a few nails.'

Later that afternoon Elizabeth painted a notice on a square of plywood and nailed it to the balance beam of the first lock.

Ruth
I'm home
Lizzie

Nine

In 1941 Waverley was requisitioned for use as an RAMC hospital. The lift was installed and many rooms were knocked together to form wards and theatres. Several rows of Nissen huts were erected beside the house, and wheelchair ramps were built about the house and gardens – the hospital specialised in prosthetics.

The huts were fitted out with work-benches and machine tools to form a factory known colloquially as 'A&L', meaning 'Arms and Legs'. Increasing demand for A&L, especially after June 1944, meant that the factory expanded to the size of a big village, overrunning the paddock and the shrubbery and encroaching halfway across the orchard.

When I came home on leave in the autumn of 1945 I found large numbers of wheelchairs lined up along Warden's Terrace – there must have been forty or fifty. They were driven outdoors in all weathers, I discovered, by Matron's ban on smoking on the wards. They looked like charioteers of an odd sort, standing ready to repel an attack. I walked along the line to see if there was anyone I knew, and found one man, an RAF man called

Andy Vines. He had been in my squadron but was transferred to night-fighters because he was a talented pilot, not just a competent bus-driver like the rest of us. He had undershot on his second night landing in a Beaufighter, hit a wall, killed his crew and lost both legs. Was it harder to remain brave if one had lost one's legs in some damnfool accident that was one's own fault? Andy Vines was a very angry man.

'Jesus, I hate my tin legs,' he said. 'I'm a fucking slave to them, and they're bloody agony to walk on.'

I saw him several times after that, and was struggling to make conversation with him when I glanced up and saw Elizabeth walking across the lawn towards the house.

'Go on, Charlie,' Andy said, seeing me get up and then sit down again. 'Don't mind me. The lady wants you.'

'All right, Andy, I'll see you tomorrow,' I said, and walked down the grassy bank towards Elizabeth. She was wearing one of those cotton dresses of hers, the sort she had worn years ago. I hadn't seen her since that glimpse in London.

'You're looking lovely,' I said. 'Tell me about Berlin.'

'You're a liar and a flatterer, Charlie,' she said. 'This is a very ancient frock, as you may remember.'

'If I'm a flatterer,' I said, 'I'm not a very good one, since you've never shown the slightest interest in me.'

She smiled vaguely and said, 'Charlie, I need a favour.'

We went into the rose garden, sat on a stone seat and she told me about her interview at Ocean Island Airways. A fortnight had gone by and she hadn't heard from anyone else.

'This Mr Savage,' I said, 'Was his name John? John M Savage?'

'Yes. A horrid man in a pinstripe.'

'I know him,' I said. 'He's genuine enough. He's already signed up a couple of people I know.'

'A couple of men, I suppose.'

'Yes. But I don't think you ought to write him off too quickly. It could be a chance for you, Lizzie. After all, if you're sitting right beside him, you'll know if something comes up. Pilots are bound to go sick from time to time. There'd be opportunities, and in time he'd forget . . .'

I paused and she said, 'Forget I'm a woman.'

'I don't mean it like that,' I said. 'I just mean that he'd start to use you when there was a difficulty and he couldn't—'

'Couldn't find anybody else. Thanks.'

'Now look, Lizzie,' I said, 'a job like that is likely to give you some opportunities, at the very least.' I looked at her straight. 'I think you're being a bit too fussy, you know. You simply have to start somewhere.'

'Charlie,' she said, 'I don't see why I can't get a proper job on my own merits. I've done the hours. I've been at it for years. I've flown almost everything there is. You know that.'

Eventually I said, 'It's just that we don't have many women pilots. It'll take a while to get used to the idea.'

'Come on, Charlie,' she said. 'Somebody's going to be first, aren't they? Somebody will be the first female airline pilot and we'll wonder what all the fuss was about. Why shouldn't it be me?'

I had no idea about Berlin and what had happened to her on the way back. I was simply trying to work out a few more possibilities. I knew there wasn't the slightest chance of her getting an airline job in England.

I said, 'Why don't you and Alice get together and set up a little firm of your own? You could carry freight to start with, and some mail, maybe. We could probably find someone to put a bit of money into that. You'd only need one aeroplane to start with.'

It wasn't a bad idea. I got interested in it, staring at the rose garden and failing to notice her silence.

'Suppose you bought a middling-size aeroplane, say a Rapide or something like that, and started a service to the Scillies or the Hebrides. There are so many aeroplanes about at the moment that you could probably get two of them. Alice could cannibalise one for spares. It needn't cost a lot.'

I was thinking I could back her myself. The more I thought about it, the more I liked the idea.

At last, I turned to her and saw that she was crying. She was sitting very upright with her hands in her lap and tears pouring down her cheeks. 'Christ, Lizzie,' I said, reaching out and holding her arms, 'whatever's the matter?'

I tried to hold her but she wouldn't allow it. Eventually she said, 'Alice is dead.'

She told me then about the flight to Berlin, their sightseeing in the jeep, the girl at the zoo, the night in the wrecked house on Unter den Linden, the faulty engine – the whole story.

I listened to it all and after a while I began to feel she was making too much of it. I wanted to ask her what she thought the war was about. She was being naïve. I wanted to say, 'Don't forget we didn't start it.'

When she got to the part about their flight back to England I saw that she felt guilty, and knew why that was. She wanted to get home, and if she hadn't been in a hurry things might have been different. That was her logic, and it wasn't the kind of logic that went anywhere useful.

'Come on, Lizzie,' I said. 'You can't make a direct connection between a whole string of decisions and Alice's death. It was just an ordinary accident, and it could have happened anywhere, any time. It's simply not right to feel guilty about it.'

In truth, I wasn't so certain. Even though it was tenuous, there was a connection of a kind between her actions and Alice's death. We both knew it.

I said, 'To be honest, I don't think you should be so concerned about what happened to Berlin and the other German cities, either. They began the bombing, didn't they? In the end they only got what was coming to them.'

Elizabeth stared at me for a moment, and then asked, 'Have you seen it? Have you seen what we and the Americans and the Russians did to Berlin? Have you actually been there, Charlie?'

'Of course I have,' I said. 'I've been to Berlin twelve times. The last time was eighteen months ago, and probably that's the last time I'll ever fly. Do you know how many aircraft my squadron lost that night? I can tell you. It was four. Four aircraft lost. Twelve went to Berlin and eight of us came back. Seven men in each aircraft, that makes twenty-eight gone in just one night. Berlin was an inferno, like it always was. That winter, my squadron lost twenty aircraft in the Berlin raids alone – that's a whole squadron lost, just because of bloody Berlin. Really, Elizabeth, you don't have the slightest idea what bombing Berlin was like.'

I hadn't meant to say anything as forceful as that. She looked down at the floor and said, 'I didn't know any of that.'

'I'm a teacher now,' I said. 'They took me off flying. I teach navigation to young lads in a classroom. I don't know why you're making such a fuss about some bloody monkey that got killed in Berlin.'

There was a long silence, during which Elizabeth went on looking at the ground.

'I'm sorry,' I said, 'I don't know why I got so angry all of a sudden.'

'I understand,' Elizabeth said. She stood up. 'Thanks for the tea, Charlie.'

'I'll see what can be done in the way of a job,' I said. 'I've still got a few connections.'

'It doesn't matter,' she said. 'I shouldn't have barged in.'

'Don't go straight away,' I said.

'It's quite all right, Charlie. It really doesn't matter.'

I walked with her to the terrace and watched her walking steadily away down the meadow. After a couple of hundred yards she turned and waved, and after that she kept going over the bridge and up the limestone track until she had gone over the crest of the hill.

The following day I walked over to Rookwood. It was a chilly November afternoon, the grass silvered with frost. As I approached I thought I saw a movement at Elizabeth's bedroom window, but when I reached the gate there was no sign of anyone.

Elizabeth's mother opened the front door. 'Oh, Mr Charles!'

'I just wondered how everything was.'

'Oh, come in, please come in. Let me take your coat. We've got a nice fire in the drawing room.' She hurried across the hall, calling, 'Lizzie! Lizzie – Mr Charles is here—'

Elizabeth was sitting in a wheelback chair by the window, her face in shadow. She was wearing a grey dress with a high collar and long sleeves – a dress that must have been her mother's. She sat still, her hands on the arms of the chair.

'Hello, Charlie,' she said, 'it's nice of you to come over.'

Frances fussed round us, arranging a chair, bringing tea and biscuits and eventually leaving us alone.

I fiddled with my teacup and started to say, 'I'm so sorry—'

Elizabeth interrupted me. 'Now, Charlie, you've come up

here like a good neighbour to see what can be done for me. Absolutely nothing needs to be done. I'm quite all right.'

'You surely don't expect me to believe that,' I said. 'It's obvious that something's not right. Besides, I can't imagine that you'd want to stay on the estate all winter. It'll be terribly dull, apart from anything.'

'I like it dull,' she said, and looked down at the floor. There was another silence, in which I could hear Frances clattering about in the kitchen.

I asked, 'Has Ruth been home?'

'No.'

'I thought she often came along the Grand Union with her boat.'

'She used to,' Elizabeth said. 'But she hasn't come this way for ages. I don't know where she is. She hasn't phoned or written or anything. She doesn't go in for writing.'

'Oh,' I said. She was silhouetted against the window, her head bowed and her hair shadowing her face.

'What happened to Alice was an accident,' I said. 'And another thing . . .' I hesitated and she lifted her head to look at me. 'Those things I said about Berlin – I know I shouldn't have said them.'

'Yes, you should,' she said. 'You were quite right to say them. I'd got things all wrong. I hadn't worked it out properly.'

'Worked out what?'

'That it was just the same for you as it was for me. The same for thousands of people, millions even.' She looked out of the window. 'It was fun, wasn't it? For a long time the war was such fun, and I didn't even notice what was going on.'

'Yes, it was fun,' I said. 'At the beginning it was fun.'

'What an easy time we've had, sitting in our little island and not knowing about most of it. We thought we were being so brave, and really the war was happening somewhere else.'

'All that's true,' I said, 'but now it's finished. We've got to get on with something else.'

'What are you going to do, Charlie?'

'I don't quite know,' I said. 'I've thought about coming home. There's plenty for me to do on the estate.'

'But you don't want to do that.'

'No, I don't. Teaching, perhaps. There's a scheme for people like me to do a degree.'

She smiled. 'You'd be a good teacher.'

She was thinking about the Gipsy Moth, of course.

'I came past the Forty Acre meadow on my way up here,' I said. 'The hangar's gone. Father got Hawkins to take it down last year. He said it was an eyesore.'

'It's a pity you haven't still got the Moth,' she said.

'Yes,' I said. Then after a moment I said, 'No, it isn't a pity at all. I've had enough flying for one lifetime.'

She didn't reply to that. I looked out of the window and said, 'It'll be dark soon. I'd better be going.'

'It's good of you to come up,' Elizabeth said, 'but really, I'm all right.' She stood up, and on the way to the front door her mother came bustling out of the kitchen, wiping her hands on a teacloth, and hovered around us while I put on my coat. I thanked her for the tea, kissed Elizabeth on the cheek and walked home to Waverley.

Ten

From the beginning my aim was only to fly with care and grace. I had no thought that my affair with flying would have its consequences, as romance does.

When the war came I immediately joined the Royal Air Force and progressed quickly through the initial training. Early in March 1940 I went through a series of tests that ended with a morning's blind flying, a pram-hood over the cockpit. We landed and the instructor took out his cigarette case and offered it to me. I shook my head and he tapped his cigarette on the silver case while he considered his decision.

'Now look, Charlie, old boy, you're a pretty fair pilot but you're the steady type, not the sort to fly fighters. You'll fly bombers, that's what you'll do. The heavy stuff. All right with you?'

Closing one eye against the cigarette smoke he wrote my name at the foot of a list on his clipboard. He had very small hands, I suddenly recall, almost girlish, the fingers stained with nicotine.

'Good,' I said. 'Thank you.'

He looked at me with one eyebrow raised, his cigarette hanging from his lips, but my pleasure was no pretence to cover disappointment. Fighter pilots were the glamour boys but I already knew I was not that sort, and I was happy to be a 'bus-driver' – that's what the fighter boys called us. The term was not inappropriate: we had our routes and timetables, we had our bus-crews and even, one could say, our passengers, their long bodies clustered close beneath us.

I was only twenty but I knew that I lacked a quality that some men possessed, an edge, an urgency, and that I wanted distance and time. And yes, those slow-moving specks so high above, so very high – I was content that mine would be the ranging view from altitude, the open earth below, the brilliance of the towering clouds, the power of the machine tracing a straight and steady track across the vast dome of blue.

That instructor told me something else that I liked the sound of, though he intended it as a palliative: bombing had become a science, and one that absolutely required careful, accurate pilots such as myself. In the nose of each bomber was a precision bombsight upon which the whole business depended. It was a bloody marvellous gadget, he said, and it would allow us to drop our bombs straight down Hitler's sodding chimney. He laughed a lot at that, laughing and coughing on his cigarette.

In my later training I took my turn at peering through the Mark IV bombsight, watching the crosswires slide across factories, roads, railways, houses, a park, a school, children in the playground, mercilessly crisp and clear. The talk was always of precision, and on the range it was sometimes possible to achieve; but over Germany it was not long before we knew that it was all nonsense.

My ignorance might seem extraordinary in retrospect, but in fact nobody knew what it would be like; the talk of the war strategists and the easy success of the Luftwaffe in Spain had made us all think the aircraft would be an irresistible weapon. Not so. At the beginning we made a few sorties by day, but immediate heavy losses forced us to withdraw into the dark – preferably the cloudy dark – and to bomb from the greatest altitude that our aircraft could achieve. Darkness, cloud, high altitude, imprecise navigation, uncertain knowledge of the winds over the target – these made all talk of precision absurd. All our work would be done from height and in darkness, and in consequence most of our bombs did not fall within three miles of the aiming point. Three miles. So much for the marvellous bombsight, and so much for the precision of our flying.

So it was night work. Hour after hour, steady on course, pitch-black, nothing to be seen. Home at dawn, cramped and cold, stepping down and unfolding oneself in the warmth of the morning sun. Hours in that tiny roaring world and never seeing one's enemy – I imagined him sometimes to be an airman or a gunner, but then I thought he was more likely an old man asleep, a schoolboy, a child. She's in my dreams, that child: a girl waking in the dark, opening her eyes in some city, gazing up at the ceiling and hearing the coming thunder, a child lying still, listening and then calling out.

The tail end of March 1943. A blustery afternoon. In the briefing hut Jacko is whispering in Alex's ear when the squadron leader comes in and flips the cover from the route map. Jacko is our rear gunner, a Welshman who'd been a miner, a small man, argumentative. I nudge him and he looks up, sees the map and cries out, 'Bloody Berlin again!'

The CO hears him and laughs. 'Bloody Berlin it is,' he says. 'You're off to the big city again, boyo.'

We called it that: the big city. The third largest city in the world, four million people, nine hundred square miles, numberless flak guns and fighters – we called it 'the big city', and the commonplace words a little reduced that mighty place, bringing its destruction within possibility.

After the briefing my crew waits for darkness. Alex Young, our navigator, lies flat on a bunk, hands behind his head, delivering one of his languid reminiscences – 'They found us in the broom cupboard, not a stitch on either of us. My dear, you should have heard what my mother said. The whole thing was truly horrible. But tremendous fun, of course. What a girl!'

Bob Rattray, bomb-aimer and farmer's son, listens and nods, lighting his pipe in that slow and careful way of his.

Jim Mackintosh looks at his watch, gets up and says to the air that he thinks he'll go and check his radios.

Jacko says, 'What, again?'

Laughter. The door blows shut behind Jim and we listen to the wind brushing round the hut, the sizzle of Bob's pipe, someone clearing his throat, turning a page.

My crew. Ah, how proud I was of that phrase, how proud of them! A boy as young as I was, unknowing and unformed, and yet such men would follow me – I could not fathom my deserving them, nor can I still.

At last someone stands up – it's Blunt, the mid-upper gunner – 'Alfred Blunt's my name. Just call me Blunt. That's what I am.' He stands up and says, 'Better get on with it.'

One by one we follow, pulling on our flying suits, sheepskin boots, perhaps a silk scarf, gloves, strapping on our parachute harnesses, stepping from the hut. Outside is the dusk. Men call to each other across the tarmac, joking, laughing, scuffling as boys do, and I glance up at the shadowy clouds. A brisk north wind comes across the open airfield. We stroll towards the aircraft in a loose group: myself, Alex Young the navigator, Bob Rattray the bomb aimer, Jim Mackintosh the wireless operator, Ted Harper the flight engineer, Alfred Blunt the mid-upper gunner and Jacko Williams – the last, Jacko, is the tail gunner, the most alone and the most at risk.

Alex, Bob, Jim, Ted, Blunt, Jacko and I. Seven of us. We stick together, my crew. We don't make friends with people who may not be here tomorrow. Only our crew matters, our team, our band, and we do not lie to each other, since we all need to know the truth. One of us is the pilot, who leads because the rest depend on him: only he can bring us all home, and they look after him, as every crew looks after their pilot, being for the most part older and wiser than he, and needing to keep him safe.

Here stand the aircraft, black-painted, their noses angled toward the sky, and in the shadows under their wings are the ground crews and the armourers with their bomb trains. A crew sits in a line on a two-ton cookie, drinking mugs of tea; one of them has told a joke and they're laughing. The cookie is not an elegant bomb, not streamlined. It is a vast tin-can packed with high explosive, a blast bomb, a weapon of brutality and desperation.

There are two kinds of bombload for Berlin: we call them 'the usual' and 'arson'. 'The usual' is a cookie plus two hundred and thirty-six incendiaries. 'Arson' is incendiaries only, hundreds of them, I forget how many.

Bombing, we all know now, is not precise work in any

sense. We scatter our cookies on a city, knocking down walls and lifting roofs, then come raining down thousands of incendiaries to light up what remains. Fire is what we want, fire does the real damage. A pitch-black night, hundreds of aircraft over the city, all those fat cookies slowly tumbling end over end, tens of thousands of the little fire bombs following. It takes twenty minutes for us to pass over: there are perhaps six or eight hundred aircraft, sometimes more, sometimes less. Twenty minutes is a short time, certainly, but long enough to light the fire and stoke it, if we do it right: we pass over and we let fall fire upon the sleeping city, and that is our brave task.

It was safer to carry 'arson'. We preferred the little incendiaries. 'The usual' was dangerous. If you were carrying a cookie and were hit by flak or fighters the aeroplane simply exploded like a big flower, a big yellow-and-red blossom that bloomed and hung there for a moment and slowly faded, its glowing fragments falling and fading. You knew they'd all gone then, that crew, the whole crew gone in that instant.

'Arson' was safer. The aircraft might burn, but you had a chance of getting out. But when you saw that sudden red bloom in the blackness you looked away and there was nothing to be said.

Our aeroplane is E-Echo, an old Lancaster that has done nearly forty operations to Germany, and we love it because it has shown that it knows the way back: since last summer it has taken us there and brought us back eleven times. The aeroplane squats heavily on its fat tyres, full and primed, our ground crew standing beneath, wiping their hands on scraps of rag. The chief ground engineer brings me the Form 700 and says 'All tickety-boo, sir.' He has an odd, lopsided face, our chief, a permanent sarcastic look that doesn't mean anything. He says again, 'All tickety-boo', and holds out the flimsy. He turns his back on me so that I can use his shoulders as a desk while I sign. We always do it that way. When I've finished he takes the form and steps over to one of the aeroplane's wheels. 'Be good, you bastard,' he says, and gives the wheel a smart kick. He always does that, too.

We stand under the nose of our black aeroplane. Ted Harper holds out a packet of Senior Service: we all take one and he is left with none. 'You poor bugger,' Jacko says, and gives him one of his, a small and cheap cigarette, a Woodbine, and we laugh some more. We stand in a circle, smoking, kicking the tarmac with our clumsy boots. The ground crew wheel up a trolley acc and plug it in. I walk round the aeroplane with Ted, a last look, checking the control locks are out.

Jacko draws deeply on his cigarette, throws down the stub and grinds it with his heel. We pick up our gear, our parachutes and climb up into the machine. It is awkward, that heave and haul up the cold metal of the ladder. The last man – it's Bob Rattray – pulls up the hatch and locks it shut. We settle in our places and begin work.

An aircrew is assembled more-or-less by chance. They put a crowd of us in a room – pilots, gunners, wireless operators, all the airborne tradesmen – and we stroll about, eyeing each other. Crews form by a process of accretion, catching someone's eye, seeing a chap you know, taking a liking to a stranger and finding he has a friend, so that's three of you already.

When I walked into the room Jacko walked straight up to me and said, 'Hallo, skip, want a gunner?' We'd never seen each other before. It was flattering, being chosen immediately like that. You couldn't turn down a chap who'd done that.

'Looks like you've got a job,' I said. 'What's your name?'

I always think of Jacko first, and not just because he was the first to join. He had the abrasiveness of small men and was not secure. He comes into my mind sharply: *Jacko*, I suddenly think, as one might notice that one's youngest child is missing.

Every so often I'd say 'You OK back there, Jacko?' and he'd say 'Don't you worry about me, skip', his breath whistling down the intercom. 'You bloody well look where you're going,' he'd say, and he'd laugh and start singing 'Men of Harlech' until someone told him to wrap it up. We were always telling him to shut up, but he didn't take much notice. He was one of those people who don't like silence, so he sang in his high tenor whenever he could.

In that crowded room I caught sight of Alex Young, whom I'd met on an astro-nav course. He was a good navigator despite his laid-back manner. He gave me an ironical half-salute and glanced at Jacko – he wasn't sure about Jacko, that was obvious. 'Alex,' I said, forestalling him, 'how about being my navigator?'

He hesitated for a moment, and then said, 'Sure. Why not, Charlie?'

They were the first two to join up. Jacko and Alex. Polar opposites, the pair of them.

On the intercom I go round the crew and make sure everyone's OK, then Ted and I work together on starting the engines. One by one they grind round, cough, puff a little smoke, catch at last and spin the propellers into silver discs.

The instruments come alive and glimmer in yellow light, and soon all four engines are warm and running nicely, sending a shimmer of vibration through the airframe. We're doing our pre-flight checks, watching the temperature gauges climbing slowly and waiting for the ground controller to call us forward.

'Looks good,' I say to Ted. He nods, checking his instruments and making notes on his pad. He's a fussy man who looks like the shopkeeper he once was. He and his wife used to run a corner shop in Chorley; since Ted was called up his wife has run it on her own. He telephones her several times a week, wanting to know about turnover, stock levels, the weekly order, things like that, and every month she sends him the accounts to check. Ted Harper. I like having a fussy flight engineer, even though he hasn't much of a sense of humour; he doesn't miss anything. Sometimes we call him 'Harpic' and he always rises to the bait – Harpic, of course, is the lavatory cleanser guaranteed to 'clean round the bend'.

In my headphones the controller says, 'E-Echo, clear to taxi.' I click the transmit button in response and look out of the window. Our crew chief is standing there with both his thumbs up. I wave to him, release the brakes and feed the engines a little power until we start to move, nosing our way heavily into the dark, following the dim tail lamp of the aircraft in front, feeling through the great wheels each crack and dip in the tarmac. Ahead is a line of five, six, seven tail-lamps, dim and yellow in the night, the squadron queuing for their turn at the runway.

A mile away, in the village, they've heard our engines running up. People stop what they're doing, look at each other, nod without saying anything. A few of the customers in the King's

Arms stand in the garden, looking towards the airfield, their pints and half-pints in their hands, cigarettes glowing.

We reach the end of the runway, turn and stop on the threshold. The lamps of the flare path stretch ahead.

'Brakes on,' I say.

'E-Echo, clear for take-off,' says the controller's voice.

'Roger,' I say, in the laconic style of the air. To the crew I say, 'Stand by for take-off', and then to Ted, 'Full flap.' We wait for the clunk of the flaps, and then I push the four throttles steadily forward, our five thousand horsepower blaring out into the night, the aircraft shuddering.

'Let's go, Ted,' I say. 'Brakes off.'

'Brakes off,' Ted repeats.

'Through the gate.'

I push the throttles to take-off power and Ted holds them there. Ahead is the flare path, the darkness. I begin talking to the aeroplane – *come along now, get a move on, that's it, let's be having you* – and nudge the control column forward, the tail coming slowly up, speed on the machine now, speed gathering, a sense, beginning now, of gathering lightness, the possibility of flight, that buoyancy, and now a sudden smoothness and the ground is gone.

Gear up. More speed. Flaps up. The slow climb, weighted down as we are, an eye on the airspeed and the engine temperatures, all the crew now looking out for other aircraft, the first hazard.

In the village below they listen to the squadron taking off, counting the aeroplanes. Some pause in their washing-up, others switch off the lights and open the curtains, a man and his wife perhaps, their arms around each other, looking through an open window. A boy lifts his head from his homework, doodles a Lancaster on the page, while in the pub garden one or two raise their glasses towards the roaring shadows, some saying *Give them hell*, others silent, watching. They stop their talk and listen, sometimes glancing at each other, and slowly the engines fade until nothing is left but the sound of the wind and a feeling of loss.

Over the North Sea, Jacko begins to sing. Tail gunners sing; it is what tail gunners do. They sing because they are alone and most at risk, and their crews allow it. Jacko is Chapel. He sings well, though I sometimes have to find a reason to stop him, because his singing tends to sadness and Jacko's songs make us think of an unremitting God, pretty girls in lace bonnets, the windy hills of Wales, the loss of love.

Alex is silent for a long time. At last he says, 'Skip, I've got the hell of a funny wind here.'

Someone laughs. I ask Alex what he means.

'According to me,' Alex says carefully, 'the wind's over a hundred miles an hour from the north. I've checked it three times. We're being blown way south of track.'

'A hundred miles an hour? Are you sure?'

I have never heard of such a thing. The forecast wind was strong, but nowhere near as strong as that.

'I've checked.'

'Can't be true, surely.'

'That's what I thought. But I've worked it out three times and it comes out the same.'

'A hundred miles an hour.'

'Yes. A hundred and five, in fact.'

'Blimey.'

'Yes.'

I think about it for a moment, and then say, 'All right, Alex, what course does that give us?'

'Zero four five,' Alex says.

The aeroplane flies through a sudden patch of rough air and we all look out into the blackness. The roughness might be the slipstream of another bomber, or that of a night-fighter, but nothing can be seen: only the black night roars on.

'Zero four five,' I say, resetting the compass and pulling the aeroplane round to the left.

It feels wrong, but Alex is correct: on this particular night a tremendous wind is blowing, and the aircraft whose navigators do not detect the strength of the wind will be scattered half across Germany. Now we are facing north-east and I feel I should turn right, eastwards, in the direction I know Berlin lies, but I must believe my navigator and the instruments: it is a rule of flying that one must do what is known to be right, what the instruments tell you, despite what you feel.

Later, Bob goes down in his bomb-aimer's position in the nose. 'Dutch coast coming up,' he says, and the darkness seems more tangible over the land. Darkness visible, I think to myself, no light, but rather darkness visible.

It comes down to a question of numbers. Berlin is far away, in the middle of a hostile country. Suppose that four hundred aircraft are sent to Berlin, and five per cent are lost – night fighters, flak gunners, accidents, one or two who get lost and fall into the sea. Five per cent of four hundred is twenty aircraft – one hundred and forty men.

Very well. In the course of a war, the loss of twenty aircraft and a hundred and forty men from time to time, for some important purpose, might well be justified.

But if the operation is repeated and the loss rate is again five per cent, the total is now forty aircraft lost, two hundred and eighty men. This is a high price, but our commanders may still think it worth paying, if what has been achieved has a sufficiently high value.

And what is the value of bombing Berlin? Ah, there's a question. Even now, so many years later, nobody knows. Yes, guns and gunners are kept from the eastern front, and fighters too. Bombing damages the fabric of Berlin and kills or injures tens of thousands of its civil population. This must have an economic cost, but there is no obvious effect on the German war effort: war production goes on rising, and the will of the people is not weakened in the slightest; perhaps the converse, indeed.

Never mind. Continue with the numbers. Send another four hundred bombers to Berlin, then another. Eighty aircraft have now been lost, and five hundred and sixty men. Four raids have been made, and the loss is equivalent to, say, five bomber squadrons. All those aeroplanes have to be replaced, all those new crews have to be found and trained.

What is the damage to Berlin now?

The answer is the same as before: nobody knows. Many thousand Berliners are dead, but the effectiveness of the raids is not obviously quantifiable. Surely the validity of such operations will be questioned now, especially when the loss rate starts rising – six, eight, even ten per cent?

Not so. Not by Air Chief Marshal Harris, the head of Bomber Command, nor by the Prime Minister, who counts Harris as a friend in belligerence and invites him for weekend chats at Chequers. In parliament, no questions. A single private letter from Lord Salisbury queries the bombing policy and is ignored. The operations continue.

Six raids on Berlin, eight, ten, twelve. On 2 December 1942,

458 aircraft are sent and 40 lost, on 16 December, 483 sent and 25 lost. The raids go on through December and into the new year: 15 aircraft lost, 20 lost, 28 lost, 26 lost, 35 lost, 33 lost, 46 lost, 33 lost, 43 lost –

But what matter; isn't this always the way of war? Who cares now that these are only numbers, and very old numbers, though once they were men?

There is nothing to see but darkness, and in time our ears adjust to the din of the engines. Motionless in our seats, we seem to fly in silence, our journey measured only by the trembling needles of the instruments. For an hour, two hours, three, the aeroplane is a place apart from light and life.

'Hey skip,' Blunt says suddenly, 'there's a star over my head.'

'Star struck, Bluntie?' – that's Alex.

Jim says, 'Bugger', because we don't like clear skies and stars and particularly hate the bright and lovely moon.

I ask Blunt, 'What star is it?'

'What star, skip?' he says, 'How the hell should I know what bloody star it is?'

Everyone laughs.

'Jacko,' I say.

'Hello, skip.'

'How about singing something jolly, eh?'

'Something vulgar, did you say?'

'No, Jacko, I said jolly.'

'There was an old monk of great renown,' he sings, 'who fucked all the women there were in the town.'

'Bloody hell, Jacko,' I protest, but he takes no notice and goes on singing.

*

Despite Alex's skill we are blown ten miles south of the target –
he cannot quite believe his own calculations of the wind
strength, and has reduced the vector a little. Getting a fix over
the south of the city, we crawl northwards into the storm. The
aiming point is the Tiergarten, already lit with the dangling
skeins of coloured light that are the Pathfinders' markers. Now
there are other aircraft above and below, many of them,
shadows that flicker into view and are gone again, and the
radio is noisy with confusing instructions.

'Fucking chaos,' Bob says calmly from his bomb-aimer's
position. He is always absolutely calm.

Eventually we find a space in the queue of aircraft, turn
steeply southwards and begin to rush with that mighty wind
towards the heart of the city. Berlin has the look of an abstract
picture, sketches for the inferno, dashed with brilliant colour,
sudden rolling shadows, flickering sparks and the drifting,
hanging jewels of the sky markers, green and yellow. Three
miles below, bombs from an unseen aircraft explode silently in
splashes of flat white light, and curving up towards us come
dotted lines of tracer, seeming slow and harmless, drawing itself
around us in sweeping curves.

The bomb doors are open.

'Steady, steady,' Bob calls. He's peering into the bombsight,
waiting for the moment that the aiming point passes beneath,
the centre of the Tiergarten. He calls, 'Right, right, steady', and
I try to hold the aeroplane straight. Something explodes close
ahead – a flak shell, and the aeroplane is kicked to the left.

'Right, right,' Bob says, more urgently, and then, 'steady,
steady.'

The run in to the aiming point takes long minutes as it
always does, but at last the aeroplane leaps upwards.

'Bombs gone,' Bob calls. 'Keep steady, skip.'

We have to keep straight until our camera flash has fired, then at last I can put the nose down and push the throttles forward: we dive away from the flames, the lights, the fire, toward the dark, the blessed dark, and our work in the cause of victory has been done.

The old aeroplane is racing now, racing home, shaking with speed. Slowly I bring the nose up, easing the pace, the angle. Alex gives me the new course and we bank to the right. Craning my neck, I can just see the blaze of Berlin behind us, seeming already far away, a few brilliant pencils of light moving elegantly among a scatter of red and green jewels.

Jim comes on the intercom and says, 'Did you hear that ass over the target?'

'I heard him,' I say.

Someone yelled on the radio over the target, the Master Bomber perhaps, telling us to give them hell, give them hell, those bastards, now we'll show them what war is like – all that sort of stuff. A bullshit merchant, that's what we called people like that, a fucking threepenny hero.

'Silly sod,' Jim says.

As he speaks, the aeroplane is filled with something strange – dust, is it? Or smoke? – and flashes of silver light, enormously bright. I feel a blow on my shoulder and then a rush of freezing air. Blunt is yelling something and I hear the shudder of his guns firing. I pull the aeroplane into a steep turn and then dive. One panel of the windscreen is shattered – that's the cause of the freezing air. I pull out of the dive, throw the aeroplane roughly to the right, dive again.

'Can you see him, Blunty?'

'No,' Blunt shouts, 'I think we've lost him.'

I pull out of the dive, try to get straight. There are holes in the floor, holes in the roof. I reach with my left hand and discover blood on my right shoulder. 'Ted,' I say, 'are you OK?' There is no reply. He's in the seat beside and below mine, a dark shape. 'Ted?' I say again. He does not move.

Alex says, 'Hang on a minute, skip, I'll come down there.'

I look down at Ted. I think he's dead, but it's too dark to be sure. I call the others.

'Blunt, are you OK?'

'OK, skip.'

'Jim?'

'Yes.'

'Bob?'

Nothing. The floor ahead of my seat is buckled and torn: Bob is down there somewhere.

Again I say, 'Bob, can you hear me?'

Still nothing.

'Jacko?'

Silence.

I call him again: 'Jacko, Jacko.'

Silence still.

The blast from the broken windscreen is beating at me and I crouch as low as I can in the seat. We'll have to slow down and ease this battering, whether or not the fighter is still about.

Alex appears with a torch, struggling along the floor on hands and knees. He crouches next to Ted, flashes the light on him, pulls himself up beside me and yells in my ear. 'He's gone, skip,' he shouts. 'He's shot to pieces.'

What must be done?

I shout to Alex, 'Can you go aft and check Jacko?'

'What about Bob?' he asks.

'Oh, Christ, yes,' I say, 'check him first.'

Alex crawls past me towards the bomb aimer's position, and

in a few moments slithers back. 'It's no good,' he yells, 'Bob's had it too. I'll go to Jacko.' He crawls away towards the rear.

Ted Harper, Bob Rattray. I feel my shoulder again. I don't think the blood is mine.

A fighter must have found us and fired upward as it passed beneath, killing Bob, killing Ted.

What about Jacko?

I try to get the aeroplane to fly straight but it wants to turn left – damage somewhere, the tail or one of the wings. I push with both feet on the right rudder pedal and it's just possible to keep straight. Airspeed, altimeter, turn-and-slip – most of the instruments are still working. I peer out, twisting my head to look behind and finding nothing but darkness. I check the compass and allow the aeroplane to turn gradually to the left until it is on course.

Alex has been gone a long time.

'Alex?'

No reply. Jim says, 'He just went past me, skip.' There is something in his voice, a tremor.

'OK,' I say to him. 'You sure you're all right, Jim?'

There is a pause. 'I think maybe something hit me.'

'All right, Jim,' I say. 'Wait until Alex comes back and get him to have a look at you.'

'Yes. All right, skipper.'

Jacko has been hit in the chest and head. He is dead and Alex can't get him out of his turret, so he leaves him there. Jim has a long, fine splinter of metal in his back. Alex and Blunt lift him from his seat and inspect the splinter but they dare not touch it. Jim is laid face-down on the floor, his head on Alex's rolled-up jacket. We block the worst hole in the windscreen with pieces of aluminium. There is damage to the instrument panel but the flying controls are working after a fashion and the engines and fuel tanks seem intact.

'We'll keep going,' I say to Alex. 'We'll try to make it home.'

We are not attacked again. For three hours Alex and I struggle to keep the Lancaster straight while Blunt keeps watch from the mid-upper turret, swivelling his guns. As we reach the North Sea the weather clears and the water is wrinkled silver under the stars. We land at Witchford and the ambulance crew tells me that Jim is dead. I don't know when he died – somewhere over the sea, I think.

*

When I climbed down from the aeroplane I found I couldn't stand up without holding on to the ladder. I thought it was just exhaustion from the struggle we'd had to keep the aeroplane flying straight, but it didn't wear off. They took me into hospital in Norwich and gave me all sorts of checks but couldn't find anything. After a few days the medics signed me off flying.

About two weeks later I began to walk again, rather slowly. Two RAF medics gave me another check-up, went into a huddle and then told me I would be transferred to ground duties with immediate effect.

It is shocking to find that one can't make one's legs work, or stop one's hands shaking. You're told your body has been shut down by your subconscious – it isn't your fault at all, old chap, absolutely not, just one of those things. Hard to believe, that is. I still feel ashamed. It wears off a bit, but it doesn't entirely go away. After I was grounded Alex Young and Alfred Blunt were transferred to another pilot and were killed in a raid on a railway yard at Rouen in June 1944.

*

The last thing Bob Rattray said was 'Keep steady, skip.' In sixty years the memory of Bob and the others has not faded – I have not wished it to fade – but for those bomber crews who survived there was another challenge to come, a challenge that we had not predicted, and made more demands on our steadiness.

As soon as the war ended something odd happened – or did not happen. No campaign medal was issued for Bomber Command, no peerage given to Air Chief Marshal Harris, our commander. Why not? The bombing campaign had cost the deaths of some fifty thousand RAF aircrew and was for years the country's principal war effort – a gigantic effort that was now being deliberately erased from history.

Those of us who had bombed Berlin began to recognise a cruel paradox: our actions had been brave and the price high, but those actions were now perceived to be wrong, very wrong, perhaps a crime, a war crime.

If one asks how it was that so many Germans were able to involve themselves in terrible crimes against millions of innocent civilians, one must also ask the same question of ourselves. The answer is the usual answer: because it did not occur to us to question orders, because we were incapable of imagining the consequences of our actions, because we accepted that all Germans were evil – the same reasons that we have heard in the mouths of so many, that we always hear.

Certainly we didn't ask questions. Certainly we did what we were told. We knew about Hamburg – that was the first proper firestorm. We knew Hamburg was exactly what Harris wanted: firestorms to obliterate German cities and destroy the German will to fight.

Bomber Harris, the newspapers called him, but in the RAF we didn't call him that; we called him Butcher Harris, Butch for short. He wanted every German city to burn like Hamburg, so he'd win the war by bombing alone, just as he'd claimed he would. He told Churchill he could do it, but we let him down; after Hamburg and Stuttgart we only managed a proper firestorm once – that was Dresden, an old wooden town, and too late in the war to matter. We burned Hamburg and Dresden but we couldn't burn Berlin, despite trying nineteen times. That last time – the night of the big winds – seventy-two aircraft were lost. We did not go there again. Berlin had beaten us. It wouldn't burn, and it had consumed too many men and aeroplanes.

I often think of Harris. There is a photograph of him standing beside the steps of an airliner with his wife and daughter, just after the war. His wife was very elegant, his daughter thin-legged, a nervous-looking little girl. Harris is jowly, unsmiling, and he is gazing off to his right, at something outside the picture. Did he ever wonder what sort of man he was? It is hard to think that he did not; he may even have thought of General Haig, another dogged man who wouldn't let go of a pet theory.

There is one more aspect of this matter about which I have often wondered: how did we manage to return to Berlin again and again, knowing the odds, defying the logic and displaying, in the conventional view, such astonishing bravery?

Here is another paradox. Our actions were not enabled by the bravery of individuals but by the bonds between us. War is a failure of humanity, of course, but war is enabled by humanity, too – enabled by affection, respect, loyalty, love and pride among and between men. If they can do this, then so can I, and each of us is one among brave men.

Oh yes, I still think about these things when I wake in the night and listen to the wind in the eaves. I had thought that flying in the defence of my country would be the grandest thing, greater even than life on earth, and I had wished that flight would take me to some high place among the stars; it did not do so, because there is no such place, but only a dream, only a foolish wish. I know this now, of course, but despite my naïvety there *was* something rare and true to be discovered, and it is enclosed in the memory of the six men whom I once knew: Alfred Blunt, Ted Harper, Jim Mackintosh, Bob Rattray, Jacko Williams and Alex Young.

Eleven

Edmund watched his sisters leave Rookwood in the canal boat. Afterwards he came back into the house and said to his mother, 'That friend of Ruth's isn't a girl. He's called Patrick.'

'I can't say I'm surprised,' Frances said.

'She's sent him packing,' Edmund said.

'What do you mean, Edmund?'

'Ruth's sent Patrick away. He's to meet her in London in a week, and she and Lizzie have gone off on their own.'

'Good,' his mother said, nodding.

The sympathetic bond between sisters was not the only element in Elizabeth's recovery. It also had to do with the slow and steady nature of their journey, its simple and repetitive routines, their exposure to rain and wind and to the isolation and calm of the canals. Certain things she never forgot – the constant presence of kingfishers, for example, keeping watch on the boat, flying ahead, settling briefly on a bare branch and moving on again, flickering blue and green and red like pinches of salt thrown on a fire. There was the absolute darkness of each night, its silence, the manner in which trees seemed to cluster close around the boat, and once, some time before dawn, Elizabeth was woken by the soft hoot of an owl.

On another morning she opened her eyes to find the stove glowing and the tiny cabin full of steam. Her sister, naked, was kneeling on the floor and washing herself in a bowl. She watched as Ruth held her hair up with one hand and soaped the back of her neck, then picked up a double handful of water and plunged her face into it, shivered and shook herself, picked up a towel, lifted her hair again and wrapped the towel about her head.

They took turns to ride the horse and steer the boat. The gait of the horse was absolutely regular and its massive strength assured their progress. From time to time Elizabeth would bend towards its neck and murmur its name, at which the horse's ears would flicker but its regular step did not falter.

'The important thing about the canals,' Ruth told her, 'is that you're always on the level.'

It was true: there is nothing more level, more steady, than a canal journey.

As they approached London Ruth began to talk about buying clothes. Elizabeth dismissed the idea. There was no reason why she needed more clothes. It was ridiculous and it was unnecessary. But she thought of herself before a tall mirror, twirling a wide skirt, trying on a red hat with a flower and a pair of shoes, also red, absurdly high-heeled – it was curious to think of such things.

Possibly, if Ruth were with her, she might try something on, just try it on merely to discover what it looked like. In the past she had always chosen the same kind of dress because that was the easy thing to do, and it didn't waste time. She imagined a black dress, close-fitting, tapered, narrow-skirted. Who were those designers that people talked about? Hartnell, Schiaparelli – that was it. Perhaps a cream dress, a long dress of some heavy, layered stuff, an evening dress, gloves to her elbows, a small sequinned purse, a silver necklace, pearls. She laughed and looked again at the busy clouds, feeling the wind against her face and the steady movement of the horse.

Tring, Watford, Cowley – as the boat worked south the clouds grew lower, the wind more chill, and the city began to enclose them. At Bull's Bridge they turned east through a clutter of factories, railway yards and bridges – Black Horse, Ballot Box, Piggery. They passed Kensal Green Cemetery and were among plane trees and streets of large, elegant houses: St John's Wood, and then Little Venice.

They moored the boat and Ruth clambered on to the roof of the cabin and waved her arms. 'Isn't it marvellous how secret the canals are! We've stolen into London, and nobody has seen us come, nobody knows we're here!'

Later, she said, 'Lizzie, we'll go into town tomorrow and look at dresses and one or two other things.'

Elizabeth continued to eat her supper.

'I had in mind a bold check,' Ruth said. 'Something quite striking, with a big collar.'

Elizabeth still said nothing.

'And we could also find a pair of high-heeled sandals. Are you still a size seven?'

'Yes,' Elizabeth said.

'And of course we ought to get a hat as well, don't you think?'

'Possibly,' Elizabeth said.

'A straw hat, perhaps, and maybe a matching scarf. I've got plenty of coupons.'

'I've got coupons of my own,' Elizabeth said.

'Oh, have you? I was going to use mine.'

'We could get you a dress as well,' Elizabeth said.

'That's not the point.'

'If you don't get yourself one, I won't have one either.'

The following day the sisters walked down the Edgware Road to Oxford Street, passed through glass doors and were surrounded by racks and tall mirrors. Elizabeth waited while her sister ran about in the maze of racks. Soon she came back. 'Let's go and look at a few of them,' she said. 'We'll just see what there is.'

Ruth was quick with the clothes, flicking through them, accepting or rejecting. 'How absurd,' she would say, pushing the hanger along the rail and then stopping for a moment to look at another – 'Oh no, certainly not!' – and going on again. But finally she found the blue and white check dress she was looking for, a dress with broad shoulders, a flaring white collar, a narrow waist and a full and swirling skirt.

Ruth stopped and lifted it from the rack, holding it against herself. 'Now there's a lovely dress.' She looked at the label. 'We don't want anything that says "utility" on it. One should have a few things that are stylish and properly made, don't you think?'

'Really, Ruth, you're awfully silly sometimes.'

Ruth laughed. 'It's such fun, looking for clothes.'

'Humph,' Elizabeth said. She stood still while her sister held the dress against her.

'Try it on, Lizzie,' Ruth said, and Elizabeth found a changing-room. She came out and stepped quickly to a mirror.

'It looks all wrong,' she said.

'Nonsense,' Ruth said. 'It looks wonderful. It's marvellous. Do a twirl.'

Elizabeth twirled.

'There you are,' Ruth said. 'It's terrific! We'll have it.' She put her head on one side and considered her sister. 'And of course,' she said, 'it will look even more wonderful with the right shoes and a fabulous hat.'

A shop assistant had been hovering and now stepped forward. 'Good morning, ladies—'

'My sister wants this dress,' Ruth said. 'And a pair of shoes, a hat and a scarf to match.'

'Of course, madam.'

When they had finished Elizabeth looked for some considerable time at the strange woman in the mirror.

'Oh, Lizzie,' Ruth said, 'you forgot the lipstick.' She stood on tiptoe and applied it.

'Perfect,' Ruth said. 'Absolutely perfect. Now we'll look for something for me.'

The sisters, wearing their new outfits, went to the Savoy, where there was the usual tea dance, were surrounded by Americans, danced for two hours and ate cream cakes.

The canal journey finished at Limehouse. After Camden eleven locks take the canal down to the Thames, and they descended slowly through the ruined landscape to Mafeking Street, where they were welcomed by Lily Attwell, who had been expecting them for some time.

Twelve

I had called at Rookwood several times. On the first occasion Elizabeth's mother told me that she had gone away with Ruth and not yet returned.

'I'm not sure exactly where they are, Mr Charles,' Frances Bowman said in her stiff way, standing in the doorway and not inviting me in.

'Please call me Charlie,' I said. 'Everyone calls me that these days.'

'Oh, I don't think I could do that,' she said.

On my next visit Frances told me that Elizabeth had telephoned her from somewhere in the Midlands. She and Ruth were on their way to London and intended to visit Elizabeth's friend Lily Attwell in the East End.

'Elizabeth sounded much happier,' her mother said. 'I'm expecting her home soon.'

'Perhaps you could ask her to telephone me when she comes home,' I said. But I heard nothing in subsequent weeks.

It was into December by the time I made my next visit.

I found that Frances was no longer certain when Elizabeth would be returning to Rookwood.

'She's staying in London for the time being, Mr Charles. I did tell her you'd called.'

'Thank you.'

'She said that you knew where she was.'

'Did she?' What did that mean?

'Actually,' I said, 'I don't know the Attwells' address.'

Frances Bowman looked vague. 'Didn't I tell you?'

'No, you didn't,' I said.

She gave me the address then. There was no telephone, she said.

'Thank you so much,' I said.

'That's quite all right,' she said.

I hesitated. 'Mrs Bowman,' I said, 'I hope you don't mind my saying that your husband was a great friend of mine when I was a boy. He was a most lovely man, and I miss him greatly, as I'm sure you must do.'

'Yes, I do,' she said, and hurried into the house.

I set out straight away for London. The train to King's Cross was delayed and it was dark and snowing heavily by the time I reached Mile End. The streets were empty – no cabs or buses. I pulled my hat down and my collar up, shoved my hands deep in my pockets and set out on foot for Mafeking Street, thinking of my old friend Ernest Bowman.

To me, Ernest was a very odd man. He liked children. I was wandering down a long corridor when we first met. He came round the corner, saw me and sat down on the carpet, something that I had never seen an adult do. I stopped, looked at him and was then drawn towards him just as I was drawn towards the warmth of the fire in Waverley's vast nursery.

'Well,' he said, 'if it isn't Young Master Charles, venturing on an exploration of the house.'

It was not magic. He simply played the ordinary games that many adults play with children, but they were new to me. On his desk Ernest kept a glass jar full of bulls' eyes. I would open the door of his room with what I imagined to be perfect stealth, and on every occasion he would say, apparently to himself, 'I'm blowed if I don't hear the footsteps of a little chap who might possibly be Young Master Charles! And here was I, just thinking that it might be time for – whatever are those things that I keep in that pot on my desk, I can never remember—'

And I, thinking what a silly man he must be who could never remember such an important fact, would yell, 'Bulls' eyes, Mr Bowman! Bulls' eyes!'

At that he would stiffen, reach for the glass jar and murmur to himself, 'Aha! Bulls' eyes! I'm blowed if that isn't an extremely edible notion! Now, I wonder – is today the sort of day that requires just a single bulls' eye, or could today be the sort of day that deserves not one but *two* bulls' eyes?'

I soon discovered that Ernest was a much more interesting father than my own; from the beginning his grin indicated that we somehow shared a mutual conspiracy against the world. Remarkably, he would ask my opinion on all sorts of topics, and evidently listened to my reply.

Most of all, Ernest was energetic. My own father began adult life as Sir St John Beevor, Baron Waverley, and for fifty-odd years gently dwindled into vagueness and obscurity; Ernest began as a Thames waterman and became the firm buttress upon which the estate depended: in that sense, they passed each other on the stairs.

'Rain and books, Young Master Charles,' he would say, patting me on the head and indicating the shelves that lined his room. 'Can you hear them murmurings?'

'No,' I said, and I never did hear his books murmuring, though I always listened hard.

'All those voices,' he'd say, 'and think of the wisdom in them pages. Just look at them now.' And he shook his head in wonder.

At the age of eighteen a downpour had driven Ernest into a library in Greenwich. For five years he had been working with his father on the river, and had never before entered a library; but while handfuls of rain clattered against the windows Ernest became engrossed in Volume N–P of the *Dictionary of National Biography*, which happened to be lying open on a table. Nelson, Newbolt, Newman, Newton, Nightingale – all those great names, and dozens more of whom he'd never heard! So much achievement by so many!

'You may say that I woke up that day, Master Charles. I awoke to the possibilities of the world.'

He discovered that a man did not have to remain content with his place, but could engineer his own destiny. Looking up from the dictionary, he saw that the means were immediately to hand: books, thousands of them, row upon row, plump with knowledge. He would become a librarian, and that would give him the key to the whole kit and caboodle!

There was no wind and the snow fell vertically and steadily. Under the street lights the falling flakes shimmered through cones of yellow light that looked like the shades of enormous table lamps; already the snow lay an inch deep on the road and pavement and had begun that neat trick of balancing in a narrow band along branches and overhead wires. From time to time a car or lorry came creeping past, the driver's face pressed close to the windscreen, and on one or two corners groups of children yelled at each other; after I'd passed them, a few snowballs sailed over my head, accompanied by shouts and laughter.

From the moment he left Rotherhithe for Waverley, at first to work as a porter in the library, later as an archive clerk and finally in the secretariat, Ernest Bowman filled his spare time with reading, and in thirty years, while climbing the hierarchy of the estate and minding my father's library, he gathered a considerable book collection of his own. His favourites were illustrated history: *Fifty Great Inventions of the Nineteenth Century*, *The Truth About Thomas Cromwell*, *The Great Navigators*, *How the British Empire Brought Peace to the World*. He was uneasy with fiction or poetry. 'Why make something up, Master Charles, when the world is already full of wonders?'

When he began reading it, history was not yet unsettling. It confirmed the status quo, and displayed for him the qualities, behaviour and knowledge required for success. He refined his manners and speech, chose as his wife a steady girl called Frances, the eldest daughter of a shopkeeper, and began a family. He did not do so in a mercenary way – though it was true that a family was a sign of stability, and stability was a desirable thing in an employee – no, he felt for his wife and children something deep and abiding that he did not question, and believed that he loved with equal strength his wife Frances, his son Edmund, his daughter Ruth and his own little Lizzie – but of course he loved Lizzie best, as everyone knew.

When Ernest had pinned down some new instance of

causality in the chain of great men, inventions, fateful battles, revolutions, discoveries, coincidences and all the stuff from which history is made, he felt a warm flood of content, slept soundly and whistled as he walked about Waverley.

'That's got that straight,' he'd say to me, 'that's why Trafalgar was won, no doubt about it.'

The logic of history was that everything had its place and purpose. Once one knew how things were arranged in the world, one's life could be adjusted to ensure success, prosperity and happiness. It was just plain silly to keep asking questions and to harbour all sorts of complicated doubts. From his books Ernest worked out that human existence was a great factory on many floors, filled with clattering looms and driven by a tangle of belts and shafts; it was complicated, certainly, but there was not the slightest doubt that pulling this lever or turning that wheel had predictable consequences. Something went in at one door and in due course something else came out of another. Of course it did! It was simply a matter of discovering which lever did what.

Ernest believed that we make our own destiny, the collective sum of which is history. His philosophy, he told me, was like the wheels and springs of his fine English clock, and worked as certainly. 'Man has life and free will, Master Charles, and his only task is to make the most of them.' As long as people did the right thing, it would all work out: he looked back, and the steadily rising slope of his own life was incontrovertible proof of the correctness of his beliefs.

A profound silence hung over the river, and the soft squeak of my own footsteps in the snow sounded absurdly loud. I began to imagine the snow as a soothing dressing for the battered streets and buildings, the sleeping city smoothed over in the darkness, its fires extinguished, its scars and gaps blended back into the living flesh. A line or two of verse drifted into my head:

> Winter kept us warm,
> Covering earth in forgetful snow . . .

We had worked for victory and wanted it with all our hearts, but when victory was declared I had not the slightest sense of it. I saw the parties in the street, the fireworks, the dancing and the speechmaking, and felt only an enormous weight of sorrow and tiredness. I suppose that human beings are designed for loss, since it is necessary to life; but so much loss, for so many years – it was not clear to me how such a thing could be repaired.

The snowflakes were falling in their millions into the brown tide and vanishing without the slightest mark. A Russian ship was unloading under brilliant arc-lights, two cranes swinging hessian-wrapped bundles across to the quay, half-a-dozen dockers stacking the bundles into neat piles. I wondered what urgent cargo it was that must be unloaded at night and in a snowstorm; but perhaps it was not urgent at all, but simply the last task of the day, after which the dockers could go home and warm their hands by the fire.

I stood and watched the ship for some considerable time, an idea slowly forming in my mind. I was looking at a scene of great simplicity, a scene entirely in black-and-white, that yet possessed a remarkable dramatic quality – it was something to do with the limits applied by the glaring light, the rhythmical movements of the men, the height and angle of the cranes. I stared at the ship for a long time, wishing that I had brought a camera with me. It might be ridiculous, my idea, but it was nevertheless an intriguing one. The more thought I gave it, the more excitement I felt; indeed, I began to think I might be seeing, in dim outline, the whole of my future life.

Suddenly conscious of the cold, I shook the accumulated snow from my hat and walked on quickly.

*

Everything comes to an end. It was the spring of 1932. Ned Garvin, a boy of about my own age, had spent all night in an unsuccessful watch for poachers in Tupman's Hanger. He saw Ernest early that morning as he walked down the Queen's Ride on his way to his duties. Ned watched him for a while, saw him greet his daughter Ruth and heard her call goodbye as she ran on her way home.

In his room at Waverley Ernest drew the tall curtains and stood for a moment before the window. He hung his hat, jacket, topcoat and umbrella on the hat-stand, sat down at his desk and began to open the post that Forbes, the senior footman, had just placed there. As he reached for the inkstand the rupture of an aneurysm within his brain caused a violent convulsion of his leg and back muscles, a spasm that threw his chair backwards and overturned the desk with an enormous crash. He fell forwards across it, several of his front teeth shattering on the embossed edge of the centre drawer.

Hearing the crash, Forbes rushed in, knelt at Ernest's side and saw that his face was fixed in a terrible contortion. He tore off Ernest's tie, opened his shirt and felt for a pulse in his neck. There was none; and there was therefore no point in haste. It might set off who knows what panic. Forbes slowly stood up, picked up the fallen chair, sat down, put his hands to his cheeks and tried to calm the terrible pounding of his heart.

At that moment I silently opened the door and stood on the threshold, waiting for Mr Bowman to recognise my presence as usual. I was wearing my first long trousers, which I wished to show off, and such is the power of expectation that I did not recognise the scene as a tragedy, but thought it some unusual activity in which Mr Bowman and Forbes were engaged.

I stood and watched Forbes. He sat still for a moment longer, allowing his arms to hang down beside the chair, then got up and knelt beside Ernest again, dragging him away from the desk and arranging his limbs more suitably. I watched him place his fingers on Ernest's face and attempt to close his eyes; that was certainly an odd thing to do. He also tried to right the desk, but it was too heavy for him to move. Finally he collected up the scattered pens and papers and turned round to discover me in the doorway.

'I thought you were Mr Bowman at first,' I said. Forbes's mouth opened and he reached out a hand to steady himself on the back of the chair. Seeing his face, I finally realised that something awful had happened. I stepped forward and looked down at Ernest's bloody face, and it was quite beyond my comprehension.

In the next few minutes a whirlwind fell upon the house. I was sent upstairs and from the landing saw strangers coming and going, the wringing of hands, men and women in uniform, white faces and people crying down the telephone. My father paced helplessly about the hall until my mother appeared and took charge, saying to him, 'St John, there is nothing we can do here. We must go to Rookwood at once. Send for the car.'

By the evening a kind of order had been restored. From my window I saw Frances Bowman and her children arrive and I wanted to go down, but was prevented. Still I did not know the true facts; those I only learned late that night when I sneaked out and encountered Ned Garvin.

He told me that he had gone to Rookwood that day for his lunch, as he often did. He was puzzled to get no reply when he knocked on the kitchen door. After a minute or two he tapped again, then pressed his ear against the door just as it opened.

Eunice Turner from the dairy stood there, holding a red chequered tea-towel to her face. 'You can't come in,' she said in a rusty-sounding voice.

Ned stood and stared at her.

'Go away, Ned. You'll have to go away.' She placed a hand flat against his chest and pushed. He stepped back. The door shut in his face. He stood there for a moment, annoyed at being ejected by a dairymaid, then picked up his gun and walked quickly round to the garden rear of the house. There was nobody there, so he strode up to the french windows and reached for the door-handle. Through the glass he saw Frances Bowman and her three children kneeling on the carpet with their arms round one another.

'I saw them, Mr Charles, and I couldn't fathom it. Was they praying or what? I was still holding the door-handle, see.'

Slowly he had released the handle, stepped away and retreated into the cover of the woods.

'Then I knew what it must be, Mr Charles. I knew Mr Bowman must be gone.'

'Gone?'

'Dead, Mr Charles. He's dead, that's what. He died that morning, didn't he?'

Ernest Bowman dead? It was not possible. I rushed into the house, found my mother and asked her directly.

'Of course he is,' my mother said. 'What on earth did you think all the fuss was about? For goodness' sake, Charles!'

At 27 Mafeking Street a woman answered the door to me, peering out into the darkness at the man standing in the driving snow.

'And who might you be?'

'My name's Charlie Beevor,' I said. 'I'm looking for Elizabeth Bowman.'

She turned and called up the stairs, 'Lizzie! Man called Charlie wants you.'

From behind her a boy peered out at me. I stood waiting on the doorstep, the open door letting fall across the pavement a beam of yellow light in which the snowflakes whirled. I could hear laughter from somewhere inside.

After a moment the woman at the door – it was Lily Attwell, I later discovered – reached for my arm and drew me into the hall, saying, 'Come in, whoever you are. You can't stay out in all that.'

Thirteen

In the East End in the winter of 1945, despite the weather and the human and material wreckage that lay everywhere about us, there was a strong sense that the future would be significantly better than the past; in particular, it would be more just. The war, by taking all classes and kinds of people and throwing them together in strange new contexts, had made the country aware of the gross injustice and inequality of British life; and now, since everyone had suffered and had contributed to victory, regardless of their status, it was right that the benefits of peace should be equally shared. There was also a gut feeling that, after such horror and such sacrifice, the future *must* be better – otherwise, what had we been fighting for?

There was at first a general sense of optimism and determination, but it did not answer the immediate difficulties that everyone faced, and in time it could be eroded by them. Things will be better, yes, but what does that mean? How will I earn my living? Who will pay for the rebuilding of my house? And when?

At Rookwood, before Elizabeth had been abducted by her

sister, we had talked for a while about such gloomy matters – probably we should not have done. She said, 'I have a theory about those big questions.'

'What is it?'

'We must begin with small things – whatever's next – and not ask that sort of question at all. We should just do what feels right, and what needs to be done, and that's all.'

'What feels right to you, Lizzie?'

'Flying, of course,' she said, and then was silent, looking away from me, out of the window and up at the clouds. I looked at her, wondering how her sorrowful logic could be unlocked and feeling, myself, the same sense of anticlimax.

Most of the time, indeed, we do as Lizzie said, and get on with the next thing. Large questions, if they ever occur, are pretty soon displaced by the ringing of the alarm-clock, the call of a child, a letter falling to the mat. But there are rare occasions, and the end of an all-consuming war is one of them, which evidently require us to ask big questions and act on the answers. In that case there is a further difficulty: having become used to novelty and challenge and danger, and done things we had never dreamed possible, peace is liable to seem lacking in significance.

After all that, many of us thought, I am not going to do anything ordinary. *I am not going back.* I am not going back to my old job, my old place, my old ways, my old role. I am not going back to my family, back to my town, back to my room. I am different now, I have learned things, I am going to make a new beginning and do something quite different, and I will live my own life according to my own choices and nobody else's.

It is a fine thought, a bold thought, but in the midst of all that wreckage it was hard to hang on to. It was vulnerable to the voice in the back of one's mind that whispers, 'So you really think such a thing is possible, do you?'

Lily Attwell shouted up the stairs again and a pair of white high-heeled shoes descended into view, followed by legs in nylon stockings, a bold blue-and-white check dress with a full skirt, narrow waist and large collar, a woman wearing a white straw hat and matching scarf – yes, I realised after a moment, it was Elizabeth, and I stared at her, I suppose, like some sort of half-wit. She saw my astonishment and stopped quite deliberately on the lowest step, one hand resting on the banister in a conscious pose, then she laughed and said, 'Charlie, don't you think you ought to take your coat off?'

A puddle was forming on the hall floor around my feet.

'Give me those,' Lily said, reaching for my snow-encrusted hat and coat.

Elizabeth stepped forward and kissed me lightly on the cheek. I was still dumbstruck and she laughed again – 'Really, Charlie, it's only a new frock.'

Lily took my arm firmly and told me I must get out of my wet clothes. Upstairs she took a pile of things from a drawer – her husband Roy Attwell's clothes, I assumed – and told me to help myself. I found some trousers and socks that fitted and went downstairs to a sitting-room crowded with people and cigarette smoke and talk. There was a great crackling fire, before which I was placed, and I was surrounded by laughter – everyone had found the sudden appearance of a large, wet snowman extremely amusing. With Lily was her boy, Arthur, Harry Nicholls, the garage owner who had once employed Alice, Ben Yossakin and George Honeysett, the landlord of the pub, and they were all laughing and saying how funny it was when the door opened and there I stood.

In a corner, large and silent, was Patrick, who was introduced by Ruth as 'My crewman and dear friend Patrick.' I am not sure whether Patrick said anything during the rest of that evening; I think not, but there were many occasions when Ruth looked at him affectionately and he smiled back at her.

In a pause in the conversation I said, 'Lizzie, you look completely different', and the inane remark caused more amusement.

'Of course she does,' Ruth said. 'She's not in uniform, for a start.'

'She looks lovely, doesn't she?' said Lily.

'What a smasher, eh?' – that was George Honeysett.

'Oh, for goodness' sake,' Lizzie said, laughing and blushing.

'Got legs,' George said. 'Legs and all that, eh?'

'Be quiet, George,' Lily said.

Yes, she must have been in uniform every time I had seen her in the last four years, perhaps five, and if she was not in uniform she would be wearing one of those plain cotton dresses of hers; certainly her legs seemed a good deal longer than I remembered, and her neck had quite a different look.

'Your hair's much shorter,' I said. 'I like it very much like that.'

'I hope the conversation isn't going to be entirely about my new clothes and whatnot,' Elizabeth said.

'New shoes, new dress, new hat, new scarf, new haircut and make-up,' Ruth said. 'Quite delightful, she looks, don't you think, Charlie?'

'Oh yes,' I said, 'she looks lovely.'

Elizabeth went pink and sat up straighter. 'Now look, Charles,' she said, 'you must tell me why you've called at Mafeking Street so late, and in the middle of a snowstorm. What do you want?'

I should have said, 'You', and left it at that, but I did not.

Instead I mumbled something about having been passing, and her mother having told me she were here, and thinking I'd call in and see how she was . . .

'You were passing?' Elizabeth said. 'Passing Limehouse? In a blizzard? In the middle of the night?'

'I was in London,' I said. 'I didn't know it was going to snow like this. Besides, it isn't the middle of the night.'

'You'll have to stay, Charlie,' Lily Attwell said. 'You can't possibly go home now. We'll find a bed for you.'

'Oh, I can find my way back to the Underground,' I said.

'I could get the van out,' Harry Nicholls said.

'You can't drive in that lot, Harry,' Lily said, and Arthur said, 'Can I come?'

'Nobody's going anywhere, Arthur,' Lily said with calm authority, 'Charlie's staying here. Aren't you, Charlie?'

'Thank you,' I said.

They had decorated the house. Paper chains were strung across the ceiling, mistletoe hung from the door lintels and a half-dressed Christmas tree stood in one corner. Arthur told me that he was in charge of balloons and I told him that was a very important job; absorbing this remark, he nodded in the slightly abstracted way that children do.

Some time later I found myself drinking a large glass of whisky – 'God bless the black market, old chap,' George Honeysett shouted, waving the bottle. Someone told a long and complex story about an official from the London County Council who was conducting a housing survey – there was a plan for the rebuilding of Mafeking Street. It was proposed to replace the houses with blocks of flats which would have every amenity. Someone else asked, 'What's an amenity, anyway?' and George Honeysett said it was what somebody else thought you needed, and you were going to get it whether you liked it or not. But what had that council fellow meant, someone else asked, by his talk of a 'green lung'?

A record was put on the gramophone – it was Benny Goodman's band, I remember, playing 'Sing, Sing, Sing' – and one or two people began to dance. Patrick and Ruth were in the hall; through the open door I saw him reach out for her, draw her towards him and kiss her for a long time, his hand on the back of her neck, his fingers reaching deep into her hair.

For a long time I couldn't see Elizabeth, then she came back into the room and sat down on the floor beside my chair.

'Lizzie,' I said, touching her shoulder, 'You're so different. You've changed so much since I saw you at Rookwood. Something must have happened, and it's not just a new dress, is it?'

She laughed. 'Ruth happened. My sister rescued me.'

'You were so unhappy.'

'Ruth took me away,' she said. 'She gave me some lessons.'

'They seem to have worked,' I said. 'You look lovely, and you look happy too.'

Perhaps I was tired. I could only think of mindless things to say.

Elizabeth looked down at the dress, then held up one foot and inspected her shoe. 'That's nice of you, Charlie, but I'm just the same as I always was.'

Some time later I woke abruptly. It was very hot and Lily was shaking me and saying, 'Charlie, wake up! I've made up a bed for you.'

She led me upstairs and I fell into the bed, only dimly aware of the sound of music and laughter below. I've no idea why I felt so tired.

*

In the middle of the night I woke again. The bedroom fire had died down, the room was cool and the square of the window showed bright in the darkness. Thinking it must be dawn, I went to the window, pulled the curtains aside and found the sky filled with stars. The ragged outlines of Mafeking Street had been smoothed by the snow and the great arches of the viaduct stood tall and brutal in the brilliant light as if they were the relics of a lost civilisation. I went back to bed, pulled the blankets around me and closed my eyes.

There were things about Elizabeth that I had never properly noticed before – the particular shade of her grey eyes, the fineness of her hair, the downy skin of her neck, the angles of her cheeks, the hollows and tendons of her ankles. Emerging from the sleeves of that new frock, her arms were slender, her hands suddenly delicate. She had a waist, she had hips and breasts. She had knelt before the fire to inspect a toy of Arthur's and I had looked across at her and noticed how vulnerable was the nape of her neck. The boy was saying something and she was intent on him, but then she glanced up, saw me looking at her and gave me the slightest smile, a minute movement of her lips, a raising of one eyebrow in a faint question.

I had spoken to Ruth, saying that she seemed to have done something remarkable with Elizabeth, and she laughed, saying 'Everyone's been locked up, don't you think? We've all been in bloody prison for such a long time.' She put her head on one side and smiled at me. 'Everyone, don't you think?'

'Oh yes,' I said, 'the way out isn't always clear, though.'

Ruth gave me a quizzical smile and I saw that the sisters had the same way of looking. She said, 'But it's worth searching for, isn't it? The way out?'

'Oh yes, of course it is,' I said. 'Sometimes one thinks the result might be rather magical.'

She laughed. 'Oh, one does, does one? Charlie, I think you just have to keep going along steadily and everything will come right in the end.'

'I know,' I said. 'I realise that.'

'I thought you probably did,' she said, and laughed.

Much later, the rattle of the coal scuttle woke me. It was morning and the brilliance of the snow shone through the open curtains. Elizabeth was on her knees before the grate. She looked up, saw I was awake and said, 'Fires are such terrific things, don't you think? I can never resist fiddling with them.'

She was working at the coals with an ancient pair of bellows. The high heels and check dress had been replaced by flat shoes, dungarees and a white shirt. I watched her and after a while the flames began to crackle and roar up the chimney. She put down the bellows and stood up.

'Charlie,' she said, 'I'm going to stay here with Lily for the time being. I don't want to go back to Rookwood yet.'

'I wondered if you might.'

She sat down on the end of the bed. 'I'm so sorry we argued about Berlin and the bombing, Charlie. It was very stupid of me. I was just looking at things from my own point of view.'

I hesitated and then said, 'Lots of things have happened to us in the last few years. We couldn't do anything much about any of it.'

'The war went on year after year,' she said, 'and then, all of a sudden, it's over. It feels so odd, don't you think? Suddenly having nothing in particular to do. One feels rather pointless.'

She gave the fire a good riddling with the poker and stood up. 'Lily's making breakfast. If you'd like some you'd better get up now.'

*

After breakfast Elizabeth, Lily, Arthur and I walked along the canal tow-path and down to the river. Most of the Mafeking Street residents had cleared the snow from their front doors and sections of the pavement, but in places there were drifts three or four feet deep across the road. Children were building snowmen and having snowball fights; a few were wobbling along the frozen canal on rusty skates. A column of smoke drifted from the chimney of Ruth's narrowboat but there was no sign of her or Patrick.

Elizabeth and I leaned on the railings beside the sea lock that allows canal traffic to leave Limehouse Basin and enter the tidal Thames. Arthur and Lily were experimenting with a tea tray and finding that it made an exciting if marginally controllable sledge. The Russian ship was still alongside the quay; in the full light of day it looked drab, and the cranes were stationary now, their grey jibs standing vertical.

'I had an idea yesterday, as I was walking past that ship,' I said. 'It was being unloaded under arc lights and looked very dramatic, as if it were on a stage. The whirling snow, brilliant lights, men like little puppets, the whole thing done in black and white. I wished I had my camera with me, and then I had an idea.'

Elizabeth looked at me, her head on one side.

'You remember the flying we did before the war.'

'Of course I do.' She turned away from me, leaned on the railing and looked out across the water.

'I've been trying to think of a way of starting again where we left off,' I said. 'There was something very simple about the flying we did in that Moth, wasn't there? There was just the aeroplane, a wooden hangar, a strip of grass and a wind-sock. That's all we needed.'

She nodded, still looking out across the water.

'I've been trying to think how one might make some kind of living from a set-up like that. Something really simple. I don't mean an airline or anything like that.'

'If you were going to carry passengers it would get complicated,' Elizabeth said. 'Licences, insurance, booking offices and all that.'

'Yes,' I said. 'I'm lucky, of course. I don't necessarily have to find a job. I could simply go back home. But I don't want to be tied to Waverley – I've decided that much, at least.'

She turned to me and said, 'Ruth made me realise that you simply have to make your own way. People have to decide things for themselves. Don't you agree?'

'Your sister is a very sensible person,' I said, and that made her laugh.

'Oh, Charlie,' she said, 'I know that perfectly well – sometimes you do say the silliest things. Anyway, what about an air taxi service? Urgent deliveries. Perishable things that aren't heavy – flowers – something like that. You talked about that before.'

'I was thinking about something simpler than that,' I said.

'What, then?'

'Pictures. Pictures taken from the air. Aerial photography.'

She thought about it for some time and then said, 'That's an interesting idea. Would you need one of those big cameras that the RAF use for reconnaissance? A camera that's built into the aeroplane?'

'No, I don't think you'd need anything like that to start with. An ordinary camera would be perfectly all right, providing it was a good one. It might need a special mounting for some purposes, but that should be easy to arrange. It could be fitted on the side of a light aircraft, I thought, beside the passenger seat, so that it looked out of the side window.'

'You'd need a high-wing aeroplane, a monoplane of some sort.'

'Yes.'

'What would you photograph?'

'Houses, factories, farms, roads, bridges, rivers, parts of the coast – cliffs and beaches for instance – mountains, ships at sea, clouds, other aeroplanes, islands, big sporting events like Goodwood and the British Grand Prix, all those pretty English towns – don't you remember Cambridge, and how lovely it looked from the Gipsy Moth?'

She laughed. 'I can see you've been working it out,' she said. 'Of course I remember the view from the Moth.' She paused and then said, 'Who would want to buy the pictures?'

'All sorts of people. People who own country houses, factories or ships, for a start. Publishers of guide books and calendars, or newspapers and magazines. Architects and town planners. Local councils, meteorologists, scientists, teachers, advertising agencies, map-makers, aircraft companies – all sorts of people. We'd have to work out the best markets, and concentrate on them.'

'You really have been thinking about this.'

I laughed. 'Yes, but only since last night.'

'Wouldn't aerial pictures be frightfully costly to do?'

'To start with, I expect they would. But in time we'd build up a library, wouldn't we? Some things don't change very fast – suppose we had aerial photographs of English country houses, for example – over several years we could sell a lot of pictures of them.'

Elizabeth was silent for a while and then said, 'When you say "we", who do you mean, exactly?'

'I mean you and I,' I said. 'I can't fly the aeroplane as well as take the pictures. You could fly and I could work the camera.'

There was another silence, and then she said, 'I didn't realise you knew that much about photography.'

'I know the basics,' I said, 'and I can learn more. I like landscapes. It's one of the reasons I used to love flying.'

She nodded at that, and said, 'I remember Cambridge, and how we circled round and round for ages while you stared down at it. Made me dizzy.'

'Did we? Well, there you are. I like to gaze at things – landscapes, buildings, the sky. And surely you agree there's something special about the view from the air. Most people have never seen it, especially in a high-quality print.'

'Of course I see that. It does sound possible, and it's interesting as well. It would take us all over the place – I suppose we might go abroad as well.'

She leaned over the railing and looked at the river again. 'The thing is,' she said. 'I like it here. I feel at home with Lily. My father worked on the river when he was a boy, and I like to be near it.'

'Yes,' I said. 'He told me that. He worked on the last of the sailing ships. The clipper ships. He was proud of that.'

'He told you about that, did he?'

'He told me about the library he went into in a rainstorm.'

'"Rain and books made me, Lizzie",' Elizabeth said, clapping her gloved hands.

'"Rain and books made me, Young Master Charles".'

'I didn't know he'd told you all that – but of course he would have done. He got on so well with children, being really a child himself.'

Lily and Arthur were going back towards the house now, and we turned to follow them.

'Your idea sounds quite good to me,' she said. 'I think it might work.'

'But you aren't sure that you want to be involved.'

'I don't know. I know I want to stay with Lily for the moment. I don't want to go back to Rookwood.'

'You wouldn't have to.'

'But surely you'd keep the aeroplane at Waverley?'

'Certainly not. It just needs a corner of a hangar. One of the airfields north or east of London would probably be best.'

'Charlie—' she said, and then stopped.

'What?'

'Last night you walked through the snow to visit me.'

'I did.'

'I'm not stupid. I know that's a very romantic thing to do, so I just thought I'd mention it.'

'I thought it would save me advertising for a pilot,' I said, and she laughed, which I took to be a promising sign.

How exciting we found the practicalities of business in those early days, how tremendous it was to focus one's attention entirely on such a project, and think of nothing else! Every few days I called at Mafeking Street and Elizabeth and I had a conference at Lily's kitchen table, making lists – they are so alluring, and give immediate substance to the most ridiculous notions. We made a great number of lists, beginning with major items – the choice of an aeroplane, of course, but also cameras, lenses, film, darkroom equipment – and ending with pencils, stationery, a telephone, a desk and two chairs, a kettle, a teapot, cups and saucers, a teaspoon, a box of matches.

'We'll need some sort of office for all this,' Elizabeth said. 'Quite a big one, in fact.'

We were discussing that question the following morning when Lily came in and told us that the archway next to hers was about to become vacant. 'There you are,' she said, 'make a perfect office, that would. I'd get in quick, if I was you.'

Sometimes things fall in place as if destined. We went at once to look at the archway. It was number 12, one of the higher arches, plenty big enough for our purposes. The previous occupants had used it for storing fruit and vegetables, and it was dry and clean.

We poked about for a while and then stood outside, looking at the white-painted wooden frontage. 'We could put "AIRBORNE PHOTOS" in big black capitals across there,' Elizabeth said.

'I quite like that name,' I said.

'Good,' she said, laughing, 'that's all right then.'

The decision to acquire the archway was the real beginning, from which we had to go forward. I took a room in the Lamb & Flag and signed up for an evening class in photography, and Elizabeth began to look for a suitable aeroplane.

The world was awash with surplus aircraft in those days – we heard of them being pushed into heaps by bulldozers and set on fire. Friends talked about bargains that had been got for a song, but they were rarely any commercial use – one chap had bought a four-engined bomber, a Halifax, in order to fly his family home to Australia; it was a terrific idea, but such a large aeroplane was impossibly expensive to operate on an everyday basis. We needed a single-engined aircraft with reasonable endurance, something more powerful and roomy than my old Gipsy Moth but simple and cheap to maintain, something sturdy and reliable. Elizabeth suggested a Fairchild Argus, several of which had been used by the ATA as taxi aircraft. 'It's sturdy,' she said. 'It cruises at over a hundred and the range is pretty good.'

It turned out that several other people had their eyes on an Argus and they were in short supply, but we eventually heard about one that had been transferred to civilian use and was about to be put on the market in Prestwick.

'Let's go up there straight away,' Elizabeth said. 'Let's go and fly it.'

As we travelled north on the train I began to fuss to myself about the wisdom of our trip. Elizabeth had not flown since the death of Alice four months earlier, and I had not flown for nearly a year. Should we have done some flying together first, at a flying club, maybe? I was staring out of the carriage window and then Elizabeth tapped me on the shoulder.

I looked round and she said, 'I know exactly what you're thinking, Charlie.'

'Do you?'

'Yes. I think you're worrying about us trying out this Argus, and whether it might remind me of Alice and all that.'

'Yes, Lizzie, that's exactly what I'm worrying about.'

'Well, you can jolly well forget it. I've thought it all out and I shall be quite all right. It would have been terrific if Alice could have been here with us, but she isn't, and that's that.'

I looked at her, she looked steadily back at me and then tears began to fall down her cheeks.

'I'm quite all right,' she said.

'So I see.'

'I do wish she could have been here. She would have enjoyed this so much.'

I put my arm around her and she put her head against my shoulder for a minute or two. Then she straightened up and blew her nose with my handkerchief.

'I'm sorry,' she said.

'You don't have to be,' I said.

'It was silly. I don't know what came over me.'

'It's allowed to happen.'

She looked out of the window and did not reply. We spoke to each other in that formal manner in those days, both of us still locked in our habit of reserve.

The owner of the aeroplane was a dealer called Freddie Chalmers, who was a sharp dresser. Several times he looked at his watch, evidently having better things to do than sell us an elderly, cheap aeroplane.

The Argus was parked at the back of a crowded hangar, covered in a layer of dust and sparrow droppings. Elizabeth walked round it and said, 'Dear me, it's a bit of a mess, isn't it? We'll have to get it out of here for a proper look. It needs a jolly good clean, for a start.' She touched the engine cowling with one finger and showed the dust to Chalmers. 'Don't you agree?'

Chalmers sighed. 'Very well,' he said, 'I'll find a couple of bods to shift everything out of the way.'

Out in the open, the Argus didn't look so bad. 'We'll wash it off,' Elizabeth said to Chalmers. 'Can you get us a bucket of water, a sponge, a clean leather and a step-ladder?'

Sighing again, Chalmers went away and we began to look the aeroplane over. It was a businesslike machine, even handsome in its way, and substantially built. It stood on a strong, wide undercarriage and its wings were well supported by multiple struts. The cabin had three seats and room for plenty of baggage. We looked through the logbooks and found that everything was up to date. In the last year it had only done forty hours flying, and plenty of hours were left on the engine and the airframe. Elizabeth climbed in, sat in the left-hand seat and began to look over the controls and instruments.

Chalmers came back with a bucket of water and asked me in a confidential tone, 'Does the lady want to fly it?'

'Certainly she does,' I said.

'Has she got the proper licences and whatnot?'

'Certainly,' I said. 'The lady's got more hours on the Argus than you've had hot dinners.'

'I was only asking,' Chalmers said, and began to wash the tailplane in a desultory manner; it was apparent that he had little experience of aircraft. Elizabeth got down from the cabin and said to him, 'We'll do that. It'll be much quicker.'

One of the Prestwick ground engineers was licensed for the engine of the Argus and had signed for its most recent checks. We found him in his workshop. 'Nice little aeroplane,' he said. 'Run her up for you if you like.'

'Thank you,' Elizabeth said.

We chocked the wheels and found a battery trolley. The engine started easily and sounded good – this particular Argus had the larger engine that had been fitted to some aircraft, giving it a better rate of climb and a slightly higher cruising speed.

'All right, Mr Chalmers,' Elizabeth said, 'let's fly her round, shall we? Do you want to sit in the back?'

'No, I don't,' Chalmers said. 'Just don't go out of sight, that's all.' He looked at his watch again. 'I'll be in my office when you get back.'

I sat beside Elizabeth while she went through the checks and taxied round to the downwind end of the airfield. It looked as though it would be a straightforward job to modify the starboard door to take a camera bracket.

A gusty north-west wind was blowing when we took off. The Argus climbed quickly and we passed the seaside town of Troon at two thousand feet, heading out over the sea towards the north end of Arran. This is the Firth of Clyde, of course, in which the island of Arran lies like an enormous sea creature, and to the north and west is a mass of mountainous peninsulas and rough-edged, precipitous islands – Arran itself, the Mull of Kintyre and the Isle of Bute, and beyond those, stretching away to the horizon, island upon island – Islay, Jura, Colonsay, Mull, Iona, Tiree and all the thousands of windy rocks that make up the Inner and Outer Hebrides. It is a beautiful place for flying; and on a winter's day such as this, a day of clear air and scudding clouds, every colour glowed, the lower slopes were warm with shades of brown and green and each hill and mountain wore a cap of the purest white.

Above Arran we turned west and ran across Kintyre towards Islay, cruising at a hundred and ten miles an hour, the Argus easily controllable although the air was bumpy.

'Let's practise,' Elizabeth said. 'Suppose we're going to photograph Gigha.'

She throttled back, letting the aeroplane fall towards the sea until the island was ahead. Now the wind was behind us; we turned and rushed along Gigha's coast at five hundred feet while I aimed an imaginary camera from the window. Close below, the waves strode along in their regular and unhurried way towards the cliffs, breaking in sharp flurries of spray that were quickly scattered by the wind. At the end of the island Elizabeth pulled the aircraft into a steep climbing turn – I looked across at her and she gave me a quick glance, grinning at the joy of it, and then turned back to the business of flying.

When we returned we found Mr Chalmers in an edgy mood, since he had watched the Argus dive out of sight behind Arran and thought he'd seen the last of it. However, he recovered when we told him we had decided to buy the aircraft, shook our hands with great eagerness and told us that the Argus was a jolly fine little plane – 'You've made the right decision and won't regret it, not in a million years you won't, squire.'

'I'm sure we won't,' I said, and Mr Chalmers folded my cheque, placed it in his wallet and hurried off to catch a train to somewhere more important. When he'd gone we walked back to the hangar and sat in our new aeroplane for a while, confirming the rightness of our decision by a discussion of its excellent features, as one is always inclined to do, having made a substantial and committing purchase.

Fourteen

In the beginning Elizabeth stayed with Lily, I took a room on the top floor of the Lamb & Flag and we found a hangar for the Argus at Rochford in Essex. That we might do as we wished was a giddy freedom, and we grinned when we caught each other's eye, as if we were children up to mischief. Was it really the case that our lives were now defined only by our own actions and choices, and that our work owed loyalty to no greater purpose than itself? It was indeed so; but it was peculiar.

We built an office beneath the arch of Number 12 Mafeking Street with the help of Lily Attwell, Ben Yossakin and one of the Honeysett girls, Angela, who shortly became our first employee. Lily supplied the smoke-darkened timber for a two-storey building with plywood walls and external stairs to the upper floor; it was not an elegant construction, just a large box, and beneath the high curve of the arch it looked like a doll's house. On the lower floor was the darkroom and above it a room for storage and display of our pictures – in that upper room, we fancied, we would hold important meetings with our clients in a whirl of cigar-smoke.

When we'd finished, Elizabeth fixed a map of Britain to the wall, stood back to look at it and said, 'We'll stick little paper flags in every place we've photographed, and one day there'll be a blessed forest of them.' Then she turned to me, saying, 'Don't you agree, Charlie?'

'Of course I do,' I said, laughing.

'I think I may have a naturally bossy nature,' she said, looking serious. 'You must tell me if I'm taking charge too often.'

'Oh, I will,' I said.

'We won't call this the office, we'll call it the *studio*,' she said. 'That sounds far better, don't you think?' She opened her arms in an expansive gesture, grinned at me and said, 'Welcome to the Airborne studio!'

Our new ambition made us happy. We worked hard and had no time for the past. In little more than six weeks in the spring of 1946 we purchased the Argus, a Morris van, two cameras and a dozen lenses, an enlarger and many items of darkroom equipment. We built the studio and the darkroom, made a list of potential clients and designed and printed a leaflet announcing our existence. In that leaflet we used our first aerial photographs – we flew in from the Thames estuary early one February morning and photographed the Pool of London in steely, angled light, the spires and towers of a mysterious city emerging from drifting patches of mist. We liked those first pictures very much, and made large prints of them to hang in the studio; they were the first piece of evidence that our plans were not entirely ridiculous.

Settling about us, in those first months, was a gradual understanding of what it meant to be released from duty. There were moments, it seemed to me, when I became aware that I had been waiting for an order, having forgotten that power over our own lives had been returned to us. We could progress at a pace and in a direction that we ourselves decided, and this extraordinary freedom had the curious effect of making the commonplace remarkable; I might look up, for example, and watch Elizabeth reaching for the telephone, dialling someone and talking about an order for photographic paper, absently twirling the phone cord with her free hand and gazing out of the window at the pigeons that fluttered in and out of the arch – perfectly ordinary behaviour, but now the consequence of her own will, and no longer bound to any other authority.

Having finished the last few jobs on the studio and darkroom, and posted our leaflets to a long list of companies and individuals, we began work on our photographic library. Of all the tasks that we undertook at the beginning – now so many years ago! – the photo library was certainly the most intriguing, the most demanding and the most enjoyable. It was also, I suppose, hopelessly self-indulgent. We began one evening with a debate over a set of maps spread across a table in the Lamb & Flag – not obviously the best place to discuss our business philosophy, but it produced a great many possibilities, since everyone in Mafeking Street felt free to join in, and none was short of an opinion. Lily was there with us that first day. We agreed that Airborne Photos ought to develop a house style, and become known for excellence in a particular kind of photography. I wanted to concentrate on natural landscapes. What was England known for, I asked, if it wasn't landscape and scenery? Lizzie told me that was old-fashioned – if we weren't careful, we'd get a reputation for dealing only in seaside postcards and views of the Lake District – 'Pretty pictures for the sitting-room wall,' she said.

'Pretty pictures? I don't mean postcard stuff, I mean proper landscapes that people will enjoy, and will want to keep, and will pay a proper price for. We've got to make a living, after all.' I was slightly hurt.

'Charlie,' Lizzie said, leaning forward with her hands flat on the table in front of her, 'Now that the war's over, something new is going to happen. Things aren't going to be the same. We ought to be looking forward, not back. England's going to change. All the old traditional things are going to be swept away. We ought to photograph new things – new towns and new bridges, new cars and new aeroplanes, new factories, new schools, new houses.'

'New, new, new,' I said. 'Just because something's new, it isn't necessarily any good.'

'If something's old it isn't necessarily any good, either.'

'I didn't say "old", Lizzie, I said "natural". Natural landscapes.'

'Natural isn't necessarily any good either.'

'No, but that's my point. If we do it well, we'll make a name for ourselves, and sell pictures.'

At this point Lily stuck out her arm between us and said, 'That's enough, you two! What I think is, you'll have to get your work where you can find it. That's what I think.'

Everyone laughed, partly because she had punctured our pretensions and partly because she was very likely right.

Discussing one's business affairs round a table in a bar would have been thought quite ridiculous by my father, and made me feel foolishly happy. If I were asked to define the opposite extreme to my own character, I would settle on the inhabitants of Mafeking Street, who were and are, among other things, warm, argumentative, vulgar and funny; it was impossible for me to be introspective for long in the company of Lily and the

Honeysetts, and that is why I became so fond of them, and eventually belonged so securely among them.

In the event the argument was simply resolved, more-or-less as Lily had said. We made lists of what we thought were possible subjects and I had my share of landscapes; but Lizzie had her railways and reservoirs, and a good many waterworks, pipelines, transmitter masts and blocks of flats as well.

We began with landscapes only because I had a romantic notion of prettiness and I thought I knew what would make a striking picture. Of course I was wrong, and soon proved so: on the way to some carefully selected location we often encountered something remarkable – the power stations along the flat and empty Trent valley, for example, crouching beneath towering columns of smoke and steam, or the steelworks at Corby on a frosty morning, or the liner *Queen Mary*, discovered a few miles off the Cornish coast in a gale of wind, long lines of foam streaking the sea, taking the grey seas over her bow and spray over the top of her funnel – oh yes, what pleasure those flights gave us! We'd get the weather forecast for the following day, take our maps into the bar and sit together, arguing the merits of one subject over another. I'd sit back and watch Lizzie talking, reaching across the map and stabbing with one finger at some feature, turning to ask me what I thought, arguing with Lily, laughing at one of George Honeysett's awful jokes or waving to someone across the crowded bar – and then, one evening, she suddenly turned to me and said, 'Charlie, look over there, it's your brother.'

So it was – my brother Gerald, whom I'd not seen for months, peering through the cigarette smoke and, when he saw me, half-raising his hand in a gesture that could be a greeting or perhaps a warning. I got up and went to him. 'Hello, Charlie,' he said, 'I thought I'd come and dig you out for a chat.'

Dig me out? I bought him a beer and after a while I took him up to my room, since he was uneasy without privacy. He sat awkwardly on the edge of my bed holding his pint of best bitter.

'I take it father sent you,' I said.

'Not exactly. We've had several little talks about you, of course, and wondered how you were getting on. That sort of thing. I said I'd find out. He's rather concerned about you, actually. We all are.'

'Concerned? You needn't be. I'm perfectly all right. In fact I'm getting on rather well.'

I suppose I must have felt guilty about walking away from Waverley, about my lack of communication with my family – all that – anyway, I was angry with Gerald.

'You could have telephoned me, or written,' I said.

'Indeed I could,' he said. 'So could you.'

I couldn't argue with that. I nodded, and Gerald said, 'What exactly are you up to, Charlie? Why have you buried yourself in the East End? And why are you keeping so bloody quiet about it?'

I sat down and wondered how to answer him. Eventually I said, 'I'm just trying to make a life for myself. I'm not trying to conceal anything.'

Gerald laughed, puffing out his cheeks at the absurdity of it. 'For God's sake! You've already got a life, Charlie. It's where it's always been, at Waverley. You don't have to make another one, especially in a place like this.' He waved his hand to indicate my bare little room and everything that lay around it. 'Charlie. You're throwing everything away. What on earth are you up to? I can't understand you. It's quite mad.'

'I'm not throwing anything away,' I said. 'I'm just making my own way – don't you understand that? I just want to make my own way.' I knew was repeating myself but I couldn't think of another form of words.

'You don't *need* to make your own bloody way, for God's sake. Is it Lizzie Bowman? Is that what it's about? That girl?'

'You're a bloody clown if you think that, Gerry,' I said. 'What kind of conversation is this? It's out of the last century, or the one before that. This is the twentieth century, for Christ's sake.'

There was the sound of footsteps on the uncarpeted stairs, and a moment later Lizzie tapped on the door and walked in. 'Hello, Gerry,' she said. He got up and shook her hand; he was, I was glad to see, considerably embarrassed. 'Hello, Miss Bowman,' he said.

'"Hello, Miss Bowman"?' Lizzie repeated his greeting, sounding puzzled. She knew what he had come for, I could see that, and she went straight on to the offensive. 'You always used to call me Lizzie. Have I done something wrong, Gerry?'

'Of course not. I haven't seen you for years, that's all.'

She looked round at me. 'Have you told Gerry about our terrific new business, Charlie?'

'Not yet,' I said.

She laughed, and looked from Gerry to me. 'Really! You two!'

'What business?' Gerry asked.

'Charlie,' Lizzie said, 'why don't we get some supper and tell Gerry all about it?'

It was nicely done: she walked in and defused our childish argument just like that, easy as winking. We had supper in the back room of the pub and she told Gerry all about Airborne Photos – how it would work, the Argus, our practice trips, the studio under the arch. She charmed him, and Gerald said he liked the sound of our plan, but he was certain that father would not. 'Father will say that it's a simple question of loyalty,' he said. 'It's a question of tradition, a question of what's right for people like us. Yes, that's what it is. A question of what's right and proper for people like us. It's the way we are, Charlie, and there's no getting round it.'

It seemed to me that once Gerald had been reduced to platitudes of that kind we had won the argument – or rather, Lizzie had won the argument. I saw that things went better if I stayed out of it and let her talk. I watched her laughing at something Gerry said, her shoulders moving under the cotton of her dress, a vein throbbing in her neck, her fingers tapping impatiently on the table. Once or twice she glanced at me, a little turn of her head and a gleam in her eye saying that she knew exactly what she was about, and that she was pleased with herself.

When Gerald had gone we went back to my room and Lizzie sat down on the edge of the bed. 'I'm exhausted,' she said.

'Thank you,' I said. 'You did wonderfully well.'

She started to check the plan for tomorrow's shoot, lying on her stomach on the bed and waving her heels in the air. I sat in the sagging easy chair and watched her.

Suddenly she looked up and said, 'Charlie', in a firm tone, and I felt suddenly anxious, knowing this wasn't going to be a conversation about tomorrow's photographs, or about Gerald.

I looked enquiringly at her, and she said, 'We're doing all right, aren't we?'

'I think we are. I think we're doing very well so far.'

'Well then,' she said, and looked down at the map again. 'I think we did rather well with Gerry too.'

'You did well,' I said. 'I listened.'

She laughed and was silent for a while, supporting her head in her hands and looking down at the map.

Eventually she said, without looking up, 'I've been reading an interesting book.'

'Oh, have you?' I said. 'What's it about?'

She didn't reply immediately but then stood up and said, 'I'll go and get it.'

She left the room and I listened to her feet pattering down the stairs. A few minutes later she came back, shut the door, dropped the book in my lap and returned to her position on the bed.

It was a small book, bound in faded brown cloth. I looked at the spine but the gold lettering was illegible. I opened it and found that it was called *Married Love*, and had been written by someone called Marie Carmichael Stopes. I looked up at Elizabeth and she was still lying on her stomach on the bed, her face supported in her hands, watching me. 'Have a look at it,' she said.

The first chapter was entitled 'The Heart's Desire', and the second 'The Broken Joy'.

'There is no doubt,' I read, 'that Love loses, in the haste and bustle of the modern turmoil, not only its charm and graces, but even some of its vital essence.'

On the next page I read: 'So many people are now born and bred in artificial and false surroundings that even the elementary fact that the act of love should be *joyous* is unknown to them.'

I felt myself becoming embarrassed. I looked at Elizabeth and she said, 'Go on. Read some more.'

The third chapter was called 'Woman's "Contrariness"'. I read another sentence at random: 'Most women have never realised intellectually, but many have been dimly half-conscious, that women's nature is set to rhythms over which man has no more control than he has over the tides of the sea.'

A page or two later there were some remarks about 'the case of a Mrs G', who was 'not exceptional'. She had married as a very ignorant girl, but often vaguely felt a sense of something lacking in her husband's love.

'It's all about love,' I said, not looking up, 'it's about how to do it properly, I think. Making love, I mean.'

'Yes,' she said. 'Exactly.'

For some moments I could not think what to say. Eventually I asked, 'Lizzie, why have you been reading about love? And why are you telling me about it?'

She laughed. 'You know perfectly well,' she said.

She got up from the bed, took one of the pillows, dropped it on the floor beside my chair and sat down on it, her legs curled up underneath her.

'What I think is' – she paused and leaned her head against the arm of my chair – 'I think you've been waiting for me, and I've been waiting for you, and we're both simply too cautious for words, and it's got ridiculous, and something has to be done about it. So I decided to make a plan, and that book is part of it.'

I reached out and touched her hair, which felt like an electric shock.

'We're going to read the book together,' she said. 'You're going to sit in that chair and read the book, and I'm going to sit here and read it over your shoulder. And when we've finished the book we'll both know what's what.'

'But, Lizzie, if you've already read it—' and she put up her hand and said, 'Read the book. I want you to read the book to me, I want us to read it together. We'll do the first chapter straight away, before we change our minds.'

I laughed at that, because I hadn't made up my mind about anything; but she had, so we began our reading that evening, in my room in the attic of the Lamb & Flag.

Fifteen

Married Love, Marie Stopes's most famous book, was first published in 1918, eventually sold millions of copies all over the world and was banned in several countries. Lizzie's copy, given to her by Ruth, is the 23rd edition, printed in 1938. It is about love, of course, and sex. In particular it's about women and sex, written from the point of view of a woman and addressed to both men and women – at times it's firmly addressed to men.

I read out the beginning of the first chapter:

Every heart desires a mate. For some reason beyond our comprehension, nature has so created us that we are incomplete in ourselves; neither man nor woman singly can know the joy of the performance of all the human functions; neither man nor woman singly can create another human being.

Lizzie said, 'Do you agree so far?'
'Yes,' I said, and went on reading.

However much he may conceal it under assumed cynicism, worldliness, or self-seeking, the heart of every young man yearns with a great longing for the fulfilment of the beautiful dream of a life-long union with a mate.

'I think she might be romanticising that a bit,' Lizzie said. 'I don't think *every* man is like that, do you?'

'No,' I said. 'I'm not sure about "yearning with a great longing", either.'

'It doesn't sound like you,' Elizabeth said, laughing.

'I don't know about that,' I said. 'But I wouldn't quarrel with the general idea. Is it all like this, or does she – well – does she get into the details after a while?'

'Yes, she does. You'll have to be patient.'

'I'm not impatient in the slightest. I just wondered.'

Chapter II discussed the difficulties of what Marie Stopes called 'physical marriage':

A girl generally has neither the theoretical knowledge nor the spontaneous physical development which might give the capacity even to imagine the basic facts of physical marriage, and her bridegroom may shock her without knowing that he is doing so.

A similar problem applied to the man:

In the early days of marriage the young man is often even more sensitive, more romantic, and he enters marriage hoping for an even higher degree of bodily unity than does the girl . . . is of the two the more profoundly wounded, with a slow corrosive wound that eats into her very being and warps all her life.

'That's true,' Lizzie said.

'Is it?'

'Yes. I've been talking to Ruth. We don't think mother was very happy at all.'

'Your mother? But surely your father – he was a kind man, I know, and loved your mother.'

'Yes, I'm sure he did. That's one of the points about this book. Being a kind and loving man may not be enough.'

'Oh, I see,' I said, not understanding at all. But towards the end of the chapter things became somewhat clearer:

Physical passion, so swiftly stimulated in man, tends to override all else, and the untutored man seeks but one thing – the accomplishment of desire. The woman forgives the crudeness, but sooner or later her love revolts, probably in secret, and then for ever after, though she may command an outward tenderness, she has nothing within but scorn and loathing for the act which should have been a perpetual entrancement.

'My mother,' Lizzie said. 'She could be talking about my mother, I'm sure.'

'But I still think that your father—'

'That's not the point. Of course my father was a loving man, but he didn't *know* anything.'

'Surely he was proud of knowing lots of things.'

'He knew lots of things that weren't useful.'

'Besides, nobody really knows much about this sort of thing, so you can't blame him.'

'Ruth knows a lot. Anyone who's read this book knows a lot.'

'You must know all about it, then.'

Lizzie blushed and said, 'That's not fair.'

'I'm sorry,' I said. 'I only mean that I'm at a bit of a disadvantage.'

'Yes, I suppose you are. I hadn't thought of that.'

'I'm not objecting. It's interesting.'

'Yes, I thought it was interesting, too.' She looked at her watch. 'But I think we'll have to go on with it tomorrow. It's getting late and we've got to be up early.'

'Lizzie,' I said, 'are we going to get married?'

'Oh yes,' she said. 'Don't you agree? I thought that was the whole point of this conversation.'

'In that case I ought to kiss you.'

She kneeled beside my chair and I kissed her – rather tentatively, no doubt. After a while we stopped kissing and she said, 'I liked you holding me like that', which was pleasing.

It was awkward, twisting round in my chair to kiss her. I said, 'Suppose you sat on my lap.'

'No,' she said, and stood up. 'I'm going to bed now.' She reached down and took the book from me. 'We'll read some more tomorrow.'

'You could leave it with me,' I said. 'I could read it for myself.'

'No, you couldn't. The whole point is that we read it together.'

I stood up and she walked over to the door. 'Goodnight, Charlie,' she said. 'See you in the morning.' And then she was gone, the door shut and only the sound of her footsteps on the stairs.

The first few times I put my arms around her she was as tense as a cat. She would say, 'Just hold me, that's all.' After a while she might put her arms around my neck and lean her head on my shoulder – we knew nothing save what we learned from Marie Stopes, and much of that made no sense for a long time. We didn't know that people commonly kissed with their mouths open; nor did we know why they did it, until we tried it.

Lizzie told me about her mother and her insistence on cleanliness and constant washing. 'Sometimes, when I have kissed you,' she said carefully, 'I feel perhaps I should wash afterwards.'

'Oh,' I said.

'I know it's wrong of me to think that. But my mother used to say all sorts of things were dirty. She was always on the lookout for dirt. She used to sniff us.'

'Sniff you?'

'Yes. If she couldn't smell the soap she'd tell us to go and wash.'

'That's incredible.'

'Is it? It didn't seem amazing as a child. It was just how she was. How does a child know what's right and what's not? Perhaps her mother had taught her to do it.'

'Getting back to kissing,' I said, 'In fact, you've only kissed me twice, so I don't think you're likely to catch anything yet.'

My fascination with her was childlike. I would take her hands, look at them, turn them over, kiss them and say, 'I love your hands.' Before long I was able to stroke her face, and hold it in my own hands. To begin with, when I did that, she'd look down, unable to look me in the eye, and as time went by she began to glance up at me, and eventually could look at me steadily. These are very simple, naïve things, but that is where we began.

On our second Marie Stopes evening I suggested that Lizzie should sit in the chair and read the next two chapters. She didn't much like the idea, but was unable to think of an excuse, so she agreed.

In Chapter III, 'Woman's "Contrariness"', we learned that a woman described as 'a highly educated lady' had suffered 'many months of agonising apprehension that she was about to have a baby', simply because a man had kissed her at a dance; it was a relief to know that some people were even more ignorant than ourselves.

But I was embarrassed, and so was Lizzie, by the case of Mrs G, whose husband, because she asked him, 'gave her one swift unrepentant kiss upon the bosom'. Mr G, Marie Stopes thought, ought to have known that 'her husband's lips upon her breast melt a wife to tenderness'.

'I didn't know that either,' I said.

'Well, you do now,' Lizzie said, keeping her head down over the book. Towards the end of the chapter Marie Stopes said that there was a widespread but quite mistaken idea that 'woman was lowered by sex-intercourse'.

'I don't think that,' I said.

'Good,' Lizzie said, and finished the chapter, and shut the book firmly. 'I'm not going to read any more,' she said.

'All right,' I said. 'Do you want me to read it?'

'No, I don't think so.'

'Good,' I said. 'It's difficult, doing this, isn't it?'

'Yes. Perhaps it wasn't such a good idea after all.' She stood up. 'I'd like to get out of here for a while.'

'We'll walk along the river,' I said.

It was the end of May, a warm evening.

'Yes,' she murmured to herself as we walked along. 'Yes, that must be right, it must be right.'

I understood that the words were not intended for me, but had escaped from the dialogue that was taking place within her.

I asked her, 'Lizzie, will you tell me what you're thinking?'

'How do people get so set in their ways, Charlie, and so awkward with each other?'

'I think we're doing rather well,' I said. 'But perhaps we've done enough of Marie Stopes.'

'I've gone off the idea of learning things like that from a book,' she said. 'It was a bloody silly idea.'

I laughed at that, and we stopped walking. I held her close to me and said, 'I don't think it was silly at all. Just think about the last few years, Lizzie. Think of what's happened in the world, and how we've got through it, and we're walking together beside the river on a May evening. There was your trip to Berlin, and what happened to Alice, and what happened to my crew – those were terrible things, but look at what we've done in the last few months – amazing things! We've begun to make a future for ourselves, we've done all sorts of things—'

'Kissing,' she said, laughing suddenly. 'We've done a bit of that.'

'Kissing, and buying the first new clothes you've had for ten years—'

'Talking about sex-tides, and buying an aeroplane, and taking dozens of photographs—'

'While being completely ignorant about it—'

'Oh, I wouldn't say *completely*. I think you'll make quite a good photographer one day.'

'Do you? I'm glad about that,' I said, suddenly anxious. 'God, Lizzie, I hope it all works out.'

'It will,' she said. 'It'll work out perfectly. You'll see.'

'We just have to keep steady, that's all.'

'Charlie.'

'What?'

'I thought perhaps I would stay in your room tonight.'

'Yes,' I said, 'I think that would be a good idea.'

'I'll have to tell Lily,' she said. 'She'll fuss otherwise.'

'Let's hope she doesn't object.'

Lizzie laughed and said, 'She won't.' She paused, and then said, 'You said something about your crew just now. I suppose you mean the crew of your Lancaster, do you?'

'Yes,' I said.

She picked up something from the tone of my voice, and said, 'What's the matter?'

'I don't think I'll talk about them now.'

'All right. But you'll tell me sometime, won't you?'

'Yes, of course I will,' I said. 'And if you're going to stay in my room tonight, perhaps I ought to borrow that book first, and do some catching up.'

She said, 'No, I don't think so, Charlie. From now on we'll just find it out for ourselves.' She paused, and I could see her thinking she might have been too assertive. 'Don't you think that would be best?'

'Going solo,' I said. She grinned at me then, holding her head on one side and blinking her eyelashes in a deliberately coquettish fashion.

It was dark when I got back to my room that evening. I switched on the light and looked at the double bed, the two chairs, the table, the chest of drawers, the square of threadbare carpet and the washbasin with a mirror on the wall above it. No pictures, and only a single bulb in the centre of the ceiling.

I spent some time moving the furniture from one place to another without making the slightest improvement. Then I walked up and down until I noticed that the window needed cleaning, so I found a cloth and did that. Finally I sat down in one of the chairs and leafed through an anthology of photographs.

After an age I heard her footsteps coming up the stairs – her light, quick, unmistakable steps. She came briskly into the room wearing her high heels and mackintosh and carrying a little suitcase, and I saw that she was blushing.

'Oh, dear,' I said. 'Of course, you had to go through the bar.'

'Harry Nicholls whistled at me, everyone looked up and saw the case, they all laughed and George called out, "Off for the weekend, lovey?"'

'Oh, I'm sorry,' I said, holding her, 'I should have thought of that.'

'It doesn't matter one jot,' she said, and put her case down on the bed. 'They would have known before long, anyway. No secrets in Mafeking Street.'

She stepped to the window and drew the curtains closed: there she is in my mind's eye, stepping briskly across the room, her coat open and swinging, reaching out for both curtains and sweeping them together.

I stepped up behind her and she held out her arms for me to take her coat off. I hung it on the hook on the back of the door, turned back to her and said, 'Shall we get into bed?'

'Yes,' she said. 'I think you should take my clothes off.'

Sometimes she had to help, because I did not always know how things worked. Each item I neatly folded and placed on a chair; of course I knew that I should be more passionate, but I could not discard my sense of the artificiality of the moment. Eventually, when I had taken all her clothes off, Lizzie shivered and got quickly into the bed.

'Turn the light off, Charlie,' she said.

I undressed in the dark, got into the bed beside her and kissed her. Her mouth tasted of toothpaste.

'I haven't washed,' I said.

'I don't think that matters at this point,' she said, and began to giggle. I was glad about that; it surely meant everything was going to be all right.

'Oh, Charlie, you're so cold,' she said, taking my hands in hers and blowing on my fingers. After a while she whispered, 'How strange this is.'

'Our being here together.'

'Yes. I do think it's strange – don't you? I don't mean *odd*, I mean . . .' she paused and thought for a moment. She was so close to me in the darkness that I could feel her breath on my face. 'I mean it's *unlikely*,' she said. 'Yes, that's it. Who would have thought that I would be lying in Charles Beevor's bed in the attic room of a pub in the East End of London?'

'Is it the pub that's unlikely, or what?'

'Don't be silly. It's *us* that's unlikely, as you know perfectly well.'

'From my point of view the whole thing seems rather fortunate.'

'"The whole thing seems rather fortunate."' She imitated my way of speaking and giggled again, then brought my fingers to her lips to show she didn't mean any harm.

'That's how I am, Lizzie. All the Beevors speak like me. You'll just have to put up with it.'

'I know what the Beevors are like, and you're nothing like the rest of them.'

'As for you and I being unlikely,' I said. 'It seems perfectly natural to me.'

'Oh, Charlie,' she said, 'I didn't mean that. You know what I meant.'

That's how it was at first, as I suppose it is with everyone. We circled around each other, trying things out, exploring each other and from time to time tripping up, and having to explain what we meant.

'I've known you for years and years,' I said. 'That's why it's natural.'

'Yes, but you haven't known me *properly*. You know perfectly well what I mean, Charlie.'

I laughed at that, and touched her cheek with my hand. She turned her head a little, pressing her face into my palm. After a while she said, 'I'm not at all used to this. Do you really think . . .' she said, and then hesitated for a long time, which did not matter at all, since it was a very slow conversation and we both understood that we could take as long as necessary.

I said, 'Yes, I really do think it will be marvellous.'

'I agree,' she said. 'And we'll go along steadily, one thing at a time, so nothing gets broken.'

'Yes,' I said. 'Lizzie, nothing will get broken. I'm certain of that.'

'Good,' she said, and for a time we said nothing. I was surprised that it felt so comfortable to lie beside her without speaking.

'It's gone very quiet downstairs,' she said suddenly, lifting her head to listen. During opening hours the murmur of conversation and laughter drifted up to my room from the public bar, but now there was silence.

'How odd,' I said. 'It's not closing time yet. Unless . . .'

'They could be plotting something, Charlie. A joke of some sort.'

'There'll be a knock at the door and someone will say we're wanted on the phone.'

'They'd better not,' she said firmly.

But in a moment we heard the sound of singing from the street below, and a handful of gravel rattled against the window. 'George Honeysett,' Lizzie said, pulling the blanket over our heads. We lay still and listened. George was leading the singing and had evidently organised a sizeable choir.

> Daisy, Daisy, give me your answer do,
> I'm half crazy all for the love of you
> It won't be a stylish marriage
> I can't afford a carriage
> But you'll look sweet
> Up on a seat
> Of a bicycle built for two.

When they'd finished they immediately began to sing, in a slow and sentimental way, 'Maybe It's Because I'm a Londoner'.

'They're going to go on and on,' Lizzie said. 'They think it's a great joke.'

'Well, it is quite funny, isn't it? I rather like it. It's touching, don't you think? They're serenading us. They're giving us a little concert.'

'I dare say they are,' Lizzie said, 'But I think they've given us enough of a concert now.'

'I don't think they'll give up for a long time, unless—'

'Unless what?'

'Unless we wave to them or something. Make an appearance on the balcony, as it were.'

'No,' Lizzie said.

'All right.'

But they showed no sign of giving up yet, and moved smartly on to 'Roll Out the Barrel'.

Eventually Lizzie said, 'You're right. We're going to have to speak to them or they'll never stop.'

I got up, put on a shirt, drew back the curtains and opened

the window. They were standing under the street-lamp like carol singers – George and all the Honeysett family, Lily and little Arthur, Ruth and her friend Patrick, Harry Nicholls, old Ben and half-a-dozen regulars from the public bar.

At the rattle of the sash they looked up, saw me and began waving and shouting – 'Hurrah! Well done, Charlie! Here he is! Here's Charlie, the man of the moment!'

I waved down to them, feeling extremely foolish. 'We're deeply grateful for your serenading, George,' I said.

'Did you hear that?' George shouted, 'they're deeply grateful for our serenading! I should think they are! Deeply grateful!'

They all laughed very loudly. I felt a movement beside me. It was Lizzie in her dressing-gown. She leaned out of the window and called, 'Thank you, George. That was lovely of you. We liked the songs and we're very touched.' She paused. 'Can we go to sleep now?'

They called out, 'Blimey! Here's the lady! And isn't she lovely!' And then, in a tone of mock astonishment, laughing all the while, 'The lady says she wants to go to sleep! Go to sleep! And it's only ten o'clock! Did you hear that? Can you believe it? Ten o'clock!'

Lizzie hid her face in my shoulder and they had some more fun with her for a few moments, but then George called for silence.

'That's enough of that,' he said, looking up at us. 'Now, we're going to stop in a minute and leave you in peace, but we've got a special treat to finish with. You'll like this. You won't have heard anything like this. This is real class, this is.'

He turned back to the singers and said, 'Step forward, young Patrick. He's a real singer, he is, and none better, so just listen to him.'

Patrick stood under the lamp and sang in a light, clear voice:

It was down by the Sally Gardens my love and I did meet –
She crossed the Sally Gardens with little snow-white feet
She bid me take love easy, as the leaves grow on the tree,
But I was young and foolish, and with her did not agree.

Lizzie and I put our arms around each other and Patrick went on singing.

In a field down by the river my love and I did stand
And on my leaning shoulder she laid her snow-white hand.
She bid me take life easy, as the grass grows on the weirs,
But I was young and foolish, and now am full of tears.

They all joined in for the last verse and by then everyone was full of tears, Lizzie and I at the window and all the others in the street below. At the end we waved and called down to Patrick, saying how marvellous the song had been, how touched we were, how kind of them it was to serenade us – and they agreed, cheering Patrick and themselves, calling goodbye to us and drifting away one by one, until the street was empty.

Lying with her in the warm darkness, nothing existed but that moment. We touched, and with those light touches began our transformation. 'Charles,' she murmured, and then 'Charlie', and again 'Charles'. I understood that she was sounding my name, testing its changing significance, and we went onward in small steps of that kind, words and sounds and caresses, until in due time even the touch of a fingertip became fire. Her skin was like nothing I had previously known, but seemed that of a sea creature, sleek and swift in the water, alive under my hands with the even pulse of her heart. The line of her waist, her hip, the way her hip rose in that curve, just so, and fell again – with all this I was entranced. She lay still, her head turned to me, and in the darkness I could just detect the gleam of her eyes. I knelt beside her, my hands shaping her neck, her shoulders, her spine, and discovered the two dimples in the small of her back, as if she had been marked by the thumbs of the sculptor who had made her – and later, when she cried out, death and life were somehow combined into that cry, and she called my name over and over – 'Charlie, Charlie, oh, Charlie—' and cried wordlessly and roughly like an animal, and all the sorrow of the earth sounded in her cry, and all the joy.

*

In the morning I woke from somewhere far away, turned over and found Lizzie lying diagonally across the bed, still abandoned to sleep. She did not wake when I kissed her, and I got up and sat in a chair beside the window, gazing down into Mafeking Street.

There had been rain in the night and early sunshine was drawing steam from the surface of the road. I pushed up the sash and heard the slow clop of hooves – a cart was coming round the corner, a rag-and-bone man leading his thin, ancient horse. The horse stopped and stood in the sun with its head drooping while the old man went from one house to the next, collecting bundles that had been left for him. Every so often, like a seabird picking its way along the edge of the tide, he gave the rag-and-bone man's cry, that once was words but now had rusted to a croak. I made a viewfinder with my hands and framed the rag-and-bone man and his horse and cart, their shadows sharp in the morning light.

I once heard a lecturer describing the response of some Australian aboriginal people to photographs of themselves. These people, he told us, were afraid of the camera on the grounds that it stole their souls – and he shook his head in amazement. I listened to the laughter of the audience and sat there for a few minutes longer. Suppose a photographer captures an image of his subject, takes it away and shows it to an unknown other, uses it for his own purposes: how is that not stealing? I got up and left.

There is a picture that Henri Cartier-Bresson took from a high window in Rouen on a wet day, a pattern of umbrellas against the cobbles of the street. It is momentarily puzzling, like the quiz pictures of everyday objects in a child's comic – a toothbrush seen from one end, or a close-up of a thimble. Cartier-Bresson looked down from his window, saw the oddness, captured it and took it away. Such oddness is present in all photographs taken from above, a consequence of the absence of perspective and the altitude that distances the photographer and makes his subject unaware of his presence. There is something cynical about such pictures – pedestrians made into a pattern of umbrellas, very droll – and the most cynical is the reconnaissance photograph, in which the photographer is certainly hostile, an intruder and a spy, and the subject's image is taken despite his objections.

I turned to look at Elizabeth, thinking that I would never photograph her, and as I watched she turned over and stretched her arms upwards, opened her eyes and saw me, sat up suddenly and said in surprise, 'Oh – Charlie – it's you!'

In a moment she had put on her dressing-gown, stepped across to my chair and surrounded me with her delicious drowsy warmth.

'Look,' I said, and showed her the rag-and-bone man. He was bending over a sack on a doorstep, picking at it with hands enclosed in rough woollen mittens. We watched him as he shuffled along the street, sometimes stopping to whistle shrilly. At the man's whistle the horse walked forward, its steps melancholy and slow, and then halted and hung its head, waiting.

As I watched the rag-and-bone man I found myself thinking yet again about Blunt and Bob Rattray, Jacko and the others – pointless, circular thoughts about chance and circumstance and blame, round and round, refusing to stop. I turned away from the window and put my arms around Lizzie.

'Charlie, what's the matter?' she whispered.

'Too much joy, I expect,' I said. 'Too many things at once, all muddled up.' I turned my head and kissed the palm of her hand. 'All this, so suddenly – you, and all that we're doing together. Leaving Waverley and coming here – I wonder why I should want to do that? Learning to take pictures. The war already over, in the distant past, long ago now, but still in my head – I'm not making any sense.'

Lizzie kept still, looking down at me and listening.

'My crew all got killed in the end, except me of course. I wasn't a brave pilot, and they took me off flying. But the others went on, and eventually they were all killed. We'd been like a family – a proper family, I mean, people who speak to each other, and are true to each other. It makes you wonder, that sort of thing. I suppose everyone hopes to be brave, and mostly we aren't. Nothing can be done about it, of course, but it's the sort of thing you carry with you, and will always carry.'

Her hand still lay warm against my cheek, and I went on talking.

'As you get older you begin to discover what's true and what isn't, and you have to decide things. You have to get rid of a lot of foolish stuff. Trappings. Things that make you feel too safe.'

She moved a little and said, 'Too safe?'

'Ways of behaving. Suppose you're always wrapped up warm – perhaps a nurse dresses you in furs in winter, a chauffeur drives you around in a warm car – if you live like that, how do you know what warmth is? If you haven't ever been cold, you can't know how good it is to be warm, can you? You simply can't know. You have to get rid of all that.'

She said, 'I think I see what you mean, Charlie, but it sounds as if you're saying we should take risks for the sake of it.'

'Does it?' I thought for a while. 'I don't think I mean that. I mean something much simpler – just trying to keep going straight, and not fall into some comfortable rut.'

'Oh, I see,' she said, laughter in her voice.

'Do you think that's funny?'

'Only moderately,' she said. 'Charlie, you're all tangled up. You need more sleep, and more kissing.'

In due course Father sent me a letter in which he expressed astonishment that 'a son of mine' – he used that infuriating phrase several times – could reject all the values and traditions of the family. 'Yes I can,' I thought, 'yes I can!' What was I doing? Living in the London slums in an immoral association. Attempting to establish a business about which you are completely ignorant. Doing permanent harm to the family, a family that has a major part to play in English life – it was a long, rambling and insulting letter, but in an odd way I was glad to get it, and it made me feel I was doing the right thing.

'Do permanent harm? That's a bit steep,' I said to Lizzie.

'By "immoral association", he means me, I suppose?'

'I suppose so.'

'How perfectly horrid of him! I think we shall have to get married at once, just to spite him.'

'Shall we invite him to the wedding?'

'Oh yes,' Lizzie said. 'I shall be tremendously gracious to

him, and he might feel a little ashamed. But I suppose he wouldn't want to go all the way to Gretna just for an hour.'

'Gretna?'

'Perhaps it ought to be the registry office. Then all of Mafeking Street can come if they want.'

'They will certainly want to come, and they'll sing, too.'

It was July, and on the morning of our wedding there was a sudden shower that washed the streets and freshened the plane trees. Lizzie looked enchanting, even Gerald was perfectly charming to everyone, as he knew he must be, and the reception at the Lamb & Flag was a jolly affair with a great deal of singing.

In the middle of it George Honeysett came up and shouted in my ear, 'What about number 17 then?'

'What about number 17?'

'Number 17,' he shouted again, amazed at my stupidity. 'Number 17 Mafeking Street. You could buy it. You and Lizzie. Get it for a song.'

'What do you mean?' I asked. 'It's a shambles, that house. It's only got half a roof and all the windows are gone.'

He laughed. 'Half a roof is better than none, innit? Timber can be found. Bricks can be found. Tiles can found. Ladders can be found, and men to climb them.' He seized my hand in his great fist. 'What about it, eh, Charlie? What do you think?'

It seemed to me, at that moment in the Lamb & Flag, that we had achieved all the happiness that could possibly be desired.

Sixteen

We established Airborne Photos on little more than a whim, sailing into it with the confidence of complete ignorance, and it nearly failed before it began. We designed what we thought was a jolly nice leaflet and sent it to every possible client we could think of. We telephoned people we knew and people we did not know, and we placed advertisements in all the right trade papers; but five months went by without a single commission.

To start with we didn't care. We were happy with our new life of flying, photography and house-repairing. We had space in which to practise our trade and establish our library. But in the end we must have customers, and at the end of the fifth month we had a formal meeting between the two of us and decided that we would continue for one more month and after that – well, we would think what to do next. Later that same day the telephone rang.

Lizzie answered it, listened for a while, then put her hand over the receiver and said, 'Would Airborne Photos care to quote for some aerial photography in the city of Bristol?'

'Certainly we would,' I said.

'It's a considerable contract, and the city needs to ensure that we have the resources and skills to do it satisfactorily.'

'Of course.'

'They want samples of vertical and oblique pictures sent immediately, both black-and-white and colour. If they are acceptable we will be asked to provide a quotation.'

'We'll send them this minute.'

Our contact was an officer of the Corporation of Bristol, a man of old-fashioned politeness and formality whose name was Rainbow. He approved our samples and invited us to quote for a set of aerial photographs covering the whole of Bristol. It had been heavily damaged by bombing, particularly in the city centre and docks; the photographs would inform the plans for rebuilding and become a permanent record of wartime.

It was a sizeable piece of work and we needed it. The price we quoted was more than keen – we would have done it for nothing. In due course we were invited to a discussion of the project. We took the Argus to the aerodrome at Whitchurch and discovered that Mr Rainbow had never been in the air. It was a fine day and we took him on a tour of the sights: the river Avon, winding into Bristol under Brunel's lovely suspension bridge; the green expanse of the Downs; the Floating Harbour, its docks still busy in those days; and finally the battered city centre and the lovely spire of St Mary Redcliffe, the church that the first Queen Elizabeth called 'the finest parish church in all England'.

Returning from a look at the Mendip hills, we flew over a pair of reservoirs straddling the main road, and Basil Rainbow, strapped into the back seat of the noisy Argus, shouted into my ear that they looked like spectacles fallen from the pocket of a giant. His delight seemed a sign that we would get the job; and in due course we did.

The Corporation wanted a set of vertical pictures that could be combined into a single large image, plus oblique views of particular features. Some four hundred vertical photographs were required, the images overlapping precisely and taken in similar light; it was photographic mapping, and we had no practice in that procedure. We flew home, spread a map of the city on the studio table, covered it with tracing paper and began to draw grids and plan how it might be done.

In due course the Corporation of Bristol arranged lodgings for us near Whitchurch and we began work. It was early in July; the weather held and we flew early each morning, spending the rest of the day processing the film in a temporary darkroom. After twelve days of anxious work we flew back to Rochford, unloaded the film, took it to Mafeking Street and began printing straight away.

Nearly a thousand large prints had to be made, checked, numbered and recorded, and in the middle of it we had a request from Australian Cargo Lines for photographs of a new ship on trials in the Irish Sea. We flew there, took the pictures, delivered them to their head office the following day and went back to work on the Bristol contract, thinking ourselves wonderfully efficient.

There wasn't room for a trial assembly of the full set of prints in our studio. We borrowed number 14 from Lily and laid them out on a table hurriedly made from sheets of plywood. The composite image was sixteen by twenty feet and was certainly impressive. Everyone in Mafeking Street came to look at this moment in the history of a city, now preserved on dozens of sheets of glossy paper. We had captured Bristol as it began the day, when people were on their way to work, taking their children to school, leaning on a spade in their allotment or talking to a neighbour. Here were the vans of the now-vanished roundsmen – baker, fishmonger, greengrocer, ironmonger and horse and cart of the rag-and-bone man. Here were the policemen on their beats, one of them evidently giving a boy a good telling-off, and on one image a man was standing in his back garden and looking up at the Argus with binoculars, spying on us as we spied on him.

As well as these everyday details the photographs showed, as intended, the consequences of the bombing that had virtually destroyed the old commercial centre of the city: the ruins of Wine Street and Corn Street, the battered docks and factories and burned-out warehouses, the houses, churches and schools that had been randomly destroyed all across the city. I had seen photographs like this a hundred times, of course, but they had never before been pictures of an English city; this was different, and it was disturbing. We gazed at the photographs for a long time, all of us crowding round the table and calling out when another intriguing feature was discovered.

In the offices of Bristol Corporation we constructed the big image again, using a room with a balcony that conveniently allowed a view from above. Many Corporation staff came to see them and the process of close examination and exclamation happened again; it is curious how photography refreshes the everyday, and makes the familiar worthy of study.

We were congratulated on our work and felt an enormous sense of relief that we had been able to do it reasonably well. The photographs of Bristol were later used in newspapers and magazines, and resulted in further contracts of a similar kind, as did our pictures for Australian Cargo Lines. We suddenly became busy, and short of staff. We took on Angela Honeysett, who volunteered to learn developing and printing and turned out to be good at it. Soon she became the darkroom supervisor and we employed her sister Julia as well.

Even my landscapes – more often sky and cloud rather than land, in fact – began slowly to sell. The first sales were to a manufacturer of greetings cards. Lizzie knew that my artistic aspirations were above the level of picture postcards, and was amused.

'Never mind, Charlie,' she said, laughing and kissing me, 'One day someone will open an old trunk and discover a whole set of early Beevors – they'll make a packet. And in the meantime, just think of the money.'

The income from this work allowed us to produce a new and rather elegant brochure, advertising Airborne Photos as an outfit with noteworthy clients and an excellent reputation, a business that was here to stay.

In such a fashion did we get started, learning as we went, and we were fortunate, and made a go of it. We did a great deal of flying, often to interesting and beautiful places, but of course we also spent much time working in the archway in Mafeking Street. Lizzie dealt with the flying and organised the library, while I did the photography and managed the darkroom; the division of labour worked perfectly well, and we were happy.

Soon we were accepted in Mafeking Street as just another of the little businesses that occupied the archways from time to time. There was a year of peace, then there was another, and we became accustomed to the fact that the war was over.

But in Berlin the war was not over, not for many years yet.

Seventeen

Julia told me that there had been an urgent telephone call for Lizzie. She was to ring a gent called Savage as soon as possible.

'I wrote down the number,' Julia said, giving me a slip of paper, 'and I tell you what, he sounded a bit of a card, he did really.'

When Lizzie came into the studio I said, 'Wasn't John Savage the chap you saw once before, the one who wanted—'

'Yes,' Lizzie said. 'He was the bloke who didn't really have an office in Oxford Street, who wanted a secretary who knew a few posh people in the aircraft business, who didn't want a woman as a pilot and who wasted my time going up and down a lot of stairs trying to find him.'

I laughed. 'Perhaps he's got a proper flying job for you now.'

'I've already got a proper flying job.'

'Well,' I said, 'it might be worth giving him a ring.'

She looked at me and after a moment picked up the telephone and dialled the number, twirling the phone cord in rapid circles while she waited for a reply.

'Is that Mr Savage? It's Elizabeth Beevor here. My surname

used to be Bowman – Elizabeth Bowman. You know my husband, Charles, I believe.'

She listened for a few moments and then said, 'Of course. I remember you perfectly well from our previous meeting in London. I'll listen to what you say, but I doubt I can help you.'

She listened for quite a long time. At one point she said, 'Of course I can. I've got a lot of hours on Dakotas, and quite a few on Yorks for that matter.'

Another long pause, and then she said with great certainty, 'No, Mr Savage. I don't want to do it. I'm sorry, but I don't care how much you're offering.'

Now she was tapping one foot on the floor with an insistent rhythm. Finally she broke into Savage's continuing argument and said, 'Look, I've got a job already and I haven't got time to do that as well. You won't persuade me. I'm sorry, but that's that. Please don't phone again.'

She put the receiver down with a clatter, said 'Horrid man' and started towards the door.

'Lizzie,' I said, taking a step after her, 'does he want you for the airlift? Is it for Berlin?'

But she went on down the stairs, past the darkroom and out into the street, the door banging shut behind her.

The campaign that won the Second World War in Europe, the Red Army's long march on Berlin, was ruthless almost beyond conception. It remained so even at the moment of victory, when the rampant troops, in a last frenzy, killed and raped without restraint, threw thousands of Germans into concentration camps and stripped the city of every movable asset.

By May 1945 the war had killed half a million Berliners – ten times the number that died in London – and one might think that they had paid sufficient price. But West Berlin, now a defiant island of democracy and capitalism, soon became the focus of a new conflict.

Early in 1948 the Russians closed the overland supply routes, threatening West Berlin's two and a half million citizens with economic collapse and ultimately with starvation. The western allies began to bring in essential supplies by air, but few thought such a tactic could succeed; no airlift on such a scale had been attempted before, and there was a shortage of military transport aircraft. Soon it was realised that civil aircraft would also have to be employed.

'Yes, of course it was Berlin,' Lizzie said that night, lying on the bed beside me, her hands behind her head. 'He's got hold of some Dakotas and a York, and he wants lots of crews to fly them round the clock, night and day. The way they've organised it, he'll probably make a fortune.'

'But you don't want to do it,' I said.

'No, I don't.'

I waited for her to say more, but she did not.

'Lizzie,' I said after a while, 'if you really want to get into commercial flying, this might be a wonderful chance, a chance you simply can't miss. Perhaps you ought to think about it, at least.'

I was at my most ponderous. She gave me a look and said, 'Don't be so bloody stupid, Charlie.' Then she rolled away from me and reached for a book from her bedside table.

I considered what she had said. Wasn't this a quite exceptional opportunity? She would get a lot of commercial experience in a short time and make a lot of contacts. People would notice her – perhaps the only woman pilot – and another job might be offered, maybe in a country that had fewer objections to women pilots – America, for example. She was certainly rejecting the job because of me and Airborne, and perhaps also because of Lily and Mafeking Street. Flying a little Argus in a tinpot photography business with her husband – it didn't compare with flying for a regular airline to Berlin, with the whole world watching.

'I shall risk further speech,' I said, 'even though I know I may infuriate my beloved wife, and she may end up thrusting a dagger through my heart. I'm going to say what I think, because this is something we ought to be absolutely clear about. You can listen or not, and then we won't say any more.'

She turned over, gave a little laugh and said, 'All right, Charlie – I've no dagger, so you're safe enough. Go on. Make your speech.'

Then I spoke about the pros and cons of Savage's offer, no doubt rather pompously. I talked about the opportunity and what it might give her and where it might lead, and about Airborne and me and Mafeking Street, and she listened, looking at me the whole time.

When I had finished she moved nearer until she could touch my cheek with her hand. 'You are a very dear man,' she said, 'and I love you very much, but Charlie, you've got this wrong. I agree it's a choice, as you say, and one choice is to stay in our little business, stay here with you and Airborne and Lily. But the other choice isn't about advancing my flying career. It's about Berlin.'

'Oh,' I said, and then, 'I don't think I understand you.'

She lay on her back again and looked up at the ceiling. 'The biggest thing I ever did was to go to Berlin. It changed the way I thought about everything. You went there too, and it changed you as well, didn't it?'

'Yes,' I said.

'I don't know how these things work,' she said. 'I don't have the faintest idea why something has a tremendous effect and something else doesn't. It's very odd, the way we keep planning our lives to be nice and neat and they suddenly go all wobbly and end up in a muddle. It's not logical at all.'

She turned her head to look at me again. 'When I was a little girl I was in love with my dear daddy and with flying – or possibly I was in love with my dear daddy and Wilbur Wright and flying.'

She laughed at that thought, and went on talking. 'I've grown up now, and I can see things a bit more clearly – some of them, anyway. I still like flying – it's a marvellous thing, and it's lovely to do it with you, Charlie. But flying isn't so muddled up with other things as it used to be. I love you, Charlie, and Lily too, and I'm going to stay in Mafeking Street and keep on with this little business that we've started, which is so much fun. I'm certain of that.'

She paused and gazed at the ceiling again. 'I'm not upset because I shall miss a chance to be a famous woman airline pilot. I'm upset for quite a different reason. If I took that job with the wretched Savage man I could give something back. Do you see? I could give something back to Berlin.'

Tears ran from her eyes and she brushed them away. 'God knows why I'm like this, Charlie – it's a long time since Alice and I went to Berlin. But it was such a sad thing, beyond anything I've ever known – all of it – the place itself, the ruins, the smoke, the smell, the people we met, everything that happened there and on the way back. Don't you see? We'd been having such a jolly little war in such a just cause, and then it all collapsed, didn't it? I suddenly saw what it was about. Killing. That's how it was in Berlin. And as for Alice dying – such a stupid thing – such a silly accident – where's the logic in that? Where's the justice in that? You can't make any sense of it.'

She sat up and leaned against a pillow.

'The reason I'm upset has to do with Berlin, and it isn't anything to do with my flying or that silly man Savage. Do you see, Charlie?'

'I think I may understand it eventually,' I said. 'Given a bit of time to work it out.'

She laughed. 'It's a bit of a muddle, I know.' She leaned over, took a handkerchief from her bedside table, and blew her nose.

'I'm sure it isn't,' I said. 'I shall work on it.'

'Good,' she said. 'Shall we go to bed now?'

When I came down next morning Lizzie was reading the paper. She looked up and said, 'That man Savage said he was going to take tinned food, dried milk, medicines and coal into Tempelhof.'

'Coal?'

'That's what he said. Sacks of coal. It looks as though he was telling the truth – Berlin's running out of coal. It says so in the paper.'

'Sounds a funny mixture to me,' I said. 'Coal and dried milk. I hope it's all clearly labelled.'

She smiled and said, 'It's all right, Charlie. I'm perfectly OK now.'

I said, 'You do know, don't you, that if you changed your mind you could go and fly for John Savage? We could find someone to help me with Airborne easily enough.'

'Don't say that again, Charlie. We've dealt with that. It's decided.'

'All right. But you can have second thoughts if you like.'

'I *am* having second thoughts, but they aren't about Savage and going back to Berlin. I'll tell you about them shortly, when I've worked them out a bit more.'

'Very well,' I said.

*

Lizzie was restless all day, and that evening I noticed that she had cut some pictures and articles from that morning's paper.

'I thought I'd keep an eye on what happens in Berlin, just for interest,' she said. 'I took a few cuttings.'

Twice that week she stayed late in the studio, pasting cuttings about the airlift into a scrapbook and writing in a large notebook with a blue marbled cover. I was curious about this, of course, but she dismissed my enquiries quite casually – 'It's just a bit of stuff I'm collecting together, Charlie.'

What did she mean by 'giving something back to Berlin'? She hadn't taken anything away. She wasn't to blame for Berlin. Was it the death of Alice that still made her feel some sort of guilt? I thought about these matters a good deal, but came to no conclusion.

Her continued concentration on Berlin, and the fact that she seemed to want to do it alone, concerned me. From the beginning there had been little that we did not do together, and nothing that either of us kept secret from the other. This was different. She organised a corner of the studio in which to store what soon became a sizeable collection of files and cardboard boxes, and did not ask me to help.

Was it possible that her interest in Berlin might be harmful to her in some way? But no, I said to myself, that's ridiculous, and one day she will surely show me what she's doing, all in good time, when she feels like it, she'll tell me about it.

Over the next few weeks Lizzie got into the habit of spending an hour on her Berlin files every day, and after a month or so she bought a filing cabinet to hold the material. 'I've got a lot of good stuff,' she said, 'and it's all got to be kept tidy.'

'That's fine,' I said. 'Let me know if you want a hand with anything.'

'I will, Charlie,' she said, but she did not.

Only once did we discuss Lizzie's researches. I saw a letter from the Red Cross on her desk and asked her what it was about.

'It's just a letter from the Red Cross. They say they found 409 on her own near a DP camp.'

'You mean the child numbered 409? The little girl you brought back?'

'Yes.'

I felt a shock at that: Lizzie was evidently chasing down every detail of her Berlin flight. I asked her if the child had come from that camp, and she said it wasn't clear. Germany was in chaos for weeks after the fall of Berlin, and some eight million refugees were wandering in Germany; the child could have come from anywhere.

'What happened to her after she got here? Was she adopted by an English family?'

'I don't know, Charlie. The records seem to be in a terrible mess. All sorts of organisations were involved with refugees and displaced persons. Some children were shipped on to America, Canada and other places across the world. She could be anywhere.'

But Lizzie was certain that 409 was alive. 'At this very minute someone could be taking her for a walk in Central Park,' she said. 'She could be on a train going through the Rockies. She could even be sitting on an African veranda. Anyway, I'll find her in the end.'

Eighteen

By the spring of the new year the constant stream of American and British aircraft was easily supporting the population of West Berlin, and appeared able to do so indefinitely. The Soviet blockade had become pointless now; indeed, it was doing considerable harm to the economy of East Germany, and East Berlin in particular. In the summer the supply routes to the western sector of the city were reopened, and soon afterwards the airlift was wound down. It had served its purpose, and West Berlin remained free from Soviet control; it had also been a tremendous propaganda coup, displaying the vast power of America and its allies and their manifest commitment to the people of the city.

I hoped that the closing down of the airlift might end Lizzie's interest in Berlin; it still made me uneasy. She had evidently assembled a great deal of information but said hardly a word to me about it. I should have asked her to make her researches a joint effort – but I had not, and after a few weeks it was too late for me to intrude on what had, by then, become a personal and private mission.

*

Some weeks later we were working in the studio when she
suddenly turned to me and said, 'Charlie, you've been very
tactful about my Berlin stuff. You've left me to get on with it,
and you haven't asked any questions, but I can see that you're
still fussing about it.'

'Fussing?'

'Yes, Charlie. I know you rather well, you know. I'm
perfectly aware that you've been worrying about me and my
Berlin stuff ever since I started cutting bits out of the paper.'

'I've certainly wondered what you were up to.'

'And why I wasn't telling you about it.'

'Well – yes.'

'When Alice and I went to Berlin at the end of the war we
met a German girl there, a girl who had worked in the Zoo,
and she told us a story.'

'Yes – the story about the orang-utan. Of course I remember
it.'

'I knew you would – we had a disagreement about it, didn't
we? Do you remember? You were angry, and said I was upset
about nothing. That's partly why I haven't told you what I was
doing. I thought it might annoy you if you knew the details.
You might have said – well, I don't know what you might have
said, but I'm sure you wouldn't have liked it.'

She pushed her fingers through her hair. 'To tell you the truth
I didn't intend to do anything much at first. I just began to keep
a few bits and pieces about the airlift, and then started to think
more and more about that last flight with Alice.'

She hesitated again. 'There were a lot of loose ends. The
more I looked at it, the more it seemed like a story that hadn't
been finished. I had a talk with Lily about it.'

'Lily?' I was surprised at that.

'Yes. It was Alice's story as much as mine, so of course I

talked to Lily about it. I told her the whole thing and she said of course I ought to find out about it, and write it down. That's what I've been doing, and now I'm beginning to tie up some of the loose ends.'

She sounded confident and perfectly cheerful about it, which was reassuring.

'I want you to look at what I've been doing,' she said. 'We won't do it now, because it would take too long and we're busy. But this evening, after supper, we'll come back here and I'll show you some of my collection.'

I heard this with great relief. It would be much better if the whole thing was out in the open.

Lizzie had laid a cloth over one of the long tables and arranged various items on it – her scrapbook, some folders and letters, a parcel wrapped in brown paper, a map, and, at the far end of the table, two or three of those blue marbled notebooks – I had thought there was only one, but there were several. Beside the table she had put a chair for herself, and there was another chair further away, in the middle of the floor, presumably for me. Clearly she was going to give a performance, and my role was to be the audience.

'Sit over there,' she said. 'I've got it all planned. We're going to go through all this stuff in the right order. We won't look at everything – just a selection.'

I did as I was told and Lizzie stood in front of the table.

'We'll begin with some photographs,' she said, picking up a folder. 'I'll hold them up one at a time and you can tell me what they are. These are just the preliminaries. They show where things began.'

She took out a photograph and held it up. 'Good Lord,' I said, 'it's your father. It's Ernest.'

Ernest Bowman? She was obviously starting a long way back. I had never seen a photograph of Ernest before; it was a large black-and-white print mounted in an oak frame. He was in full morning dress including top hat, beaming at the camera.

'It's my mother's picture, the one she keeps beside her bed. I borrowed it.'

She turned the picture round to look at it herself. 'It was their wedding day, of course. What a handsome man he is! He looks so proud, so confident—' She gazed at the picture for some moments, then said, 'I think we'll leave him on view,' and propped the picture against her pile of folders.

I laughed when she held the next one up. 'It's us,' I said, 'it's you and I in the Gipsy Moth. Gerald took that at one of the racecourses – I think it was Taunton. It's a lovely picture. I haven't seen it for ages.'

'Far too easy, that one,' Lizzie said. 'Next.' This one showed a canal boat and two figures.

'Ruth and Patrick.'

'Another easy one. Next.' This was another framed picture.

'That's – I think that's Wilbur Wright, isn't it?'

'Yes. That is the incomparable Wilbur Wright.' She propped it next to the photograph of Ernest, saying, 'I think there's a likeness between them, don't you? Yes, I'm sure there is.' She was edgy, moving quickly, full of nervous energy.

'That was the overture,' she said. 'Now the first act.' She walked to the far end of the table, reached under the cloth, pulled out a wooden box and lifted it on to the table. It was clearly heavy.

'This box' she rested one hand on it. 'Do you know what it is?'

I looked at it – a rectangular beechwood box about two feet wide, eighteen inches high and a foot deep, very nicely made with neat dovetailing and a substantial leather handle. For a moment I had not the slightest idea what it might be, but then it came to me.

'Oh, it's Alice's box,' I said. 'It's Alice's toolbox, of course.'

'Yes,' Lizzie said, 'that's exactly what it is.'

She lifted the box from the table, put it on the floor in front of me and knelt beside it. 'Just look at this,' she said, opening the front panel and displaying a set of drawers of varying sizes. 'Have you ever seen anything so neat?' She pulled out one of the drawers. 'Look – this one's full of taps and dies – all the way from the smallest BA to three-eighth Whitworth.'

She pulled out a larger drawer. 'Callipers and micrometers. Various reamers. Isn't it wonderful?'

'It is,' I said. 'Everything has its place. Everything fits exactly.'

'That's Alice,' Lizzie said, closing the box and returning it to the table. 'She made the box herself, of course. She was amazingly neat and methodical. She always checked everything three times and never made a single mistake.'

She took one of the envelopes from the table and brought it across to me. It contained a set of ground engineer's certificates in the name of Miss A. Attwell, certifying that she was licensed to work on various types of engine and airframe. I leafed through them – Merlin, Hercules and Twin Wasp engine certificates, and among the airframe licences, the Fairchild Argus.

'Oh, Alice was licensed for the Argus,' I said.

'Of course she was,' Lizzie said, taking the envelope from me. 'We had them in the ATA. We used them as taxi aircraft, for carrying our pilots around. Didn't you know that? Now the next thing is another photograph.'

She passed me a small print of four men in RAF uniform. They were all grinning and one of them was waving his cap at the camera. I had never seen them before, but it wasn't difficult to guess.

'They're the four prisoners of war that you and Alice brought back from Berlin,' I said.

'You're not supposed to know that.'

'I didn't know,' I said. 'I just guessed.'

'Well, that's very clever of you. But you won't know their names. John Stevens – that's the tall one with the stick. Bill Jones is next to him, then it's David Bryant and Jack Scott waving his hat. John Stevens sent me the photograph.'

She unfolded a letter and read aloud: '"Dear Mrs Beevor, of course we remember you very well. We'll always be grateful to you and Miss Attwell for getting us back."'

Lizzie paused for a moment, shook her head and then went on reading. '"I enclose a photograph of all four of us, with our grateful thanks. Yours sincerely, John Stevens." And he's written a PS that says they put their uniforms on specially for the picture, and found they didn't fit so well these days.'

She turned away from me and I stood up, wanting to go to her, but she turned and said, 'Sit down, Charlie. This is my show and I'm in the middle of it.'

I sat down and asked, 'How did you find the prisoners of war?'

'RAF records, of course.'

'What about the nun and the child? Have you found them too?'

Lizzie ignored me and said, 'Sergeant Frank Oldfield is married and lives in Aspen, Colorado. I have a letter from him. His wife is expecting another baby in the autumn.'

'Lizzie—'

'I haven't finished yet.'

'I know, but I'm not sure—'

'Just wait, Charlie. I found the German woman who worked at the zoo.'

'Anna.'

'Yes. Anna Schwarz is her name. She was easy to find. I just wrote to the zoo in Berlin and they sent me her address. It's in East Berlin. I've written to her but she hasn't replied yet.'

Lizzie picked up the scrapbook. 'I've got a lot of cuttings about the airlift,' she said. 'I'm not going to show you them all now, but look at this one.'

She held out a page with a large photograph of parked aircraft. 'Dakotas,' I said, 'Four Dakotas parked at Templehof, I think.'

'Yes, but look at them closely.'

I did so, and saw that four of the aircraft were marked 'Ocean Island Airways'.

'John Savage's aeroplanes,' I said.

'Yes,' she said. 'I was quite surprised to see them. You never quite knew whether he was telling the truth. He must have found some pilots from somewhere.'

She looked again at the picture of Templehof – a blurred newspaper picture, but it was good enough to show the elegant curve of the airport buildings and the dozens of aircraft that were parked in neat rows before it.

'Perhaps I should—' She started to say something and then broke off.

'Perhaps you should what?' I asked.

'Oh, nothing.' She turned to put the scrapbook back and leaned against the edge of the table. 'Charlie, if you don't mind, I don't think I'll do any more of this tonight. It's getting late and I feel tired.'

'That's all right,' I said. 'Lizzie, this display of yours, all these things that you've organised to show me—'

'You want to know why I did it.'

'Well – the way you've chosen to do it, and all the work that you've put into it—'

'You want to know what I'm up to. Of course you do. Well, it's perfectly simple.' She walked across to her own chair and sat down, and I suddenly felt a curious sense that time was slowing down.

'It's perfectly simple,' Lizzie said again, lifting one hand towards her face. 'I thought it would be a way of – of working it out. I thought I could – I thought I could—'

She reached up, touched her lips delicately with her fingers in a strange, dreamy gesture and said, 'I thought that when Alice and I went – when we went – when we went to Berlin—'

'Lizzie,' I said, and started to go towards her.

'No,' she said, putting up her hands, 'I'm quite all right. Really I am. But I just feel – suddenly I think perhaps I can't—'

I knelt in front of her chair and she slipped towards me and began to sob, saying over and over, 'I'm sorry, I'm so sorry, Charlie, I'm sorry, I'm sorry.'

I held her for a long time, and her sobbing gradually faded. At last, with great difficulty, I got her to stand and took her to the house, her feet dragging as if she were drunk. I laid her on the bed, covered her with a blanket and sat down beside her. Slowly the light faded, the city grew silent around us and the street lights cast their pale light across the ceiling. After an hour, perhaps longer, Lizzie's eyes were fast shut and her breathing deep and steady.

I went downstairs and across Mafeking Street to the studio. Something that Lizzie had discovered in the course of her researches had caused this sudden breakdown, and I wanted to know what it was.

The lights were still on in the studio. I began to leaf through the papers, letters and photographs until I reached the parcel I had noticed earlier. It contained a bible – in fact, a copy of the Vulgate, the Latin version of the bible intended for popular use. Inside the front cover was a letter in Polish, and clipped to it, an English translation of the letter.

The letter had been written by a nun called Sister Julia. It was she who had brought the child numbered 409 from a DP camp near Sachsenhausen and then from Berlin to England. The child's Christian name was Rosa and her surname was unknown. Rosa spoke Polish and was thought to be about four years old. Sister Julia had taken Rosa to the Sisters of Mercy in Gloucestershire, where several other Polish children had been collected; all were thought to be orphans, and had been found in the same area of Germany.

When Rosa arrived she had been found to have a rash on her chest, possibly a symptom of typhoid. She was immediately isolated, and soon became seriously ill. On the 22nd September 1945, at 6.15 in the evening, the letter said, Rosa was taken into the eternal care of Almighty God, our Lord and Father in Heaven. Her grave could be found in the churchyard of the Sisters of Mercy, marked with a stone bearing the child's name, her age, the date of her death and the words *A child harmed by war: let her rest in peace.*

Lizzie, my darling Lizzie – she had dug into the past until her relentless spade had brought up the body of this child, another fragment of the war's harm. She had been trying to make it safe, this history of hers – collating it, annotating it, filing it, in the belief that she might secure herself from the dangers of the past – but it had all gone wrong, and would not be ordered, and she had been harmed after all, Lizzie, my dear Lizzie.

*

I knew that I should have done something earlier. I should have diverted Lizzie from her quest altogether, or joined it myself, or at least diverted the agonising show that she put on for me – surely I should have done something – I knew, or thought I knew, what she was doing – that she was applying her father's principles to the events of Berlin, and I knew that in those events no sense could be discovered – I knew what she was doing, and I had done nothing about it.

And why had Sister Julia sent Lizzie this weighty bible? Because she wished to show sympathy by a gift, perhaps, and a bible was one of the few gifts that a nun might make – indeed, the greatest thing that she might give, being the source of her faith, her love and all her hopes – 'Only love God, and all will be well.' I felt for a moment the tremendous tug and draw of faith, such a tempting invention – but the war had cured me of that and the lure of it made me angry, so I took the bible and threw it whirling across the studio, its pages fluttering like a frantic bird.

Nineteen

Knowing nothing of such things, I thought that Lizzie would shortly be herself again. But in the next few days I found I was wrong. Abruptly, at that moment in the studio, Lizzie had gone beyond my reach, and although I sat and talked to her by the hour, brought her food and drink, washed her, combed her hair and kept her warm, she did not respond. For much of the time – perhaps twenty hours a day – she was asleep, or seemed so. She ate almost nothing. When she was awake she looked at me dully, as though I was of no account to her, and responded only with a few flat words.

Lily came visiting and was puzzled when I sent her away with vague excuses. The word quickly went round and most of Mafeking Street, being both sympathetic and curious, came knocking and were sent away, which was strange behaviour for those parts.

Soon Lily called again and I realised it was wrong to keep this secret; I took her up to Lizzie and she saw the dull look and heard the monotonous voice.

'Charlie, she's ill. Get a doctor,' Lily said.

Of course she was ill – I saw it at once. I had not believed such a change possible, and had denied it to myself. I sent for Doctor MacDonald. He was a bluff and rotund man, his thumbs hooked into the pockets of a brown tweed waistcoat. He sat on a chair beside the bed and took Lizzie's hand in his large, plump fingers.

'My dear young lady,' he said, 'you must learn not to be so melancholy. After all, you're very young, and have your life before you, and you can't spend it in such gloom. These days, I'm afraid, tragedy is commonplace, and we all have to live with it. It's a matter of determination, d'you see? The human spirit is exceptionally robust, my dear, and if you set your mind to it, you'll soon be on the mend. You need no intervention by medical science, let me assure you of that.'

Lizzie stared blankly at him, then turned her head away and closed her eyes.

'I'm not sure that's the right approach,' I said. 'I think my wife needs some kind of help to get over this.'

'You mean psychiatry,' he said, and gave a short laugh.

'Perhaps. Someone who has experience of this sort of thing, anyway.'

'I can assure you that I see patients like Mrs Beevor all the time. There's just been a war, my dear fellow.'

'I know that,' I said, 'but there are specialists in this sort of thing, aren't there? Perhaps she could see one of those.'

Dr MacDonald stared at me and laughed again – a curious snort that I suppose was a laugh – then evidently decided that an argument was not worthwhile. He drew a sheet of paper from his case and I waited, listening to the slow scratch of his pen. Eventually he blotted the sheet, looked up and said he would refer Mrs Beevor to Mrs Rachel Moss, a psychiatrist, for assessment.

'You will no doubt hear from her in due course,' he said. 'Good morning.'

We heard from Rachel Moss by return of post, and I took Lizzie to see her at Park Manor a few days later. The atmosphere of the place was subdued and melancholy. It was a beautiful house in fine grounds but the interior smelt of cigarettes and stale food, and the manner of the nurse on the reception desk was severe.

'Yes?' she demanded as we walked in, 'Name?'

But Rachel Moss, when we reached her, was not at all severe.

'Oh, dear me yes,' she said, after she had tried the labour of talking to Lizzie, 'this must be sorted out as quickly as possible. We'll take you in as soon as we can.'

Lizzie gave a slow nod, and it was not clear that she understood.

I said, 'You're going to stay here for a while, Lizzie. Here at Park Manor.'

She looked at me and asked, 'What is it?'

'It's a hospital,' Rachel Moss said. 'A psychiatric hospital, we call it.'

Lizzie looked away at that, as if she did not care one way or the other. I found it hard to watch her when she did that, the change from her former self seeming incredible to me.

Rachel Moss talked to us then about trauma and neurosis, saying that neurosis was a relatively mild condition from which recovery could soon be expected.

'You will understand,' Rachel said to me, 'that what Lizzie is suffering from is far beyond the ordinary level of sadness, and has become what we call neurosis. I think she feels depressed and anxious, and guilty about certain events, and that she has somehow failed.'

'Yes,' Lizzie said in her flat voice.

'What is absolutely certain, Lizzie, is that you have not failed in any way, and bear no guilt for anything, and certainly none for any of the horrors of the war. You just need time to get back to normal, that's all, and we'll help you to do so.'

I thought that the warmth and certainty of Rachel Moss was encouraging and I believed her; but Lizzie remained expressionless, and gave me no idea what she might be thinking.

And so began a very curious time, a kind of pause, in which our lives seemed suspended motionless in the calm August air. It was decided that Lizzie would remain at Park Manor at least for three weeks. I took her there with a suitcase and helped her to settle into a tiny room with a view across gardens towards woods and fields. She was sitting on the bed when I left. I kissed her and walked to the end of the corridor, where I stopped and thought I would go back – but I would only have to leave her again, so I turned and went on, down the stairs, out of the hospital and across the gardens to the car park. I looked up as I opened the door of the car and saw her at the window. She moved her hand in what might be a wave and I waved back, got into the car and drove away. It felt wrong to leave her, but it was also a relief that something might now be done, since it was clear that I could do nothing to help her myself.

At Mafeking Street everyone worked hard to keep the business going – and also, I expect, to keep my own gloominess at bay. I found another pilot – Adrian West, whom I'd known before the war – and we flew together most mornings. In the afternoons I visited Lizzie at Park Manor between two-thirty and four on weekdays and between three and five at weekends.

The weather being steadily fine, Lizzie spent most of the day in the gardens. She was there the first time I visited her, sitting on a garden seat in the shade of a large cedar, an unopened book beside her.

'Charlie,' she said, and I felt ridiculously pleased that she knew me, and could say my name. She leaned against me and I put my arm round her; I think she was pleased at my presence.

So it was on many subsequent visits. I came to know where she would be, and went straight to her, and held her for the prescribed time, and went away. I felt during those days an immense sense of danger which is hard to express; it had to do, I think, with my sense of our having made our lives so very closely together, each being part of the other, that I was unable to imagine any other kind of being. It wasn't, in other words, entirely a fear for her, but a fear for myself also.

And then one day when I arrived she said, looking up, 'This tree – I've been wondering how long it's been here.'

I kissed her and looked up at the wide, graceful branches of the cedar. Certainly it was a massive tree, and presumably ancient. I said, 'Two hundred years? Three hundred, perhaps? An oak of this size would be that sort of age, but I don't know about cedars.'

In truth I had no care about the tree, but I had a strong sense of delight about the sentence she had uttered. A whole sentence! It became our principal topic, that cedar, and during subsequent days she seemed to draw from it endurance and strength.

'Is it a cedar of Lebanon?'

'I believe so, but I'm not good on trees, Lizzie.'

After two discussions of the tree I went to the library and looked up *Cedrus libani*, so that I would be prepared.

'It has enormous cones hidden among its branches – look.'

I looked up again. This cedar was certainly a fine tree for

such a place as this, a calm and gracious tree, a tree that had endured, come what may.

'If this cedar were three hundred years old,' Lizzie said one day, 'it would have been a sapling in sixteen forty-nine.' She laughed.

She had laughed! I hugged her, and she looked puzzled, as if she had felt something that she did not entirely understand, which was, I suppose, a spasm of happiness.

On another day she said, 'Isn't history short, when you think of it in terms of trees? Sixteen forty-nine – that was Cromwell's time, wasn't it?

'Yes,' I said, feeling the need for another visit to the library.

'I've seen squirrels in its branches, pigeons, crows and smaller birds too – starlings, a blackbird, sparrows, even some great black beetles. It's like a village, sheltering such a large population, a village in layers, higher and higher. And it smells so lovely, too.' She gestured with both hands at the branches.

Our conversations were inconsequential, cautious, concentrating on innocuous subjects immediately before us – the cedar, the gardens, the sky. She seemed not to want to talk about Mafeking Street, about Lily, Arthur or anyone else, nor about our business, but to keep her mind at some distance from the everyday. I did not object to that, of course, but when she talked in that curiously dreamy way, as she had about the village in the branches of the cedar, I knew that this was not quite as she had been, and she would not be coming home in the next day or two, or even in the next week.

August, September – the original three weeks stretched to four, then six, then eight. I'd come in past the fierce receptionist and go looking for Lizzie in the grounds where the patients wandered, some in their night clothes, some sitting alone, smoking and gazing at nothing while pigeons fluttered round them. Occasionally I would see someone sitting and crying, or rocking with their arms round their knees, but there was rarely any sign of extravagant behaviour. It seemed to me that most of the residents of Park Manor were suffering from varieties of depression, from anxiety and loss of spirit.

'Nobody adds up the psychological damage of a war,' Rachel Moss said. 'There are thousands of patients like ours, but they might as well be invisible.'

I asked Lizzie what kind of treatment she was getting, and she was vague about it; she was being given drugs of some sort, and saw Rachel Moss twice a week. I asked her what she talked about when she saw Rachel, and she said, 'Everything.'

We had been so close that I found it difficult to give Lizzie to this institution, and to trust it with her. The interior of Park Manor was shabby, and the airless building with its endless shuffle of slippers was sometimes dispiriting; however, as I became accustomed to it I began to see that the hospital had an underlying tenderness, and was committed to its difficult and unfashionable task. It was enormously accepting, no matter what behaviour was displayed, and it kept on at its work, though it was a task often lengthy and dispiriting.

And Park Manor was having its effect. Lizzie was recovering. She was getting closer, day by slow day, to her old self. One afternoon she suddenly asked whether I'd ask if Lily would like to come and see her.

'Of course I will,' I said.

'Charlie, if she wants to come, tell her to bring little Arthur too, and anyone else from Mafeking Street.'

When I left Park Manor that day I was whistling, and the subsequent visit was a great success. They all came, of course, needing no further asking – Lily and Arthur, all the Honeysetts, old Ben and Harry Nicholls, a procession that brought not only a ridiculous quantity of flowers and chocolates but a bottle of fine sherry that George, as he told us several times, considered just the right present for a lady as wanted cheering up.

Rachel Moss saw Lizzie and I the following day, and said to Lizzie, 'What do you think?'

Lizzie said, 'I think I would like to go home.'

'Good,' said Rachel Moss, taking her hands, 'I shall miss you.'

When she came home our life together was different. I was cautious with her and she was cautious with herself, her energy and joyfulness less visible, her certainty not so obvious.

While she was away a letter had arrived for her, a letter whose stamp bore the bold black eagle of East Germany. I had not taken it to the hospital, but now it must be given to her.

'It will be from Anna Schwartz,' she said.

I watched her as she turned the letter over in her hands. 'I'm afraid of it,' she said.

'I know you are,' I said.

'What do you think I should do?'

'Whatever you want to do.'

'I shall put it away.'

'Very well.'

I had placed all the materials that Lizzie had collected in a tea-chest. The letter from Germany was added, and the whole lot taken up to the attic, where it remained undisturbed for many years.

Twenty

When the war ended the two of us began to construct for ourselves a confined, measured and marvellous life. It was interrupted by Lizzie's discovery of the death of the child whom we now knew to be Rosa, and afterwards it began again, in a somewhat different and more cautious fashion.

We did not venture any distance, but turned inward and built our lives from the materials that were close at hand – each other, our aerial photography and the people of Mafeking Street, who had no expectations of us and with whom we shared no history – except the history of Elizabeth and Alice Attwell, which was indeed a strong and essential bond.

All those years – each morning, waking to discover her again, each day spent in making our life together – that was all I wanted, and all she wanted too, as far as I could tell.

'I have an exact view of things,' Lizzie said, not long after she had come back from Park Manor.

'Do you, indeed,' I said, and she laughed.

'I can see how our life will be, years and years into the future.

I see our prosperous little business, well established in a year or two and venturing all sorts of new things.'

'What sort of new things?'

'Don't interrupt. I am engaged in speculation.' She laughed very gaily at that, both of us knowing it was a parody of the way I spoke myself.

She put on a more serious face and said, 'After a few years, Charlie, perhaps three or four, we'll decide to have children, one of each. We'll have to move house to have enough room for the pram and the play-pen. In due course the children will learn to fly with us, and in our old grey age we will be able to take up a life of deck-chairs and pottering in the garden.'

'It doesn't sound like you, pottering in the garden,' I said. 'You've never shown the slightest interest in gardening.'

'I will,' she said, kissing me, 'I'll become intensely interested in gardening, and singularly keen on pot-plants.'

'You have your father's energy and his optimism,' I said, and she looked sad for a moment.

'I would so like him back,' she said. 'I would so very much like him back.'

But then she smiled and said, 'He was so *hopeless* at flying a kite! He hadn't the slightest idea how it worked, but when it was up there – oh, how he loved it! He lay on his back in the grass, waving his bowler and shouting "Higher! Higher!"'

A set of chance elements – among them, my father's present of a Gipsy Moth, our flights to Berlin, Lizzie's friendship with Alice, Mafeking Street, a snowy evening and a Russian ship – had drawn us together, and had determined the place and manner of our life. We set out to ensure that it would be a success, and we had no particular setbacks, except that we had no children. We never knew why. In those days such things were regarded as a matter of chance or God's grace, according to your philosophy, and it did not occur to us to investigate the reasons or search for a cure. For a time the prospect of having no children about the house made us sad, but we accepted it; and there were, at the time, a great many children running around Mafeking Street, most of whom regarded our property as equally theirs.

Years went by and little changed. There was just us, just Mafeking Street, just the photography and the flying. In the nineteen-fifties we began to look for a bigger house, and eventually bought one that was five minutes' walk from the studio. Looking east from its attic window now, I can just see the river and one of the cranes that have been allowed to remain as decoration for the waterside. To the north-west the railway that was the L&BR still runs along above the arches.

The business expanded sufficiently to employ two pilots, so we hired Adrian West permanently and bought a second aeroplane, a smart little Cessna. In the nineteen-sixties we sold the old Argus and bought an Islander, a larger aeroplane with twin engines – it was ideal for our work, easy to fly, stable and roomy.

The mapping side of the business had grown steadily. We eventually employed more than twenty people on that alone. The photo library had also grown. We kept it up to date, changing to colour film for most of our work but using black-and-white when it seemed right to do so. The growth in travel and magazine publishing resulted in plenty of demand for skyscapes, landscapes and coastal pictures. We developed some specialised lines – photographs of English country houses, archaeological sites and illustrations of long-distance paths like the Pennine Way. I held one or two exhibitions of the black-and-white skyscapes that were my particular interest; the shows were positively received and the prints sold steadily.

In the seventies we continued to extend the photo library, reaching out to the coasts of Belgium, France and Spain. We began to sell a great many coastal pictures to travel companies; at some time or other we must have photographed every one of the thousands of seaside hotels that blight the European coasts. We used the Cessna for that sort of thing. It was a great pleasure to fly south into the sunshine, and the Cessna was a good aeroplane for that sort of work – fast, stable and quiet. Adrian had done well, and we began to leave the management of the business to him.

The aerial photography went well and we went well, Lizzie and I. We took delight in each other. Lizzie enjoyed my slow and deliberate way of thinking – which might well have enraged another person – and I remained enchanted by her beauty and her energy.

She told me the story of the fighter pilot, Tom Anderson, whom she had met in 1940, and showed me a letter he had written to her – he said that he expected to be killed, and had left the letter with his brother so that she would know that he had loved her. We talked about the other young men who had been interested in her, and the fact that she had rejected almost all of them.

'One of them grabbed me once and tried to kiss me,' she told me. 'I hated that sort of thing.'

'It doesn't seem unreasonable to want to kiss you,' I said. 'You are rather beautiful, after all. I expect the young man just got carried away.'

'I know,' she said. 'I can see that now. I was very foolish to be so afraid of men.'

She took hold of my hands and said, 'I didn't want to be touched. I didn't want to be kissed. I felt it was wrong.' She brought my hands up to her lips and kissed them. 'It was my mother who taught me such things were wrong, but there was also some inner fear of my own. Ruth didn't have such a fear, and was free of that wretched anxiety. What a nuisance that was! Charlie, I'm glad about the book – Marie Stopes's book.'

'I think we would have found a way without it, in the end.'

'Do you?'

She kissed my hands again. 'Still, I found a fairly decent chap in the end.'

Ruth came to stay with us from time to time, and she and Lizzie spent a long time discussing their childhood and the reserved character of their mother, puzzling about her match with their extrovert father.

Little Arthur Attwell became a successful businessman; he had inherited his mother's energy and turned the family's timber business into a builder's merchant. He often came to see Lizzie, bringing his wife, who was a relative of the long-dead Ben Yossakin.

Those are the bones of it, but they do not convey the intensity of our life together, as generalisations never do. There is something curious here; history is surely made from small stuff, from moments, yet that real stuff is lost in the telling, and with it a true sense of the past. There is another kind of history, something that is not a full record nor a proper one, but is focused on small truths. It is not concerned to draw morals, nor to discover new facts, nor to identify causes, but only with capturing a moment or two, and getting them right.

One night, many years ago, I was lying awake when Lizzie suddenly whispered something to me – I had thought she was asleep. I turned my head towards her, saw the glint of her eyes and asked, 'What did you say, darling?'

'Charlie, please fuck me,' she whispered. 'Fuck me now, Charlie, please.'

I reached for her and found she was crying – I had no idea why – and we made love as if we were about to die, urgently and violently, and lay entangled for a long time, until at last we fell asleep.

What a shock that was, her whisper in the dark! And how intense were the feelings she generated – lust for her, joy in her, love for her – I cannot catch the force of it. That was an abrupt descent to particularity, if you like, and was one of those moments that stamps one's life as true and real.

In the morning I asked her why she had been crying. She put her arms around my neck and said, 'I don't know what it is, but sometimes I get afraid. I feel such love for you, but sometimes fear comes over me in a rush. What is it? Is it the thought of dying? Of losing you? What? Why am I afraid, Charlie?'

I could not answer her question, but it was a particularity, a moment of our history together, which is otherwise blurred and lost among the days and years.

Yes – all my particular moments have to do with her. There is nothing of more value in my life. I want to return to her as she was then, and that is the sole reason for this work. I want to keep her alive because she fills me with such emotion as, before her, I had not known existed, and can only feel now because of her, because she was once alive beside me. She did that for me – oh, for so long, so many times and in so many ways – for all those years she gave me life, and then she died, and her death was drawn out fine as a wire.

Twenty-one

Throughout the 1950s the Soviet pressure on Berlin steadily increased. In 1953 the Berlin Rising, a protest against state-controlled low pay in East Berlin, was crushed by tanks. In that year more than 300,000 East German refugees crossed to the west, and that was not an exceptionally high figure: during that period the river of escapers averaged a quarter of a million annually. In 1958 Khrushchev called for the west to renounce their 'occupation' of West Berlin, and Willy Brandt predicted the building of a wall between the two Berlins.

The number of refugees doubled in the first half of 1961. It was the consequence of growing 'Torschlusspanik' – terror of the gate closing – which was well founded. On Sunday 12th August soldiers appeared along the whole length of the East German border, and the 28 miles that lay within the city of Berlin were blocked with barbed wire, soon to be replaced by concrete, minefields and watchtowers. It was a remarkably quick and efficient job, done under the command of a man named Honecker, who evidently had a talent for such things. During August nearly fifty thousand refugees left the east, and even in September, despite the new hazards, fifteen thousand managed to escape.

In the west the 1960s were a period of exceptional prosperity. Suddenly we began to rebuild on the old bomb-sites, to have money in our pockets and to explore new freedoms. One of those freedoms was foreign travel, and Lizzie and I were increasingly asked to work abroad for airlines, hotel chains and the fast-expanding holiday companies.

In September of 1961 Lizzie told me she had decided to read Anna's letter. We were in France at the time, sitting on a hotel balcony that overlooked a calm sea. I felt a shock when Lizzie said the name Anna Schwartz – we had not discussed her, nor anything to do with Berlin, since Lizzie returned from Park Manor.

'Anna Schwartz,' I said. 'The letter you put in the tea-chest in the attic.'

'Yes.'

'Because of the wall? Is that why you've decided to read it?'

'Of course. It's bound to have affected her. She lives on one side and works on the other – or she did, once.'

'When did she send you that letter? Lizzie, it was years and years ago!'

'It was 1949,' Lizzie said. 'Twelve years ago. Not such a long time.'

'Will she still be at the same address?'

'I don't know, but I'll try it.'

'Very well,' I said, and hesitated.

She looked at me. 'Charlie, it's all right – I'm not getting obsessional again. But from time to time I think of her, and I suddenly decided I would find out what's happened to her.'

She thought for a moment. 'I suppose I might not be able to

tell if I was getting ill again. Perhaps we ought to write together, you and I.'

'No, Lizzie. You met her in Berlin, and you must write to her. If you find that you're uneasy about it—'

'I'll tell you, Charlie.'

'Anna Schwartz.' I said the name again and we began to talk about her, and about the meeting of the three of them among the ruins of Berlin. We talked in an open way, it seemed to me, and there was a sense of unlocking the past, and allowing it freedom, which had never been the case before. The sun slowly fell into the Mediterranean and we sat there until it was dark, talking easily about Anna and Lizzie's flight to Berlin, with long, meditative pauses and without any sense of the danger that had once surrounded those memories.

So Lizzie read Anna Schwartz's letter after a gap of twelve years, and found that it was not something to be feared, but an ordinary letter of response and enquiry, written somewhat formally and in excellent English. Anna said that she remembered her meeting with Lizzie and Miss Attwell very well, and had often thought about it. Their conversation had lasted only a few minutes, she said, and at the time she had been very angry; afterwards she had wondered what these two Englishwomen were doing in the ruins of Berlin, and what they had thought of her fury. She had been very young at the time, she said, and that sounded almost like an apology. It was a cautious and intelligent letter, inviting the continuation of the correspondence but allowing the possibility that such a thing might not be appropriate. It was noticeable that the letter said nothing about herself or her current way of life.

'I shall reply,' Lizzie said. 'I shall ask about her, and tell her something about us.'

'Good,' I said, still being somewhat anxious about the whole matter, and hoping that this revival of interest would not awake the trauma of the past.

Lizzie wrote a letter to Anna, a letter intended to be short, polite and cautious in the style of Anna's but eventually, as she got into the task, becoming long and detailed. It described our way of life since the war but said nothing about the flight to Berlin and back all those years before. I think Lizzie wished to get to know Anna first, and learn something about her, and then she might become more open.

Lizzie waited eagerly for a reply, and after a week she said, 'I don't expect we'll get a quick response.'

'There'll be all sorts of difficulties,' I said. 'There might be interference with her post – censorship of some sort – all sorts of things.'

'Or she might just decide not to reply.'

'I don't think she'd do that,' I said. 'She wrote to you, after all, and it would surely be intriguing to receive a sudden letter from someone you'd met, and written to, so long ago.'

Ten days and then two weeks went by. We were busy, and our busyness was a good reason to avoid the topic. After three weeks Lizzie said, 'I suppose my letter didn't reach her.'

'I suppose not,' I said. 'Maybe she's moved.'

It was like a love letter sent on impulse after a romantic encounter: there was excitement and a feeling of risk as it slipped into the post-box, then anxiety mixed with hope, then a growing and ever more certain sense of disappointment.

'She might just be busy,' Lizzie said.

'She might never have received the letter.'

'She might have decided not to reply for some reason.'

'It might be dangerous for her.'

The possible reasons for the lack of a response were infinite and might well be perfectly commonplace; but as time went by Anna's silence seemed to grow, and caused in us a kind of hollowness.

On that hotel balcony in France we had discovered that the topic of Berlin was no longer dangerous, and had begun cautiously to explore it, and to fill in what seemed like missing pieces of the pattern of our lives. But now there was a loose end again, an awkwardness, a piece of unfinished business that cast a shadow across our new freedom. Our talk inevitably returned to Anna Schwartz and what might have happened to her, the girl whom Lizzie and Alice had met near the zoo, and was passionate with a kind of rage that was now familiar, the rage of loss. The absence of a reply from her always made us pause, and tended to silence our conversation, and gave us a slight sense of sorrow. As the days and weeks and months passed, and eventually the years, the more certain it was that, without Anna, the pattern could never be completed.

Twenty-two

Lizzie's illness was first suspected in the autumn of 1989. She seemed perfectly all right to me – a little forgetful sometimes, but so was I, and neither of us thought anything of it. We were perfectly healthy and had never had any difficulty with the medical checks we needed for our licences.

Towards the end of October Lizzie had her usual check-up and her doctor asked her to have some extra tests with a specialist – from what he said, it sounded as though there might be a problem with her eyesight. It turned out that the specialist was not an ophthalmologist, as we had expected, but a neurologist, whose name was Richard Chapman.

On that first visit Richard asked Lizzie to do various tests of hand and eye co-ordination, reasoning and memory. Afterwards he sat down to talk to us both, and said that Lizzie had been referred because there were slight aberrations in her sight and physical co-ordination, and there might be a problem in her brain.

Lizzie asked, 'Do you mean a tumour or something like that?'

'I don't think it's a tumour,' Richard said. 'But we'll have to do a few more tests to be certain. I'm going to send you for an EEG and a brain scan.'

'If there's anything wrong with me I want to know what it is,' Lizzie said. 'You won't keep anything from me, will you?'

'Of course not,' Richard was a straightforward person, another good doctor. At the end of the consultation he looked at his notes and said, 'I see that you were referred by a doctor who was doing a medical for your flying licence.'

Lizzie sat up straight and clasped her hands together. 'Yes,' she said, 'I've been flying for a long time. It's what Charlie and I do for a living.'

Richard said, 'I'm very sorry, but I think it's likely you won't meet the requirements for renewing your licence.'

'Yes,' Lizzie said briskly. 'We've thought about that, of course. We know we can't go on flying for ever. That's obvious. We've been lucky to go on as long as we have.'

'Well,' Richard said. 'I think perhaps you ought to make some plans now, because I don't think your licence will be renewed.'

We drove home to Mafeking Street, had supper and sat talking for a long time. Someone we knew, terminally ill with cancer, had recently been given a ride in a racing car at Silverstone. A group of friends had clubbed together to raise the money.

'It's bizarre, that,' Lizzie said. 'What were they thinking of? Did they really think a racing car would take his mind off dying?'

'Perhaps it did. He was *very* keen on racing cars, after all.'

Lizzie laughed, and said, 'I think they did it because they felt they had to do something – anything. It was really for them, not for him at all, just so they'd feel they'd done something. Perhaps we ought to carry little cards that say, "In the event of terminal illness I do NOT wish to have a go in a Ferrari."'

She laughed and then looked down at the carpet, perhaps remembering that she might never fly again.

I said, 'Even if your licence isn't renewed, you could keep on flying with me – as long as I keep my licence, anyway.'

'No, I couldn't,' she said. 'I wouldn't want to be there on sufferance.'

'It wouldn't be like that, Lizzie.'

'Oh yes it would. You'd be worrying if I could cope. I wouldn't be able to do any landings or take-offs, would I? We couldn't risk the aeroplane. The insurance wouldn't cover it.' She laughed. 'We couldn't risk you, either. Anyway, I don't want to fly if I'm not able to be in charge. I'd just be a passenger, and you'd let me have a go when you felt like it. I couldn't do that. And I don't know what's going to happen to me, Charlie – I don't want to start feeling funny in the air. I've done enough flying for a lifetime, anyway.'

I'm not sure whether a person can ever do enough flying for a lifetime – not someone as addicted to flying as Lizzie was. But I just said, 'All right, we'll just take it steady and see how things go.'

We had been flying for fifty years – it was astonishing, when you counted it up. We had first flown in the little Moth before the war, and then Lizzie had flown almost every type of wartime aircraft while I was busy with Wellingtons and then Lancasters. After the war she had flown regularly in the Argus, the Cessna and the Islander. She liked the Islander enormously – 'It's a proper aeroplane, Charlie, a real tough, hard-working aeroplane.'

When she said that I remembered how she had loved my Moth, and used to run her hands along its wing all those years ago.

*

We were told that the EEG and the scan would take two weeks to be processed. It was the beginning of November. We had little work to do that week and I was raking leaves from the lawn when Lizzie came rushing out of the house, calling, 'Charlie, Charlie, I've had a terrific idea – come and look at this – quickly – come on!'

She grabbed my arm and tugged me into the sitting-room. The television news was on. 'It's about Berlin,' she said. 'The Berlin wall is coming down any minute.'

That year, 1989, had been a year of marvels. The western nations had once feared that countries around the world would fall one after another to communism; but no, it was the communist countries that were the dominoes, and they fell quickly. The map of Europe, fixed for so long – fixed for ever, so we had assumed – cracked and split apart in a few months. By the end of the year the process was well advanced; once Hungary had become democratic the population of East Germany began streaming across the open border, and Honecker's East German regime was clearly going to be the next to collapse. The Berlin wall might fall at any moment. There was already doubt in the minds of the border police, and increasing numbers of people were being allowed to move both ways through the checkpoints.

When the news ended Lizzie turned to me and said, 'I want to go there, Charlie. The wall's coming down and we must go to Berlin straight away. I want to go there and see if we can find Anna. Can we go tomorrow?'

'Tomorrow!' Oh yes, Berlin had always been at the back of my mind, but going there now, this moment – and as for Lizzie finding Anna—

'Charlie,' Lizzie said, 'You've got your serious face on. This isn't something to be serious about.'

'Well,' I said, 'it's such a sudden idea – I feel nervous about it, Lizzie. Is this the right moment? Can't we wait and see what happens? Wouldn't it be better to let everything settle down? There'll be all sorts of chaos when the wall comes down—'

She clapped her hands. 'This is the perfect moment! Oh Charlie, don't you see – the wall's going to come down, it's the end of the war, the real end of it, and we must go there and see it happen, and at last I can see Anna again!'

'Anna,' I said.

Lizzie put her arms round my neck. 'Charlie, I know what you're going to say. You're going to tell me all sorts of things about how it isn't sensible to try to find Anna. You'll say we didn't find her before, so how will we find her now? You'll say she's likely to have moved, or she might be dead. Charlie, I know all those things and I don't care. I want us to fly to Berlin before it's too late, and I want us to find Anna if we can. Don't you see? It would finish everything off.'

There was a pause after she'd finished talking, and then I said, 'We'll take the Islander, shall we? I'll get a weather forecast later on.'

Lizzie did a little dance on the damp lawn then, a twirl or two of her skirt, and went rushing into the house, saying she was going to begin looking for Anna right this minute, and for a start she would phone Berlin Zoo.

I went back to my raking of the leaves. If she was alive, Anna Schwartz must surely be a similar age to us – in her seventies. She would have lived most of her adult life under communism. She wrote good English, so she would probably speak it also, and if Lizzie found her we would be able to talk together. I wondered about her anger, the anger that she had displayed when she was telling the story about Muschi. What had she done with it? It was the same anger that Lily had displayed, anger that was a form of energy, and might be focused on some purpose. But she would know nothing about Lizzie and her journey to Berlin and back, nor about Alice, and there was no telling what significance their meeting might have for her. She would have no knowledge of me or my participation in the destruction of her city, the killing of tens of thousands of people and the creatures that had been in her care and had moved her so much.

It was not many minutes before Lizzie came sauntering out of the house wearing an expression of great glee.

'Very well,' I said, leaning on my rake, 'You've found her already, just like that. Where is she?'

'According to the administrative director of the Zoologische Garten in Berlin,' Lizzie said, speaking with elaborate precision, 'Fraulein Anna Schwartz lives in the same apartment in East Berlin that she has occupied all her life. She has not worked for the zoo for many years, but she is a recognised authority on apes, and particularly the orang-utan. Unfortunately she does not possess a telephone, but the director will get a message to her today or tomorrow, asking her to telephone me as soon as possible.'

'Dear Lizzie,' I said, and stepped towards her.

'Get rid of that rake,' she said. 'Come inside and start planning the flight. We'll need clearances across Holland and Germany, won't we? I don't think we'll go tomorrow, but we'll go early the following morning.'

And she did another little dance on the lawn, another twirl of the flowered cotton skirt she was wearing that day.

I went inside and phoned for a forecast. The weather was going to be cold but stable across Europe for the next few days, with occasional snow showers and a light easterly wind. There was no reason not to go.

And that evening the phone rang. I answered it and Lizzie came running from the sitting-room.

'I am Anna Schwartz,' said a clear, crisp voice. 'I wish to speak to Elizabeth Beevor, if I may.'

'Certainly,' I said. 'Here she is.'

I went away and left Lizzie to talk to her, but once or twice I heard laughter, and that told me we would be meeting Anna in Berlin.

When Lizzie came back into the sitting-room, fizzing with excitement, I asked her, 'And why was there no reply to your letter?'

'She never got my letter,' Lizzie said, sitting on the arm of my chair. 'It was lost in the post, or the secret police took it – she never got my letter! And we spent such a long time thinking about it! Why on earth didn't I write again?'

'Because you weren't certain, and neither was I.'

'Yes, of course. But this time I was certain, and she was there.'

'And we shall meet her.'

'Oh yes, we'll meet her. We're going to her apartment. She told me the way, and I've drawn a little map.'

After so many years it was all arranged in a few moments. That night I lay awake, still wondering whether if the journey was sensible. Lizzie said sleepily, 'Charlie, I can hear you fussing. Stop it at once. We are going to Berlin to see Anna, and that's that. And I've had another idea.'

'What's that?'

'We must take her some photographs. Some of our own and a few others. Tomorrow I'll make a selection. Now go to sleep.'

Twenty-three

At the start Lizzie flew the Islander and I sat in the right-hand seat, gazing at the landscape. The weather was settled and the sky clear when we left Rochford. We headed north of east across the corner of East Anglia towards the Hook of Holland, a hundred and sixty miles away. The deep windscreen of the Islander gives a fine view; it was a luxury to have no work to do, and to be able to gaze out across the flat lands that I had first known in wartime and remained familiar still, nearly fifty years later – dozens of wartime airfields are still visible in East Anglia, some of their outlines now blurred by crops and buildings and roads, though I have forgotten most of their names. We passed south of Norwich, the Broads glinting below, and then the coast lay ahead, fringed with yellow sand.

Right from the start it had been the view from height that I had found intoxicating, the way in which the world wheeled and turned, seeming to display itself to me; and now, flying with my wife across this curious diagram of roads and rivers and railways, I felt enormous joy.

I said to Lizzie, 'Come to think of it, I've never flown to Berlin in daylight before.'

'I have,' Lizzie said, 'but it was a while back.'

'You're very happy,' I said.

'Of course I am.' She looked across at me and grinned. 'And so are you. What could be nicer than a decent long trip in our lovely Islander?'

She flew a gentle 'S' turn, a wiggle left and right just for the fun of it, and then straightened on course again. Soon we had crossed the coast and the grey sea, unmarked and still, stretched before us into infinity, the air a little misty and so calm that we seemed to hang motionless in a globe of silver light.

'Rotterdam,' I said. 'Rotterdam, Utrecht, Amersfoort. I remember the way.'

Lizzie was as beautiful as ever, her hair now white as the sky. She wore glasses, rimless glasses of a narrow, oval shape, over which she liked to peer, and she held the controls lightly, with the ends of her fingers. I could look all day at her profile, her lovely nose, the angles of her cheek-bones, the upright way she held her head.

She turned and said, 'Charlie, you're gawping at me.'

'Why not? Doesn't a husband have a right to gawp?'

'You're my co-pilot, Mr Beevor, and I hope you know your place.'

'Yes, skipper,' I said. 'Anything you say.'

She laughed, and said, 'Take her for a minute, would you?'

I reached for the controls and she left her seat and came to stand behind me.

'Charlie,' she said, her mouth close to my ear, 'This is the right thing to do, isn't it?'

'Oh yes,' I said. 'I was doubtful, but I'm not any more.'

She laughed. 'You're quite often doubtful.'

'I know. It's a failing in my character.'

'I'm a bit impetuous and you're a bit cautious. Doesn't that make us a perfect match?'

'I think it does,' I said.

She put her arms round my neck and rested her head against mine. We flew on like that for a long time, course a little north of east, altitude three thousand feet, airspeed one hundred and forty knots. It's about five hundred and fifty miles from Rochford to Berlin, about four hours flying in the Islander, via Rotterdam, Utrecht, Amersfoort, Enschede, Osnabruck, Minden, Hannover, Wolfsburg, Stendahl, Brandenburg, Potsdam and Berlin.

Later, Lizzie dozed in one of the passenger seats while I flew the Islander across the Dutch coast and onwards across Germany. Somewhere near Munster, she came back into the cockpit and said, 'Charlie, I'm sorry, I had a little snooze. Is everything all right?'

'It's fine,' I said, putting my arm around her. 'It's a very strange journey, this.'

'I know that, darling,' she said. 'It's a kind of – what's that word? I've forgotten.'

'A mission?'

'No, not that.'

'A quest?'

'Perhaps that's what I was thinking. We're going to find Anna, but that's not all, is it? I don't think I'll do much flying after this trip . . . In a way, it's – yes, I know, it's a *celebration* of all our flying together. A celebration. That's what it is.'

I was delighted with that. 'A celebration! Lizzie, what a lovely word that is! Yes, let's call it a celebration! How many years are we celebrating?'

'Oh, about fifty.'

'Fifty years!'

'Yes. Can we really be that old?'

'I've forgotten,' she said. 'Am I seventy, or seventy-one?'

'You're about twenty-five,' I said. 'And another thing to celebrate is that we're doing this journey together, and it's marvellous to be doing it with you.'

'Good,' Lizzie said, tucking her head more closely into my shoulder. 'You always were a rather serious man, but I love you anyway.'

These days you have to do what you're told in an aeroplane. The German controller routed us straight into Templehof between two 737s, and we had no chance to look at the city from the air. We parked the Islander in a corner and took a train into town.

Berlin glittered with frost and the crystal decorations of fine falling snow. It was high on money, crowds, shopping, Christmas, East Germans, the autumn fashions and above all the wall, *die Mauer*. It still stood, but the city held its breath.

As we walked into our hotel an Australian girl was saying to the receptionist, 'Italy was OK, but the spaghetti was crap. It's better in Melbourne. We have a helluva lot of Italians in Melbourne.' She was short and tough-looking, one of the shoals of young people drifting everywhere, their plump rucksacks gaudy with maroon, purple and lime green: the world had come here to wait and talk and drink and dance.

After a meal we went out into the crowds and discovered the Kaiser Wilhelm Gedachtniskirche a preserved ruin, a ragged black tooth. I looked up at it and seemed to hear the roar of aero-engines, but there was no melancholy reflection in Berlin now; shops and market stalls jostled round the walls of the church that we had knocked down in 1942, and every window and counter was piled with treasures. We edged through a family standing in front of a kitchen shop, holding hands and staring silently at the stainless steel, the gleaming knives and pans, the sieves and scourers – they must be East Berliners, we guessed, from their astonishment.

Berlin was exhausting. Soon we retreated to the hotel bar and sat in a corner with glasses of beer. There was an American woman there, a tall, thin woman with glasses on a string, looking like a schoolmarm. She told us how she'd got lost in the crowds, how confused she'd been. I showed her our guidebook.

'Why, say, that's real kind,' she said.

'Years ago I met an American in Berlin,' Lizzie said. 'He was a tall, handsome man and his name was—' She turned to me and said, 'What was that American's name? The one that Alice and I met at Gatow?'

'Frank Oldfield,' I said. 'Sergeant Frank Oldfield, US Air Force.'

'Frank Oldfield,' Lizzie said. 'That's right.'

'I can't say I know anyone by that name,' the American woman said.

Lizzie thought for a while and said, ' Do you know, for a moment I thought I might marry him? It passed through my mind.' She laughed. 'But I married Charlie instead, and that worked out pretty well, didn't it, Charlie?'

'I never did marry,' the American said. 'Where was he from, the guy you met in Berlin?'

'Now I did know that once,' Lizzie said. 'It was a long, long time ago, at the end of the war, and I've forgotten.'

'That sure is a long time back.'

'Sure is,' Lizzie said.

*

Soon after that we went up to our room. I opened the window and listened to the tremendous buzz and chatter of the city, music drifting up, car horns, people calling, while down from the dark sky came drifting that fine snow, so fine that it was no more than white dust.

Europe was changing beyond all imagining, and so quickly that it was hard to grasp. In England change happened rarely and slowly. The country was exhaustively mapped, and our parents, our schools, our jobs and our landscapes cast us again and again in the same forms: to be English was to know who you were and where you stood. But now, after fifty years, something fundamental had snapped in Europe; surely we would now be carried to new places of which we had not dreamed.

'Lizzie,' I said the next morning, 'I really did get this all wrong. I thought it would be sad to be here in Berlin, but it's not sad at all. The place is buzzing. The place is hopping.'

She was sitting on the edge of the bed and brushing her hair. 'Sad? No it's not sad, it's terrific!' She turned round and grinned, and I reached out for her. She lay in my arms and said, 'Charlie, today I shall see Anna again, forty-four years and a few weeks after I first saw her.'

We walked eastwards through the icy woods of the Tiergarten, past the golden statue of Winged Victory and on towards the Brandenburg Gate. Somewhere here was the grand house in which Lizzie had stayed that night in 1945; we looked at several possibilities but she could not decide.

The Gate was surrounded by television vans but nothing was happening. Border guards walked along the top of the wall in thin sunlight, chatting, waiting. It was not clear to which side they belonged, nor whether such things mattered any more.

Crowds strolled and talked, their pockets and shopping bags bulging with lumps of reinforced concrete. The wall was disappearing. People stood beside it, chipping away with nail files, penknives and scissors. I prised off a chunk for Lizzie and a piece for myself, but a tall woman in a fur coat looked so longingly at the fragments that we gave them to her.

At Checkpoint Charlie a multitude of West Berliners was heading east with parcels, flowers and dozens of children. We went down corridors and through a great many doors and joined a long queue. In front of us some Americans were making a fuss, insisting their papers were stamped so they could show the folks back home the black eagle of the Deutsche Demokratische Republik. I waved our passports in the air and the guards shoved us irritably through a door and out into East Berlin.

I hugged Lizzie. 'We're in East Berlin!'

'I know that, Charlie,' she said. 'Where's my map?'

East Berlin seemed preoccupied, silent and gloomy, and the thin snow that had glittered in the west seemed here like a shroud falling across the empty squares and the grand, solitary statues. We were early and we wandered the misty streets for an hour, trying to spend our compulsory allocation of Ostmarks; but the museums and galleries were closed, the shelves almost empty in the shops.

'That's quite enough wandering about,' Lizzie said, 'It's nearly three o'clock. We'll go to Anna's apartment now, even if we're a few minutes early.'

It was a tall apartment block with seven flights of concrete steps and a plain white door with a tintacked file card saying *A Schwartz.*

I knocked and there was Anna, a woman in her sixties

wearing a black dress and knitted cardigan, grey hair tied up in a bun, glasses dangling on a cord round her neck.

Lizzie said, 'Anna, I'm Elizabeth,' and immediately the two of them had their arms around each other and their heads together, grey hair against the white, Anna saying 'Elizabeth, oh Elizabeth' over and over, and Lizzie saying nothing, being too overwhelmed to speak.

Eventually they unwrapped themselves and held each others' hands, grinning and laughing, tears on their cheeks, still saying their names, saying how amazing it was, how long it had been, saying 'My dear Elizabeth,' 'My dear Anna'.

Over her shoulder Lizzie said, 'Isn't it amazing – oh, Charlie, I'm so glad we came!' and Anna, letting go of Lizzie's hands, shook both my hands too, and then we all held hands, standing in a ring and smiling and laughing, all of us.

Anna drew us into the apartment and shut the door. 'You would like coffee, I am sure, Elizabeth and Charles,' she said over her shoulder, her shoes pattering quickly along a corridor and into a small, hot room crammed with tropical life – photographs, masks, paintings, sculptures of stone and wood, rugs, pot-plants and small tables cluttered with books.

Anna Schwartz turned and said formally, 'I am so glad that you have come to see me, and that you, Elizabeth, have remembered me for such a long time.'

Lizzie said, 'Anna, you have been on my mind all those years since we met by the ruins of the zoo, and I am so glad to be here. Please call me Lizzie – everyone does. And Charles – he is called Charlie.'

'Elizabeth and Charles,' Anna said, 'that is so English! But I shall call you Lizzie and Charlie now. Please sit down. I will get some coffee.'

She left the room and we looked at the dozens of images of

apes, individual animals and groups, that hung around the walls and stood on every flat surface. Directly in front of us, hanging over the fireplace, near life-size and dominating the room, was a large framed print of a female adult orang-utan, red-haired, staring calmly at the camera, her hooked fingers hanging loosely.

In a moment Anna returned with a tray, saw us looking at the picture and asked Lizzie, 'Do you know who she is?'

Lizzie immediately said, 'Muschi.'

'Yes,' Anna said, very pleased. 'You are quite right. It is Muschi.' She put the tray down and turned to face the picture.

Lizzie said, 'You told me that Muschi was rescued by a gun-crew. What happened to her after that?'

'She lived for many years in the zoo,' Anna said. 'Then she became sick. It was in 1968, and she died the same year. Sometimes orang-utans live to a great age, perhaps fifty years, but in captivity they may get many diseases.'

Lizzie said, 'You were Muschi's keeper all her life, were you?'

'Oh no. For sixteen years, yes. But after the wall was built I could no longer work in West Berlin. It was not permitted any more. A few times I went to see Muschi, but it was not good – she did not understand why I was gone so long, I think. It was better not to see her. Then she became sick, and I did not see her any more after that.'

She paused, still looking at the photograph, then said, 'I did not mind so much that I could not work at the zoo after Muschi died. Die Zoologische Garten – I had begun to see that it was not so good after all. It is not right to keep animals in cages for us to look at, I think. The purpose of animals is not to entertain us, or even to educate us. They should have their own lives, and be free. People come and look at them – no, there is another English word that is better than "look" – what is that word?'

Lizzie said, 'Perhaps you mean "stare"? People do stare at animals in zoos.'

'Yes, exactly. People stare at the orang-utans in a zoo for some time, and when they are bored with that they go to buy an ice-cream and maybe stare at some lions. It is completely foolish to say that people learn about animals at a zoo. If you want to know about animals you must do more work than that.'

Lizzie laughed and clapped her hands – this was the fierce Anna whom she remembered.

In a moment Anna laughed too, and said, 'I am sorry. I have not many visitors, and I spend too much time thinking.' She waved her hand at the photographs around her. 'I know these animals better than people, I am sure. But—' she hesitated and smiled. 'In these weeks it has been strange. Many people have come here to East Berlin, people from the west, come to look at us—'

'Just like a zoo,' Lizzie said. 'Staring at you. But we have come here too, of course.'

Anna waved her hand. 'You have not come only to stare. It is something like a zoo now, I think. We are the strange people of the east, who will soon be extinct. Perhaps they will come and see us, and then they can tell their friends. People just like me will write books about us and our strange behaviour.'

I had a sudden sense then that our lives had come to a focus upon this small, hot, shadowy room, the apes looking down, this woman with her dark, intense eyes and the stillness of her gaze. It was easy to see why Lizzie had remembered her.

'You are just the same,' Lizzie said. 'How old were you when we first met?'

'In 1945 I was twenty-two,' Anna said. 'I thought the world was a simple place then, black and white, right and wrong. But now—'

'I'm sure you know what is right,' Lizzie said.

'Sometimes. I will show you something.' She got up, went to a chest and took out a photograph album. 'Here are some pictures of me in 1934 and 1937.'

Lizzie and I looked at the pictures. There was young Anna in a uniform like that of the Girl Guides.

'I was a member of the Jungmadelbund,' Anna said, 'and when I was a little older, the Bund Deutscher Mädel. I was very enthusiastic about it. I think you would call it the Hitler Youth.'

We looked at the picture of the bright-eyed girl in her immaculate uniform and I said, 'We don't always know what is right, especially when we are young.'

Anna said to me, 'I think you were in the Royal Air Force. Lizzie already told me that. You flew one of the bombers that came here—' and she pointed upwards.

'Yes. I did what I was told. I know that's the usual excuse. I'm sorry.'

'When a war begins it is even more difficult to tell what is right. People must follow orders – there is a difficulty. My father and mother died in the bombing, but—'

I started to say something, but Anna went on. 'All these things are a long way in the past. They must not be forgotten entirely, because there are lessons for the future. But I do not think that blame is useful, or guilt is useful. What we did in the camps, and what the Russians did when they came here – perhaps those are the hardest to forgive. But in the end it must all be forgiven.'

She laughed. 'I am sorry – I am making a speech, or perhaps a lecture. But I have been sitting here, waiting for you and thinking that nothing is simple. The wall is coming down, and that is good, I suppose. Of course I know that the regime of Honecker was corrupt and it has failed, but not all of us thought as Honecker did. At first some people in the DDR were trying to find another way of living, according to some principle of equality. I do not see a principle of equality in the west. Many others have this opinion. Many of us will not be having a party in the street when the wall comes down. There is sorrow because we have failed, and we have to begin again. It is a victory for you, but victory never comes without loss.'

There was a long pause, in which the hissing of the gas fire seemed very loud.

'I understand that,' Lizzie said at last. 'It will be another difficult time for you. In England we had an easy time, during the war and afterwards. I didn't realise that at first, but when I saw the ruins of Berlin I began to see the truth. Sometimes it takes a long time to find out what is true.'

Lizzie got out the photographs she had brought, and showed Anna a picture of us in the Moth – it was taken by my brother at Taunton Races – and an aerial shot of Limehouse taken in the late afternoon. The shadows are long and snow has rounded the angles of the roofs and walls and the tumbled outlines of the bomb sites. Smoke trails from a dozen chimneys, diagonally across the print.

'This is Mafeking Street,' Lizzie said. 'We still live nearby, of course. We took this photograph in the bad winter after the war – when was it, Charlie?'

'1946,' I said. 'The winter of 1946.'

'Here's the railway,' Lizzie said. 'It runs above our archway, where we have the studio and darkroom. Here's the canal and Limehouse Basin, and that's the Thames.'

'There is nobody in this picture,' Anna said. 'It is an abstract picture. But I know there are people in the houses because there is smoke from the fires.'

'Yes,' I said. 'It's tea-time. You can imagine them in their sitting-rooms, putting the kettle on. It's a picture of people, even though they're not visible.'

Anna laughed. 'I have to change my argument, I think. We can learn something from looking at this picture. But we are surely not staring.'

We discovered that Anna had taken most of the pictures in her apartment.

'Oh yes,' she said. 'I have been to Borneo and Sumatra many times and taken many pictures, sometimes also film and video of special kinds of behaviour.'

'It must have been difficult for you to travel so much,' I said. 'I mean, under Honecker.'

She looked at me and said, 'It was not so difficult.'

Anna was spiky and the conversation from time to time ran into a prickly patch; but the wounds were slight, and were repaired, and the talk continued, I suppose, for two hours. There had been an immediate bond between Lizzie and Anna, and it was obvious that they wanted to sustain it, and develop it. Soon they were discussing ways in which they might meet again, and laughing over the lost letter, and the absurd anxiety that had prevented her from writing again when there had been no reply.

Towards the end Lizzie told Anna about the possibility of her illness, which might soon make travel difficult, and Anna said, 'But of course I shall come and stay with you in London! I shall spend hours in the British Museum!'

We were on the way out of the apartment when Anna said to Lizzie, 'I remember your friend Alice very well. She was a small woman with her hair – what would you say—'

She pushed her fingers upwards through her own severe hair and Lizzie said, 'Bushy.'

There was a pause, and then Lizzie went on, 'At that time we took our aircraft wherever we were needed. We carried whatever we were told to carry. It was just an ordinary journey, except that it was to Berlin. After we met you we went back to England with some prisoners of war and a refugee child. That was when Alice was killed. It was an accident. Also the child died soon after we got her to England. There was nothing good about that journey, except one thing: meeting you, Anna, in Berlin. That was a very good thing.'

Anna said, 'Perhaps we will talk more about your flight, and about your friend Alice, the next time we meet.'

'Yes,' Lizzie said. 'I would like do that.'

Soon afterwards we left the apartment and walked through the empty streets to the Fernsehturm TV tower. We swayed several hundred feet into the night sky in a creaky lift to the restaurant and had a poor and hurried meal while rotating. We were only allowed one revolution.

'You stay one time only,' the waitress said, 'And then you go. Understand?'

The restaurant jerked slowly round and far below the orange lights of the Alexanderplatz fun-fair in West Berlin glittered like trinkets against the absolute darkness of the city to the east.

It was a celebration, as Lizzie had said, but another of our purposes had been to glimpse Berlin at the moment of decisive change, the moment that might mark the real end of a long war; and our journey was other things too, among them an act of remembrance and an act of absolution.

That evening, shortly after we returned to our hotel, there was a tremendous outburst of noise – car horns, fireworks, people shouting and singing. We went downstairs and found there had been an announcement on the radio: the wall was down, the city once again united.

Twenty-four

Lizzie flew the Islander all the way back. We reached the English coast in the early afternoon and got clearance to fly into Rochford across the Essex rivers and the Thames Estuary. Dozens of seals lay on the sandbanks and flocks of Brent geese were feeding along the edges of the marshes. We flew low across the mudflats, turned north to the airfield and Lizzie touched the Islander down exactly on the centre of the runway, taxied it to the hanger and shut down the engines.

An envelope was waiting for Lizzie when we got home. It contained her pilot's licence, a worn blue booklet with a photograph of her at the front of it. She had surrendered it, and now it had been returned, each page stamped CANCELLED. I don't know why they have to do that. It doesn't seem necessary. Why don't they just take it away and file it? People use the word 'grounded' in a very casual way these days – children use it to describe petty restrictions put on them by their parents – and the word has almost lost its original meaning. For a pilot to be permanently grounded is an almost unimaginable condition; knowing that, I fussed round Lizzie for several days until she became quite irritated with me.

At the end of the week we went to the hospital and got the results of the scan and the EEG. Richard Chapman said there was indeed something wrong. Lizzie did not have a brain tumour but she had suffered a loss of brain cells. Further loss of cells could not be stopped entirely, though it might be slowed by certain drugs. In due course the loss of cells would cause the symptoms known under the general heading of dementia, which is to say, loss of memory, declining reasoning powers and loss of control of bodily functions.

Lizzie asked, 'How long will it take to affect me?'

'It's already affecting you,' Richard said, 'but I think it may be some years before it has very serious effects.'

'Years?'

'Yes. Two or three years.'

'So I'll be able to do things for a while?'

'Some things, yes.'

'Good,' she said. 'I've got a lot to do.'

And indeed she did do a lot in those three years, among other things making a substantial record of our work together, with maps and photographs, which was eventually produced in a dozen copies, all beautifully bound. Anna often stayed in our house and several times we went to Berlin to see her, though not in our own aircraft. Anna and Lizzie became the greatest of friends. There was no subject that they did not explore at great length and with considerable argument.

But life became very difficult for Lizzie towards the end. She became steadily more childlike, and went beyond childlike to somewhere that is impossible to conceive. I shall not describe the process because it would be a betrayal, but in the end she did not recognise me, and was afraid of every shadow.

There is not much more that I can say, except for one curious thing. When Lizzie had become, in the last months of her life, like a small child, unable to speak, I found that I could bring her back by showing her photographs, and in particular, photographs of aeroplanes. Her speech would suddenly return and she would name them with some accuracy. That gave me the idea of taking her to see the Shuttleworth Collection of vintage aeroplanes. There's a big rally at a grass airfield called Old Warden every summer. I still go there – to see the Moths, mainly. There's always at least one Gipsy Moth. It's amazing how quiet it sounds, what a gentle, slow aeroplane it is, and so elegant. I wheeled Lizzie across the soft grass towards the parked aeroplanes and when she saw the Moth I knew that she recognised it from the way she moved her hands and smiled.

Acknowledgements

I'm grateful for the help I've had from my agent, Derek Johns, and my editors Tim Binding and Lee Boudreaux, who have stayed with me during the enormously long time I have taken to complete this book.

Hilary and our daughters, Georgia and Freya, have been supportive in many ways, as have Annie Woolland, Frances Clarke and Keiren Phelan.

Wing Commander Eric Viles, secretary of the Air Transport Auxiliary Association, gave a lot of time to my enquiries about the ATA's activities in Europe at the end of the war.

The story of the Berlin orang-utan I found in Martin Middlebrook's excellent history of the bombing of that city, and I took the liberty of borrowing it for this fiction.

As the wall was beginning to fall in November 1989 I went to Berlin with Georgia, then a teenager; since it was to be her new world, we thought she should see its beginning. My subsequent discussions with Georgia, her help with research and her readings of the many drafts of this book have been particularly valuable.

Martin Corrick
August 2004